W9-BKZ-442

# THE 'LUIS ORTEGA' SURVIVAL CLUB

AUTAUGA PRATTVILLE
PUBLIC LIBRARIES
254 Doster Street
Prattville, AL 36067

# THE 'LUIS ORTEGA' SURVIVAL CLUB

## SONORA REYES

BALZER + BRAY
*An Imprint of* HarperCollins*Publishers*

KAF
Reyes, S

While my writing draws inspiration from events I have experienced,
this book is a work of fiction. Any references to real people, places, or
events are intended only to give the book a sense of authenticity and are
used fictitiously. All other characters, places, dialogue, and incidents
portrayed in this book are the product of my imagination.

Balzer + Bray is an imprint of HarperCollins Publishers.

The Luis Ortega Survival Club
Copyright © 2023 by Sonora Reyes
All rights reserved. Printed in the United States of America.
No part of this book may be used or reproduced in any manner whatsoever without
written permission except in the case of brief quotations embodied in critical
articles and reviews. For information address HarperCollins Children's Books,
a division of HarperCollins Publishers, 195 Broadway, New York, NY 10007.
www.epicreads.com

Library of Congress Control Number: 2023930683
ISBN 978-0-06-306030-2

Typography by Jessie Gang
23 24 25 26 27  LBC  5 4 3 2 1

First Edition

For the neurodivergent darlings,
your brain is lovely and so are you.

# A NOTE FROM THE AUTHOR

This book deals with issues of bullying, slut shaming, sexual harassment, rape culture, and the aftermath of an off-page rape. I have done my best to depict these topics with care and sensitivity. If these are difficult subjects for you, please look after yourself and know that your mental and emotional well-being comes first.

I want to mention why I chose to name a rapist in the title of my book. I believe there is power in naming predators. It holds them accountable for what they did and ensures no one will ever forget it. So many people can't name their Luis Ortegas in real life, so I wanted to give my main character the catharsis that comes with naming and shaming her abuser.

When I first started writing this book, I had no idea how many of my own scars would come to light. But scars are a beautiful sign of a healed wound. I found that by telling Ari's story, I was healing myself. I hope this story provides healing for other readers out there as well.

# ONE

The driver looks at me like he knows exactly what I just did. I run my fingers through my cold, sweaty hair and smooth out my black dress for the millionth time since I walked out of that party. The cute wrap dress with slits revealing some of the skin on my ribcage gave me the confidence to break out of my shell, which I'm now wishing I never did. I've been waiting outside for a while now, numb to the music thumping from inside the house behind me. Numb to the chatter from the backyard and to the buzzing on my phone from Luis texting me to forget the ride and come back inside.

Waiting in the cold was better than spending one more second at that sensory hell of a party. Besides, it's not like Phoenix gets freezing cold, even in February. I step in the car, and the driver sizes me up through the rearview mirror.

"Uh . . . Luis, is it?"

I break eye contact with the mirror and stare at the cup holder in the backseat filled with breath mints—he must really want a five-star rating. I'm definitely not Luis, but he doesn't need to know that. Luis called a rideshare for me since he's eighteen and I wanted to leave. I know I'm not technically allowed to be in this car without an adult, but I'll take whatever trouble I might get in for taking this ride over being that close to Luis again. All I want to do is go home and sleep. No, I want to shower first. I smell like Luis, and for once, I'm not enjoying that smell.

The driver clears his throat. I force myself to make eye contact with his reflection in the mirror and nod.

Can the driver see your picture when you use the app? Aside from our similar medium-brown skin tones, I look nothing like Luis. I don't have his pretty gray eyes, and my straight-haired bob looks nothing like his curly fade. Plus, he's tall and fit while I'm five one and thick as hell with big ole scoliosis boobs. But I could be Luis, as far as this driver knows. Hopefully he can't tell I'm only sixteen.

After another quick look down from the mirror, he finally chuckles and starts driving. Thank God.

"Okay, *Luis*. Where are we headed?"

I don't answer. Isn't the driver supposed to know where they're going? Luis put my address in. Does he want to know if we're going to my house? The thought of a random driver knowing where I live makes my skin crawl.

"So . . . how was your night?" the driver asks. I look out the window instead of answering and watch the party house disappear as we turn the corner. I hope I never have to see that house again.

If I could bring myself to answer his question, I'd say my

night sucked. Like, *really* sucked. I'd say I had sex for the first time, and I hated every second of it. I made an enemy out of Shawni, too. *Shawni*, aka the nicest girl I've ever met. She lent me a pencil last month when I forgot to bring one to class, and she sometimes holds the door open for me. Okay, she holds it open for lots of people, but still. Now she probably wants to kill me. She told me to stay away from Luis and I didn't, even though I knew she wasn't over him after their breakup.

I'm a terrible person.

"Quiet type, huh?" the driver asks. He has no idea. If he keeps asking questions, this will be an awkward ride, because I literally don't talk.

My mom says I won't, but I just don't. Not to anyone besides my parents and sometimes my journalism teacher, Mrs. Jones— but other times I can't even talk to any of them. My parents don't believe in psychiatrists or therapy or doctors or any of that "big pharma" crap, so Google diagnosed me. Autism with a heavy dose of selective mutism, I'm pretty sure.

I used to think of myself as the Little Mermaid, whose voice was stolen by a sea witch. My voice comes back when I feel completely safe, which is really only ever at home. It makes having a social life in high school pretty much impossible. Which is why this party was such a big deal. No one ever expected me to actually show up.

Luis is the only person who ever tries to talk to me. He says he doesn't mind that I don't talk back. He's always been so nice to me.

I wish he hadn't been.

It would make hating him right now a lot easier. But he's always made me feel special somehow, ever since the first time he spoke to me. The first time *anyone* at school did.

I remember the day he first introduced himself to me at the beginning of the school year. I was sitting alone at lunch and he took the seat across from me.

"Ariana, right?" he'd said. "I'm Luis." He'd said my name with a hard *r*, like my mom always insists on.

I blushed and nodded.

"You look lonely." The dimple on his left cheek deepened. "Are you?"

I shook my head no and smiled. Not then, I wasn't.

"You don't have to say anything, Ariana. I just want to look at you."

At the time, I thought it was sweet that he didn't mind my silence. Now I feel like that's the *reason* he liked me.

He didn't even ask me if I wanted to have sex with him. Just kind of assumed. I mean, I did . . . I think. Maybe not, I don't know. He should have asked. Is that a thing? Don't people ask before having sex? It should be a thing if it's not.

"Rough night?" the driver asks. I almost forgot he was there.

He probably wasn't expecting me to burst into tears at the question. I don't even know why I'm crying. I had a crush on Luis before he ever spoke to me. Everyone does. This is all I wanted, for someone to pay attention to me. And he did more than pay attention to me. So why do I hate myself right now?

"Woah, look, it's going to be alright . . ." He gives me an awkward smile like someone is holding him at gunpoint to make him comfort me. I wipe my nose with my arm and cry into my hands as the car slows down.

We pull up to my apartment complex, and I'm out of the car the second it stops. I wave a quick goodbye and run to my building, not bothering to wipe the tears flooding from my eyes. I'm sure I would be making a scene if there were anyone around to see, but the apartment complex is dead right now. When I reach my building, I can't bring myself to go up the stairs. I hope my parents are already asleep because I don't want to face their questions. I don't want to talk about any of this, ever.

Instead of going up, I sit on the steps in the cold and throw up between my knees on the cement.

# TWO

When I finally gather the courage to go inside, the lights are already out. I can hear my mom snoring from her spot on the couch, where she's been sleeping on and off for the last year or so, ever since my dad caught her cheating. The only one who greets me is my black cat, Boo, who mews and rubs herself on my calf.

"Shhh . . ." I whisper as I crouch down to pet her. If I don't, she won't stop meowing and it'll wake up my mom. It's too dark to see, so I use my phone to light the way to the bathroom. I tiptoe across the living room and down the hall to keep the floorboards from creaking as I make my way to the safety of the bathroom and quietly shut the door.

I'm so not looking forward to tomorrow when my parents will ask me about the party and the first boy—person—I ever brought over to the house. I'm not looking forward to Monday when I'll see Luis at school. And I'm *really* not looking forward to seeing Shawni.

If she didn't hate me before the party, she definitely does now. I think she put together what was happening before I did. The music and all the people at the party were giving me a sensory overload, making my skin crawl and my ears burn. I thought Luis was being considerate by taking me to a quiet room. When we were heading into the room together, Shawni happened to be coming out of the bathroom. She looked like she was going to cry when she saw Luis and me. Then she looked angry.

"What are you doing with *her*?" she had asked. Ouch.

"We're just gonna talk," he'd said.

And I believed him.

Shawni clearly didn't. She just ran out the door and left. I didn't get why she was upset then. I thought we were just getting away from the noise.

No one saw us go in the room but Shawni. Maybe no one else has to find out.

I don't see Luis as the type to go running his mouth, but I text him anyway.

**Me:** Please don't tell anyone what happened, okay?

I put my phone down on the sink and take off my clothes, ready to wash Luis's touch off my body. I stare at what *would* have been the bathroom mirror but is now completely hidden by a sheet taped to the edges. My mom covered all the mirrors in the house about a year ago. It annoyed me for a while, but tonight, I'm grateful to not have to look at my naked body. Somehow I think seeing myself the way Luis saw me tonight would just make me throw up again.

I hop in the shower and turn on the water as hot as it'll go. It takes a while to warm up, but when it does, it's hot enough to singe Luis's smell from my skin. I should have listened to Shawni. She tried to warn me. Whether she did it out of jealousy or to look out for me, she was right.

"In case you didn't already know, he's using you." Shawni had come up to me the moment Luis left to get a drink at the party.

I rolled my eyes. She thought I was a rebound. And maybe she was right. But I'd never been anyone's anything before, so being someone's rebound was actually kind of exciting. If it turned out he had real feelings, I would probably die from exploding into glitter and rainbows. Especially when Luis could be with *Shawni*. I wasn't exactly in her league.

Shawni was gorgeous in a really effortless way. Her long box braids were tied in a low ponytail under her left ear. She didn't wear makeup or dress fancy or anything, but she was so hard to look away from. You could tell she was a dancer just by her appearance. Her posture, plus the shadows of muscle shaping her dark skin, gave her away. I looked at the ground instead of at Shawni when I realized I was staring, and tried not to think about how I was competing with *her* right now.

She kept talking, so I didn't bother getting out my phone to type out a response.

"Stay away from him, okay? I'm serious." I thought it was weird how she threatened me and gave me a sympathetic look at the same time. I didn't need her fake pity.

Shawni's going to kill me.

The look she gave me made me feel like she didn't believe I could be with someone like Luis. But the truth was that I could. She just didn't want me to be. Yesterday, being with Luis was all I could think about, but now thinking about him makes me sick.

I scrub everywhere Luis touched. My face. Hips. Thighs. Breasts. And . . .

I scrub so hard it hurts, but I still don't feel clean. When my hands are too tired to keep scrubbing, I fall onto the shower floor and hug my knees, letting the hot water hit my back. I don't know how long I'm sitting there like that, but by the time I get up, my skin is pruned and the water is cold. When I finally turn the water off and take a step out of the shower, my foot slides on the shower floor and I end up on my back.

"Fuck!" I shout. I don't mean to be so loud. Sometimes I can't help it. When I go so long without making a sound, it has to come out in little bursts. And right now, I need to let it out. I pull a towel over my face and cover my mouth with it. Then I scream, hoping the towel will muffle the sound enough to keep from waking up my parents, if I haven't woken them already.

My phone dings, and I'm scrambling out of the shower a second time. Luis's name is on my screen. If he doesn't agree to keep quiet, I don't know what I'll do. I'm afraid of what he might say: "Oops, too late, I already told everyone including Shawni and she's going to murder you."

My shoulders tighten and my throat dries at the thought. I open my lock screen to assess the damage.

Luis: Tell anyone what? ;)

I sigh out loud and sink back onto the floor in relief. No one has to know about this. I can just pretend like it never happened.

# THREE

I spend Saturday locked in my room, not even getting out of
bed to eat. Usually, when something's bothering me, I get up
and dance until I feel better. Or at least until I'm too tired to be
upset. Today, though, I just can't bring myself to move. I can
barely get up to go to the bathroom. Today is not a dancing day.
It's a sulking day, and that's okay. My dad knocks on my door
around noon.

"You hungry, mija?" he asks. He's rarely home on the
weekends, and if it were any other day, I'd be jumping at the
opportunity to spend time with him. He's always been so good
at making me feel better. He's really easy to talk to—at least
about problems that aren't his own. Talking to him about what
happened with my mom is like pulling teeth. I guess it's not a
problem he thinks he can solve. But I can't move. I can't even
talk. Papi opens the door and peeks inside when I don't answer.
"You okay?"

I can't look at him right now or I'll cry again, so I pull my sheets over my face and roll over.

He sighs. "I guess you want to be left alone. 'Stá bien, mija. I'll be here when you want to talk about it," he says gently. The problem is, he won't be. He's never home, and I'm wasting my chance to take advantage of him being here.

I shut my eyes when the door closes, but it opens again just a few minutes later, and my mom walks in, sitting herself on the edge of my bed.

"Well?" she asks with an anticipatory smile on her face.

"Well what?" I ask.

"How was the party? How are you and Luis? He seems like such a nice boy!"

The mention of his name clogs my throat, and I can't bring myself to utter another word, so I repeat what I did with my dad, pulling the covers over my head and rolling over.

My mom does not take the hint.

"May I?" she asks.

I let out an "aagh!" instead of the word *no*. She's asking me if she can touch me, probably to rub my back through the blanket, but I can't be touched right now.

There's a long pause. "Okay, mija. Let me know when you want to talk . . ." She sounds sad, but I can't think about her feelings right now.

I don't pull the blanket off myself until she gets up and leaves my room, clicking the door closed behind her.

I don't even bother feeling sorry for myself. I'm just numb. Just tired.

I'm not sure how much time I lose dissociating in my bed. Boo is sitting on my chest purring like she does when she's worried about me. I heard cats don't just purr when they're happy, but they also purr when they're stressed as a way of self-soothing. When I'm stressed, Boo sometimes snuggles up and purrs on my chest, and I think it's her way of trying to make me feel better.

I stare at the dark spot in the ceiling where the white paint is peeling. And even though it doesn't feel like that much time has passed, the setting sun lights my room with an orange tint from my bedroom window. The sounds of rush hour traffic outside are already dying down, and I still can't move.

So I sleep.

Or try to. The sun goes down and the lights go out, but my mind won't rest. I stay laying restlessly in bed for hours until I finally check my phone. It's almost three in the morning. Thank God tomorrow's Sunday. Today. Whatever.

I stretch out my leg, looking for Boo at the foot of it to bring me comfort, but she's not there. I sigh and hunch over the side of my bed, peeking underneath it. Boo's big green eyes stare back. Sometimes she sleeps underneath my bed, but I wish she'd just stay consistent.

"It's okay, Boo," I say, making kissy noises to try to coax her out from under the bed, but she doesn't budge. I flop back down in bed and close my eyes, trying my best to fall back asleep, but it's no use. My mind is too loud for sleep. All I can think about is last night. I keep replaying it in my head, wondering if there was something I could have done differently, but I come up blank every time. There's no way I can sleep if I can't get *him* out of my head.

I reach for my headphones on my nightstand and start playing my emo playlist on Spotify. This is what I usually listen to when I'm feeling shitty for any reason. After two songs I'm fully awake and fully emo, and I need to get it out somehow. I usually don't just get up and dance in the middle of the night— it's mostly a "get out my pent-up after-school anxiety" kind of thing, but I'm tired of lying in bed sulking, and a good dance vent seems like the only thing to get it all out of my head right now.

I sit up in bed, starting out just using my upper body, waving my arms around and throwing my head from side to side. But eventually my whole body wants to move, so I crawl out of bed. I put my hands on my knees and start flipping my hair wildly, and then I throw myself on the floor into a somersault. I get back on my feet and attack the air in front of me, punching and kicking and swinging my arms as close to on beat as I can manage. I pretend Luis is standing there, and that I wouldn't feel guilty beating the shit out of him for how he made me feel last night.

For the first time, I give myself permission to fight. To feel my feelings where no one else can see. I throw myself onto the floor again and kick my foot in the air, then roll so I'm on my belly on the floor. I throw my head back and close my eyes, and then I let myself fall to the ground, and I just lie there for the rest of the song. I don't realize I'm crying until the music fades out.

I let myself sob until I finally fall asleep, right there on the floor.

It isn't until Monday rolls around that I'm forced to get out of bed. I snooze my alarm again and again until I completely run out of time to get ready. There's no point in waking up early today. Besides, Boo is cuddled up next to me, and isn't it against some kind of law to move a sleeping cat?

Usually, I wake up at least an hour before I have to leave for school so I can pick out an outfit and straighten my hair. Normally, I try to wear something that will get me noticed, to make up for my lack of talking, even though it never really works. People ignore me no matter what I wear.

I don't care about that today, though. I lay in bed staring at the plastic stars stuck to the corner of my bedroom ceiling. Two of them are still glowing, but most of them lost their glow years ago.

It's almost as if Boo knows I'm running late, because she stretches and hops off my bed, freeing me to get up. I usually look forward to going to school. I'm good at it, and something about the structure and predictable schedule makes my little autistic heart happy. But today, I'm dreading it. I finally force myself to throw my comforter off and roll out of bed. Posters and articles of Jose Antonio Vargas, Ida B. Wells, Janna Jihad, and other journalists I look up to line my walls. Janna

Jihad (a young Palestinian journalist and my current biggest inspiration) would tell me to get up and make my mark today. But that's what I thought I was doing when I went to that party . . .

I head toward my closet and push through all the rompers and colorful dresses. Nothing feels right. Today isn't like other days. Today, I don't want to be noticed, let alone look in a mirror.

I throw on a pair of sweatpants and a baggy sweater, then grab my pocketknife and stick it in my sweatpants pocket. My mom gave it to me about a year ago, when I started regularly walking around by myself. She said you can never be too careful, and I think she's right. I always take it with me since I walk to and from school alone. Our apartment is only a five-minute walk from school, but it still makes me feel safer.

Part of me wishes I pulled the knife on Luis at that party. I dig my nails into my palms. I totally had the power to make him stop, and I just . . . didn't. What is wrong with me?

I force myself to stop thinking about it by making eggs on toast for myself and Mom and Dad. I set both their plates down on the kitchen counter for them to find later. Mami's still sleeping on the couch. I try to leave before my dad comes out of his room for work. I shovel down my own toast and walk quietly toward the door. Just as I reach for the knob, his bedroom door opens.

"Morning, mija. How was that party? Do you want to talk about it?" he asks. I knew he'd bring it up eventually since he knows *something* happened based on my behavior over the weekend.

"It was . . . fine." I shrug. I wish he wouldn't ask because I don't like lying to my dad. I reach for the doorknob again so he doesn't try to prolong the conversation. Instead of asking more questions, he rushes over to me and kisses my forehead.

"Thanks for breakfast. Have a good day at school, mija."

"You're welcome. Thanks, Papi."

I walk the entire way to school with my hands in my pockets, secretly clutching my knife. This is normal for me since I've always been paranoid about getting mugged. It's cold out, for Arizona—which means it's about sixty degrees. That's enough for most people here to assume my hands are in my pockets to keep warm. Usually I keep my eyes peeled the whole walk in case anyone comes near me, but today I can't bring myself to care. Two kids pass me, and I don't even notice they're behind me until they breeze by. If someone were going to try to mug me, today would be their lucky day.

When I get to school, I weave through the students standing around outside, cutting through the courtyard and walking through the way-too-green fake grass until I make it to the safety of indoors. I head for the biggest building on campus, where there is a good number of kids walking the halls. Usually when I come in here in the mornings it's completely empty, but since I woke up late today, I don't get to be alone.

But there is one room I know that's always safe. I go straight for the journalism classroom minutes before the bell rings. Mrs.

Jones is usually here early. She says I'm always welcome to hang out in here before school, so I come before the bell when I wake up early enough. She encourages me since she knows I want to be an investigative journalist one day. Mami says I can't be a journalist if I don't learn how to talk, but so many interviews are over email now. I don't think I'll have to do a lot of talking. Ironically, one of the few places I feel safe enough to use my voice is in this room with Mrs. Jones. Well, before anyone else gets here, at least.

Mrs. Jones sits behind her desk and doesn't take her eyes off the paper in front of her when I walk in the room. She clicks her pen and writes something down.

"What's on your mind, Ariana?" she asks without lifting her eyes as I settle into my desk. This is how she usually greets me.

"Bad weekend," I mumble, letting my eyes wander to the wall next to me where student articles are plastered all over, most of them mine.

A smile betrays my sour mood when I see the article I wrote about the dress codes here being sexist. That article actually got the school's attention, and they amended the language in the rule book.

"Everything all right?" Mrs. Jones glances up from the paper and looks at me, eyebrows raised.

"No," I admit, the question pulling me back down to reality. I've never really been able to bring myself to lie to Mrs. Jones, and today is no exception.

"Well, if you want to talk about it, I'm here." She smiles at me and puts down her pen. I make myself smile back. I appreciate her, but I don't want to talk about what happened with Luis.

But no matter how little I want to think about him, I can't avoid him much longer, since I have class with both Luis and Shawni. My chest gets tight and it's hard to breathe when I think about him now, but I still find myself counting down the minutes before the first bell. What is wrong with me?

The fact that I'm still craving his attention pisses me off. I just want to be mad at him like a normal person. But do I even have the right to be mad at him?

I should have the right. Sex might not be important to him, but it's a big deal to me, and he's acting like it's not. Any kind of physical contact at *all* is hard for me. He should have figured that out after the first time he tried to hug me.

He had just walked me home from school for the first time, and apparently goodbye hugs are A Thing. When he put his hands on me without warning, I screamed and pulled my knife on him. It was a really embarrassing overreaction, but it was true to how much I hate being touched without some kind of warning. He laughed and apologized, but he still went for another hug. My scream and knife didn't stop him because I couldn't actually say the word "no."

I wanted to be able to hug him. I hated that I overreacted. Maybe I'm overreacting now, too.

I don't want to think about it. I just want to go back to how it was before, when his smile gave me butterflies and not a pit in my stomach.

Hearing Shawni's name pulls me out of my thoughts. Jessica and Melanie walk into class early and they're talking about her. People talk about Shawni a lot. Especially them—probably because they're close friends with Luis.

I start eavesdropping.

"Did you hear Shawni got Manny to cheat on his girlfriend with her at that party?" Jessica says in a tone that sounds like she's trying to be discreet, but she's clearly talking loud enough for anyone who came to class early to hear.

If I had my voice right now, I would correct them. Shawni left right after she saw me go in the room with Luis. She didn't have sex with anyone at that party, not that it's anyone's business who did or didn't have sex . . . I'm just surprised they aren't talking about *me*.

But whether anyone had sex with anyone is not the point. It annoys me that they're implying Manny cheating on his girlfriend is somehow not Manny's fault.

"Yeah, I heard about that. She just lets anyone with a heartbeat get in her pants. Like, have some self-respect!" Melanie says.

That one hits harder. I know they aren't talking about me, but they might as well be. I *do* have self-respect. So does Shawni, I'm sure. I feel guilty for not sticking up for her, even if she hates me. But I can't just make myself speak at will. It doesn't work like that.

The bell rings, and it's a minute before anyone else comes in the room. I bounce my leg, watching the door. Ugh, why the hell am I so eager? Shawni comes in, and she's not with Luis. I hate that I care if she's with Luis. I don't want to care about him, or her. I look away but keep her in my peripheral vision to try to see if she's giving me a murder stare or something. She's walking right toward me.

My heart beats three times as fast as her footsteps. Shit shit shit shit shit shit. I glue my eyes to my desk as she sits down right in front of me and turns around.

She pulls her notebook out of her bag and rips a page out of it, then puts it on my desk with a pencil. She checks the time on her smartwatch, then looks back at me, probably deciding there's enough time to chew me out properly.

"Hey." She leans forward, and I can't help but look. Her lips curve upward a tiny bit, and her eyes flicker down to the pencil and back up at me. She looks so pleased with herself. Honestly, I can't believe she's talking to me. I take the pencil.

*Hey*, I write on the paper. She adjusts her beanie before responding.

"So . . . about Saturday. I have some questions."

I can't tell if she's messing with me, or if she actually wants to know. Is she just trying to find out for sure what happened with me and Luis? I'm sure she's already put it together, but maybe she wants some kind of confirmation? I raise an eyebrow, waiting for her to go on.

Her nostrils flare when she speaks. "About Luis—"

Luis walks in before she gets a chance to ask. My stomach drops. I try not to give anything away in my body language or my face, but it's hard. Luis is wearing jeans and a gray T-shirt tight enough to show off his lean chest muscles. He looks right at me and grins, dimple on full display. I hate that cute little dimple so much. Shawni looks at me, then at him, and sends him a glare that could pierce skin.

He's about to walk over when he notices her glare, and then he turns around and takes a seat across the room with Jessica and Melanie, who both seem more than happy to cozy up to him. Shawni looks back at me, her glare melting away into a sad look. Probably because I betrayed her. Then her eyes go intense again. "You know what I'm trying to ask, right?"

Oh God. She's going to kill me.

I take the easy way out and play the fool, shaking my head innocently.

She frowns. "Okay. It's like I said at the party. You need to stay away from him. For your own good. He's m—"

But the next bell rings before she can finish. Was that a threat? She takes the paper from my desk and starts writing. And writing, and writing. Is she writing a freaking novel? She finally folds it up and turns around to give it to me.

"Shanaya, no passing notes in class. Hand it over." Mrs. Jones stops writing on the board and walks in front of Shawni's desk, holding out her hand. Shawni slumps forward and puts the folded-up paper in her palm. I guess the world will never know what her little novel was about. Though I have a feeling it was some kind of long-winded threat about what she'll do to me if I go near Luis again. Even though the thought of Luis makes me sick now, the idea of being threatened about it doesn't sit right with me.

Shawni looks back at me and mouths the words "we'll talk later," then turns back around.

I spend the day stressing about when "later" is. When I'm walking to my third class of the day, I feel like everyone's staring at me. No, I don't *feel* like it, they *are*. But it feels all wrong. I'm in sweats and a hoodie, not my usual "look at me" clothes. And no one was looking at me in the beginning of the day.

For a moment, I wonder if they noticed that I didn't put effort into my outfit today. But then I start to hear the murmurs, see them nudging each other and gesturing at me instead like I'm some kind of circus attraction. I check the bottoms of my sneakers for toilet paper or something. I smooth out the top of my short hair in case there's something sticking out from it. There's nothing, but they stare anyway.

Oh no.

What if they know what happened between me and Luis? It's the only reason I can think of, but how can it be true? The only person who might even suspect it is Shawni, but she doesn't even know anything for sure, does she? All she knows is that we went in the bedroom together. Alone.

Shit.

She must have told everyone, or even just someone, and the rumor spread.

I turn on my heel and head to the bathroom instead of to

my next class. How am I supposed to face Shawni for the "talk later" today? How am I supposed to face Luis?

I tell myself I might just be overreacting. Maybe no one knows and I just have something in my teeth. Everyone's stares bore into me as I walk. I clutch the straps of my backpack and look forward. I walk faster, and faster, until I end up breaking out into a sprint to the bathroom. No one moves for me, so I have to shove past people who give me dirty looks as I run by. When I get to the bathroom, I lock myself in a stall and sit on the toilet with the seat down.

The door opens again, and there are two familiar voices. I pull my legs up and hug my knees so they don't see me.

"I can't believe I missed Manny's party," Jessica whines. "Did they really do it in his room?"

"That's what I heard."

"Oh, my God, who would have guessed *she'd* be such a slut . . ."

My chest tightens and I hold my breath. Are they talking about me? Who else could they be talking about? Maybe they're talking about Shawni, like this morning . . .

The bell rings, and the girls leave me alone. I stay put. I can't bring myself to go to my next class. I just can't. So I sit on the toilet alone for the rest of the hour, carefully watching the time pass on my phone.

The time ticks by slower and slower, like it's slowing down just for me so I can catch my breath. Okay, breathe. I don't have any proof Jessica and Melanie were talking about me. Maybe this is all just in my head. Besides, I'm hungry as hell, and it's almost lunch. I decide I'm going to go for round two of the staring just so I can eat something.

When the bell rings for lunch, I leave the bathroom in a hurry and book it for the cafeteria. That way I don't have to notice anyone staring. I sit in my usual table all by myself, hoping Shawni doesn't ambush me when she gets here. I'm glad Mom made one of my safe foods over the weekend, so I can have plain chicken flautas for lunch without having a panic attack. We have an open campus for lunch, but I always eat at school. I scan the cafeteria looking for Shawni, and I notice more than just a few people are still looking at me.

I ignore them and find Shawni standing alone in the lunch line, like she normally does. The kids standing in front and behind her are both in little groups, so Shawni looks extra alone today, even though she almost always is, even before Luis. She never had the greatest reputation at school, since she kind of gets painted as this really promiscuous girl just because she's bi. Which is really shitty.

She hasn't exactly been nice to me recently. I might have once considered her my only friend, but I guess being sort of friends in second grade doesn't mean much when you steal someone's boyfriend. Ex. Still.

Well, I don't know if you could actually have called us friends, but I always liked her back then. In second grade, we were the only two kids who never talked. Shawni's English wasn't that great yet since Spanish was her first language, and I just . . . didn't talk. Teachers always assumed I only spoke Spanish, too, because I'm Mexican. So I would always get paired with Shawni. Our teacher probably thought we would talk to each other, but that didn't happen. She tried talking to me, but I couldn't talk in English or Spanish. Not outside of the comfort of my home. Still, there was a kind of solidarity that came from always being partnered together. I didn't mind it, and neither did she. We were silent buddies that year and some of the next. Eventually, Shawni's English got better and she stopped getting paired with me. Maybe that relationship never meant anything to Shawni, but for me, she was my first and only friend. And now she hates me. I guess that part is deserved.

I'm pretty sure Luis was Shawni's only friend. Even though I'm not her biggest fan anymore, I don't really get why she doesn't have other friends. She's talented, gorgeous, and nice to everyone. It doesn't make sense.

When she gets her food, I hang my head so we don't make eye contact. I'm not in a hurry to see Shawni in dance next period, but I don't know how much longer I can stretch out avoiding her. Someone sits across from me, and I look up expecting to see Luis or Shawni. It's neither of them, and I hate that I'm disappointed it's not Luis. What the hell is wrong with me?

I don't know this guy. All I know is he used to be on the football team with Luis, and I've seen them hanging out before.

"Hey, baby. I'm Jesus." He looks me up and down way too slowly.

I just stare at him. Why is he talking to me?

"You look pretty." He grins.

I try to tell him to go away with my eyes, but when he doesn't listen, I look back down. I feel my face burning up.

"My parents don't come home until late . . . Want to come over after school?"

I feel like throwing up. Why would he think . . . Does *everyone* know? Maybe it's just a coincidence.

I get up to leave, but he grabs my hand. The fire from his touch sears through my skin and into the bones, and I'm frozen.

"Hey, I'm just trying to be nice."

I'm about to run out of the cafeteria when a freshman girl with green hair grabs him firmly by the shoulders. Jesus looks just as thrown off as I am.

"Why aren't you with your friends, Jesus?"

"Um, do I know you?" he asks, then gets a better look at her. "Ohhh, you're the girl from that list! Nina, right?" He laughs meanly. That's when I recognize her.

Earlier this year, a list went around on Instagram. The "100 sluttiest girls at Westview" list. Nina was the number one spot. Shawni was top ten.

Somehow, she doesn't look bothered by his laughter. "That's me," she says with a smirk. "Now are you going to leave Ariana alone?" she asks, hands still on his shoulders.

He tries to shrug them off, but she digs her fingers in and starts giving him this really threatening-looking massage. He finally swats her hands off and walks away.

"Not so fun when it happens to you, is it!" Nina calls out as he leaves, giving her a disgusted look.

"Hi, I'm Nina." She leans in and holds her hand out enthusiastically. When she gets closer, I realize how moisture starved her green hair is. Which isn't surprising, since every time I've seen her before she's had a different hair color. Her outstretched arm is covered in bracelets and rubber bands. I take her hand and shake it. She did save me, after all.

There's no awkward pause like there usually is when people wait for me to respond. She just keeps talking.

"That pendejo is a huge dick with a tiny dick. You don't want to have sex with him, trust me."

My eyes widen and I shake my head to tell her there's no way I was going to anyway. Does she know, too? How would this freshman girl even find out?

"Oh, don't worry, there's no slut-shaming in my house! Anyways, nice meeting you." She waves and leaves me alone again as quickly as she came. I want to run after her and set things straight. If Jesus and this random freshman girl know I had sex, who else does? Who told them? I get out my phone to text Luis.

Me: Did you say anything?

Luis: say anything about what? ;)

Me: I'm serious.

Luis: no, I wouldn't do that to you love.

If Luis didn't tell anyone, that leaves only one other culprit. Shawni.

All this time I was afraid I had hurt her feelings.

I knew she was mad, and I was prepared for some kind of retaliation, but not *this*. I didn't think she would go so far as to tell everyone, because she knows exactly what it's like to have these kinds of rumors spread. She must really hate me.

I have dance soon, but I can't see her right now. I can't. I can't.

If I make it off campus before lunch is over, no one can stop me from running all the way home.

So I run.

# FOUR

I don't want to go back to school. Not ever. Not when Shawni's there. And everyone else who now knows about what I did at that party. What Luis did.

Is this a good enough reason to drop out of school? Mom and Dad would laugh in my face for even suggesting it, but it feels like a damn good reason to me.

I shoot my mom a text saying I went home sick so I don't get in trouble if she comes home early, and then I just curl up in bed lazily petting Boo. So, it's clear now that people know what happened between me and Luis. But no one's heard *my* side of the story. And no one probably cares to.

Before long, I hear the apartment door opening. Before I can panic about someone potentially breaking in, Mami calls out, "I brought you some caldo de pollo, mija!"

Then the door to my room opens, and in she comes. She sits on the edge of my bed with a takeout bag from El Rancho Market, then pulls out a to-go bowl of soup and places it on my nightstand.

"I didn't know if you missed lunch or not, so I thought I'd bring you some sopa just in case."

"Thank you, Mami." For some reason, the simple gesture makes me want to cry. She doesn't know what's going on with me or why I came home "sick," but she's doing what she can to look after me, and I appreciate it so, so much.

She leans forward and kisses my forehead. "I have to go back to work, now. I'm working a double today, so I had some time between shifts to drop by. I'll be back in a few hours!"

A small twinge knots my stomach at the mention of her newish job. She used to work as a marketing manager at a big corporate office, but after she cheated on Papi with her boss there, she quit. I guess the guilt ate her up, and now she works as a server at a restaurant and has to hustle three times as hard to make half the money. I shoo the unpleasant feeling away. At least she's trying. All I can do is give her a small smile as thanks as she leaves, since my voice is caught in my throat.

Even though I already ate, I decide to enjoy the soup Mami brought me. I don't know what it is about caldo de pollo, but it always makes me feel better. Sure, it's better when Mami is the one who makes it, but takeout will have to do for today.

When I'm finished, I avoid thinking about everything with a good, long depression nap. I wish I could just sleep through the night into tomorrow, or better yet, into next week or next month when all of this blows over. But, no, I wake up only three short hours later.

I open my laptop and go to my comfort website, Expose-TheMierda. It's a blog dedicated to featuring stories that "expose the shit" that usually gets buried or covered up by those in power. These are the kinds of stories I want to tell when I'm a journalist. My dream is to one day write a story good enough to be featured on the site. I've submitted every article and essay I've ever written, and while Mrs. Jones is always so impressed, I've never gotten anything more than a form rejection from ExposeTheMierda. I was hoping they'd post my dress code article at least, but I got the same form rejection as always.

I scroll through the blog, hoping they've posted a new story since I last checked. The latest one is from an anonymous whistleblower about an abusive politician. It was one of the bigger stories on the blog, blowing up so much that the politician actually issued an apology. So, it makes sense that it would take a while for them to post another story.

I sigh and pull up Instagram to distract myself with the usual mindless scrolling. But I have more notifications than I've had in my entire life—which, to be fair, aren't many.

I brace myself for the hate comments, but they aren't there. I guess I'm a little paranoid. Since Shawni doesn't really have any friends, I don't know why I was expecting a mob. What I do have is thirty new followers, which is double my previous count. Mostly boys. And Shawni, and a few others I don't recognize. What the hell is going on?

I also have a few messages, so I go through those. One of them is from the guy who threw that hell party. Manny, I think his name was. I open that one first.

Didn't know you had it in you . . .

I block him. Next message.

Hey beautiful :)

Blocked. Next message.

How come we never talked before cutie?

If I'd gotten this kind of attention a week ago, I would have melted. I would have felt important and beautiful and *seen*. But now I know better. The only reason they're all talking to me is because they know I had sex with Luis. Do they think just because I had sex with Luis that I would do it with them, too? Would it kill people to be nice without having ulterior motives?

I open the next message. It's from the guy from lunch today. Jesus.

Jesus: Hey, sorry if I made you uncomfortable today. I didn't mean to scare you.

He seems sorry enough right now, so against all instinct, I respond.

Me: Thanks for saying that. But you shouldn't just go around hitting on girls you don't know.

Jesus: So let me get to know you mija ;)

I roll my eyes so hard it gives me a headache. "Mija," really? Does he think it's cute to call me that or something? Because it's not. My parents call me mija. Jesus and I are the same age, so it just feels condescending. I have no desire to "get to know him," especially because I know exactly what he wants from me. What apparently everyone wants from me now. I'd like to think I wouldn't have given Luis the time of day if I'd known from the beginning that's what he wanted. But I'm not sure if that's true. I don't respond to Jesus, but after a few minutes, he's in my DMs again.

**Jesus:** ????

**Me:** No thank you.

**Jesus:** I heard all it takes is a couple of compliments. If that's true I don't want you anyway . . .

No. *No.* That's not true at all. Is it? Is my self-esteem so low that I fell for Luis just because he said some nice things to me? Because he *looked* at me? All Luis did was tell me I didn't have to talk. He told me what I wanted—needed—to hear and I was wrapped around his finger.

Did he know how badly I needed someone to treat me like a person? Did he know it would be that easy from the start?

No, that can't be right. That would make me pretty pathetic. I must have had other reasons for liking Luis. I might not be able to think of them right now, but I had them, I swear. I don't need some guy to tell me I'm worth loving. Not even worth loving. Just a little attention.

Bile threatens to rise in my throat. Is this what it's going to be like now? Maybe I can fix this. Shawni is Luis's ex, so people will probably believe me over her anyway. I can get her back. I can just say she's lying. I can pretend it never happened. It never happened . . .

I grab my laptop and start typing furiously in my notes. Heat flows to my ears as I type. It's almost an out-of-body experience. I'm not the type of person to lie about myself online. Except I am. I'm lying right now, and I can't say I feel too bad about it. The truth is no one's business anyway. I write what I wish had happened, instead of what actually did. Once I'm happy with what I've written, I screenshot it and post it to Instagram.

*I just want to come forward and clear my name. I did NOT have sex with Luis. Nothing happened between us. He is a friend to me and that is the extent of our relationship. We went in the room together to get away from all the noise, and we talked. That's it. Any other fuckboys who take this RUMOR as an excuse to be disgusting need to stay away from me. I did not have sex with Luis, and I am not going to have sex with anyone else. Please leave me alone.*

It isn't long before I get my first passive-aggressive like, from Shawni. It pisses me off so much that I have to get up and pace my room. Boo meows her annoyance at my getting off the bed, but I ignore her. Does Shawni not know I KNOW it was her? Maybe it's just her way of acknowledging that she *does* know? I wish she would just tell me what she's thinking instead of me having to try to decode this freaking Instagram like.

Then my phone buzzes with my first reply, and I scramble back to the bed to grab my phone and check what it says. It's from Luis.

Friends huh? Good to know . . .

Heat pours through my face, ears, and chest. Dammit. Part of me is angry with him for not just going along with it, at least on my public post, but I also feel guilty. Was I more than just a rebound after all? Why would that even *matter* to me? I don't want to want Luis, but I do, and I hate myself for it. I hate myself for ruining it, and I hate myself for caring that I ruined it. But I also hate Luis for making me feel this way.

The front door opens before I can think too hard about it. Mami's home from work. I wait while the sounds of her footsteps near my room. She knocks on my door but opens it before I get a chance to respond to the knock.

"Come in, Mami," I say, and sit up straight in my bed. I'm surprised I can even talk at all right now after the day I just had. Maybe I'm just feeling emboldened by the post I made. It was pretty ballsy of me, if I do say so myself.

My mom walks in and sits at the edge of the bed like she does every day after she gets home from work.

"How was your day, mija?" she asks.

"It sucked ass," I say, for some reason incapable of lying anymore.

"Language." She gives me a disapproving look but wraps her arms around me.

"Sorry," I say, and lean into her embrace.

"Would you mind?" she asks, and after I nod my approval, she starts rubbing my back. I soak up the moment, letting her touch melt away the anxieties left over from that post. "So, ¿que te pasa? How are you and Luis? Did something happen with you two?"

"I don't want to talk about Luis," I say grumpily. "How are you and Dad?" I shoot back, knowing I'm out of line, since we both know their relationship is a sore subject. But she should know how it feels.

"I don't want to talk about your papi," she echoes. I feel a little guilty, but at least I got her off my back about Luis.

For a while, she just sits there, rubbing my back, waiting for me to open up, but I don't do it. If I don't say anything, maybe she'll keep rubbing my back. Mami's touches aren't like Luis's. Hers are safe. I could fall asleep like this, even though I just woke up. I'd rather fall back asleep than talk about any of it.

"*Manos*," she scolds, and pulls my hand away from my face. I don't usually realize I'm sucking on my knuckles until she makes me stop. It's a self-soothing habit I've had since I was little. I guess it's sort of like sucking your thumb, but I never grew out of it. I get why she doesn't want me to do it in public since it's not "socially acceptable" or whatever, but I don't understand why she won't let me comfort myself in my own home. I wrap my arms around myself instead.

My phone buzzes, but I ignore it. Mami wouldn't be happy if I checked it while we were having a moment.

"So, don't you want to know about your mama's day?" she asks with a grin, and part of me thinks she's just trying to cheer me up, but the other part knows she doesn't really have anyone else to talk to about these kinds of things.

I honestly don't really feel like I have the capacity to offer my mom any kind of support right now, but she's so lonely I can't turn her down. Since she doesn't really have any other friends, and she and my dad don't always get along, she says I'm her best friend. I guess she's my best friend, too, but sometimes I kind of wish we both had more than just each other to talk to.

It would probably hurt her feelings if I let her comfort me and bring me soup only to not let her tell me about her day, so I give in. "How was your day, Mami?"

She goes on to tell me all about her work drama. Apparently two other servers quit on the spot, leaving my mom and the others to pick up their slack. Which means she got paid barely anything today since they were so understaffed and no one wanted to tip for the "poor service." Then she goes on to talk shit about the people who quit. I guess they were a couple of white people complaining about "forced diversity" or whatever, as if that's even a thing. I won't lie, I do like hearing *some* of my mom's gossip. She's funny and a really entertaining storyteller.

My phone keeps buzzing, and my fingers itch to check it, but I leave it. When Mami's finally worn herself out, she sighs and gets up.

"Well, I guess dinner won't make itself, will it?" She laughs and kisses me on my forehead before leaving the room.

Now that I can finally check my phone, I'm not sure I want to. But my anxiety won't go away until I do, so I check my notifications. There are so many responses. Some of them are supportive, but most aren't. One of them in particular stares me down harder than the rest . . .

Shut up and face the consequences of your slut actions.

# FIVE

I don't know what I was expecting. I guess I was hoping everyone would just believe me and then leave me alone. But that's definitely not what's happening. Most of my comments at this point are people calling me a liar and a slut. My chest tightens so it's harder to breathe with every notification I get.

I can't read them. I lied about this whole thing so people would leave me alone, but what if I hadn't said anything? I ended up making things so much worse.

The screen gets blurry every time I even try to look, and I don't know if it's because I'm tearing up or dissociating again. Either way, it doesn't stop the notifications from coming.

I can't deal with it, so I do something that *will* stop the notifications. I deactivate my Instagram before anyone else gets a chance to say something.

There. It only got twenty likes and a few comments. Hopefully people will just forget about it. The only thing worse than everyone knowing I had sex with Luis is everyone knowing I lied about *not* having sex with Luis.

I'm pulled out of my thoughts when my mom knocks on my door again. She doesn't wait for a response before opening it.

"Mija, dinner's ready."

"Coming," I say in a fake cheery voice. I can pretend none of the other stuff is happening. That nothing happened. I get up and walk over to the kitchen to grab my plate.

"Ahh, this smells so good!" my dad exclaims as he serves himself a bowl of posole, sounding just as fake as me. My parents are always putting on this act in front of me—that everything is fine. Great, even. But I've seen them when they think I'm not paying attention. They're distant. They barely talk unless they think I'm listening, and then it's all smiles and cheer.

Well, I learned from the best.

"It does. Thank you, Mami!" I say, serving a bowl for myself and taking it to the table to meet my parents, who are already seated.

"How are you feeling, mija?" Papi asks.

"Better," I say between spoonfuls of posole. "How was work?" I ask to get the attention off myself.

"It was great!" he says, but I know we're both lying. Papi pretends like he loves his job cleaning up after rich kids as a janitor at a private school, and I pretend I didn't just make the biggest mistake of my life on Instagram.

We go through the motions while we eat, all three of us, laughing and joking and smiling. But none of us are actually happy. I should be, since my dad is actually home for dinner for once. He works late most days. I think it's his way of avoiding Mom, but it also means he's been avoiding *me*.

He and I force a laugh at a joke my mom tells, but I can't stop thinking about the post I made. I hope deactivating my account actually solved the problem and that no one is talking shit about me right this second, gossiping about what a slut and a liar I am.

But somehow I doubt it.

Eventually I excuse myself because I don't think I can keep up this act much longer. So I go to bed, where I can cuddle with Boo, the only one I never have to pretend with.

The next morning, I decide I'm done sulking. Even if inside I want to shrivel up and embrace my natural invisibility, I know it won't make me feel better. I don't want Luis to have power over me and make me hide away. No, there's no way I'm giving him that satisfaction.

I get up early to straighten my hair, and I pick out a floral shirt and tie it off at my waist, just above my tan paperbag shorts.

I'm used to acting like everything is fine with my parents, so school should be no problem for me. When I get to campus, I keep my chin up and my chest out and walk as confidently as I can fake. I pretend the stares I'm getting are the ones I've always wanted. They're all whispering to each other, and my mind blurs out what they say, replacing them with the fantasy.

*Look how cute Ariana is!*

*I wish I could pull off that outfit.*

*She's just so effortlessly gorgeous, isn't she?*

I fake a smile and march on, staring ahead and basking in all the stares, pretending I don't know what they're actually saying about me. But even with my chest out, the air in my lungs gets thinner, like I've just hiked to the top of Camelback Mountain.

I can feel the fantasy cracking. It's only a matter of time before my ears betray me and I hear the words people are actually saying. Only a matter of time before the illusion shatters. I just need to make it to the main building so I can hide in Mrs. Jones's room before that happens. In order to get there, though, I have to walk past everyone in front of the cafeteria. I grip my backpack straps tightly while I make my way. People stare at me but don't move for me to walk past, so I have to weave my way through and around everyone. It's early enough that there isn't anyone inside the building just yet. But when I get past the doors and into the empty hallway, I feel firm hands on my hips pulling me backward.

I scream and whip around, my hand zips to my pocket for the knife that I *forgot at home*. I didn't notice anyone following me. My eyes are closed tight, because anyone that touches me like that probably wants to kill me. The hands let go.

"Whoa, it's just me." Luis laughs at my reaction. I personally don't think it's very funny at all.

He grins at me, and I realize he's alone. Come to think of it, he's almost always alone when he talks to me. When he's with his friends, he barely acknowledges I exist. I glare back. Can he just get the message that I don't want to be touched like that?

"So, we're friends, huh? Nothing happened . . ." He steps closer. Too close.

I nod my head. Nothing happened.

Nothing happened.

"You know no one is buying that right?" Can't he just go along with the lie? Why does he have to go and make this harder?

His mouth is too close to mine. I purse my lips. He's worse at reading body language than I am because he's only getting closer. I can't breathe. I put a hand on his chest and push him back to keep him from getting any closer. Then I get out my phone with my other hand to type a message for him. I show him my screen.

*You're not exactly helping . . .*

"Sorry, baby. I won't say anything. Cross my heart." He winks and makes an *x* on his chest with his index finger. Then he walks away, finally leaving me to catch my breath.

I make my way to my locker and find a sliver of a piece of paper peeking out of the crack in my locker door. My throat closes up as I prepare myself for whatever mean message someone might have left me. Was it another Jesus? I'm ready to just crumple it up without reading, but there's a little voice in my head that tells me I shouldn't.

*Read it.*

Once I gather the courage, I put in my combination on the

lock and open the door. The paper almost falls out when the door opens, and I catch it. I brace myself and unfold it, slowly.

*Me too.*

There's a Tumblr handle written below the note: TLOSC.

I immediately fold the paper to hide the words, as if anyone might see what it says. I stare at the folded note much longer than I need to. What is "me too" supposed to mean? My heart races as I rack my brain trying to figure out who left it.

I mean, I don't live under a rock. I know what the Me Too movement is. But is that what this is referring to? And if so, why? Why would that apply to me? Especially when everyone probably thinks I lied about not having sex with Luis. But "me too" is hardly a threatening message. And they left me a way to contact them.

I hug the note to my heart. I don't know why it brings me comfort because I don't even know what it means. It shouldn't be possible, but the feeling of this little piece of paper warms my chest. This note is the closest thing to a real friend I have right now. And I really need a friend.

# SIX

At lunch time, I sit down at my usual table and unpack the sandwich I made this morning. Usually I stare at my food while I eat—to make sure I get the best possible bite each time. But today, I'm on high alert. Shawni's in line alone, as usual. Seems like she's forgotten all about our "talk later," which I'm perfectly fine with. Then I catch a glimpse of Luis from the other side of the cafeteria, everyone around him laughing at whatever unfunny joke he probably just told.

We lock eyes for a split second, and he gives me a simple smile, then turns away. I don't know why I expected him to approach me. All year, he's been pretty hot and cold with me. Some days, he would ignore me, or only give me a little smile, and others he'd make me feel like the center of the universe. I guess it's good that right now I'm practically invisible to him.

Just as I'm about to take another bite of my sandwich, I notice Shawni walking in my direction from across the cafeteria. Before she has a chance to come over to my table for the "talk later," I collect my things, get up, and rush to the bathroom. It might make me a coward, but I'm just not ready for that talk. I spend the rest of lunch sitting on the toilet.

I'm going to have to get up and go to my next class when the bell rings, which I'm dreading. I have dance with Shawni, but I'm still determined to avoid her. The dance teacher, Ms. M, doesn't usually pay attention to anything that happens after the first ten minutes of class unless she has something special for us to work on. She guides our stretches and across-the-floor warm-ups, where we learn things like chassés, pirouettes, and leaps. Then she's usually off in the corner choreographing her own stuff and expecting us to do the same. It's the easiest class I've ever taken, since you get an A for showing up, and you can get extra credit for any dance events you go to outside of school. Not that I ever had the spoons to go to one. The dance room is right above the gym, so she lets us leave and "dance" down there if it's empty.

Shawni and I are usually the only two people left in the room since we both like dancing with the mirrors. I like having the room almost to myself. I can't dance out in the gym with everyone else, or people will make fun of me, because I suck. I don't have any dance vocabulary or anything—I just like music, and I like moving. It doesn't always look good, and I'm okay with that. Actually, it almost always looks really bad, but it makes me feel good. Today, though, I intend to leave with the rest of the class. No thank you, confrontation.

After we finish our warm-ups, everyone else files out of the room. Ms. M already has her headphones in and is in her own little world in the corner, and I accidentally make eye contact with Shawni through the mirror as I'm rushing out. She looks annoyed that I'm leaving, but she takes dancing so seriously that I doubt she'd ditch dance just to commit a teeny little murder.

I immediately start walking to the door to go down to the gym again. Before I reach the handle, I flinch at the hand touching my shoulder. I tense up so hard I bite my tongue.

"Fuck!" I don't mean to shout it so loud, but I can't always control my outbursts. Ms. M spins around to see what's wrong. She must have heard me even through her headphones. People only ever hear my voice around here when it's an outburst, and sometimes not even then. I'm so, so sick of being touched without permission.

"Whoa, sorry." Shawni lets go of my shoulder and takes a step back. "I wanted to talk to you, remember?"

I shake my head. Not because I don't remember, but because I want to be left alone, *especially* by Shawni. I still can't relax my muscles enough to get myself to the door.

"Hey, what's your problem with me?" she asks, as if she doesn't already fucking know.

My problem is that I don't want her to kill me, and I also kind of want to kill her. Of course I have a fucking problem with her. She told everyone about me and Luis. My feet finally take over, and I run for the door. She doesn't follow me.

After dance, I keep my eyes down while I walk to my next

class to avoid making eye contact with any of the people staring at me. The fantasy has been sufficiently cracked. Or at least, the shine has worn off. I'd gladly trade all the stares I've been getting today for being invisible again. When you're invisible, you can do what you want in peace. I feel like people are watching my every move now, and it's so overwhelming I just want to go back home. Just being aware of how other people see me has cost me more energy than I'd usually spend in a month.

I start walking faster, trying to mind my own business, when someone pinches my left butt cheek, making me jump. My whole body tenses up as heat flushes through me from where I was touched up to my ears.

When I turn around, there's a group of boys behind me, but they aren't even looking at me, just walking. My eyes dart around for another culprit, but there's no one else close enough to have done it. None of the boys behind me acknowledge me as they walk right past me.

I want to scream at them to never touch me again. Or at least to stop walking and *look* at me. But my vocal cords are tight and the words don't come.

My face gets so hot I don't know what to do. One of the boys finally looks back at me and winks. I rush toward him and shove him, desperate for some kind of retribution. I push hard enough for him to acknowledge me with more than a wink. If he wants to treat me like an object, he needs to really see my face and own it.

"What?" He turns around, throwing his hands up in fake innocence.

He *knows* what. He looks like one of those guys that messaged me on Instagram yesterday. Manny, I think his name was. One of his friends laughs into his knuckle, and the other two pretend they didn't see anything.

"Oh, this?" He reaches for my butt again, but I jump back with a yelp and swat his arm away. He laughs. They all do. "What? Nothing happened, right?" He holds my gaze.

Nothing happened.

One of his friends steps forward.

"So, Ariana, you wanna ditch fifth and . . . you know. We'll just say nothing happened." He chuckles, and they all laugh again. Their laughs feel like a bullhorn pointed right in my face. Everything in my body screams at me to run. Not safe.

I cover my ears. I know it won't make them stop, but it's a reflex. I'm left with only the sound of my own breath, which is really hard to catch right now.

It's not like whether or not I had sex with Luis is anyone's business, but I hate that they're right. I hate that nothing *didn't* happen. Something happened, and lying about it definitely didn't help my situation.

I open my mouth again, to yell at them or scream or cry, but nothing comes out. I just push past them and keep walking to class with tears stinging my lashes. People around me still stare and whisper, but I keep my eyes ahead of me, blinking fast to stop the tears from rushing down my face. My hands are shaking, so I clutch the straps of my backpack for dear life.

When I hear the sharp clap of hand on skin and feel the newly familiar sting on my backside, my arm automatically swings behind me, meeting Manny's cheek hard enough to make him stumble. I shake the sting out of my hand, proud of the fact that I hit him hard enough for it to hurt *me*. The crowd around us grows.

"Bitch!" he shouts, cradling his cheek.

"Excuse me?" A teacher pushes through the crowd.

"She slapped me!"

The teacher looks at me for an explanation I physically can't give. I look around to see if anyone will defend me. Maybe someone saw him touch me and can vouch for me. No one does. The teacher looks defeated when I don't say anything, like he wants to side with me but can't, because I can't vouch for myself. Tears still push at my tear ducts, but I blink them away, refusing to let them come out. Not here, not in front of everyone.

"Alright, come with me," he says, and I reluctantly follow him to the office.

When we get there, the office lady looks at me and sighs.

"Have a seat, Ms. Ruiz."

I sit down in the chair closest to the door in the office and wait. I usually get sent here a few times at the beginning of every year, so the office lady knows me. Mostly, I get sent here for not responding to a teacher who calls on me. Eventually, though, they realize that's just how I am and they stop trying to get me to talk.

The principal's office door opens and someone walks out. I know this guy, Angel. He used to hang out with Luis a lot. Not anymore, though. All I know is that last year Angel was one of the popular guys in Luis's circle, but one day he picked a fight with Luis and kind of got his ass kicked. Since then, he's been a bit of a loner. Luis told me he's a traitor, but he never elaborated on why.

Angel acknowledges me with a nod but doesn't say anything, which I appreciate because I'm so tired of the shit that's been coming out of people's mouths today.

"Ariana?" Principal Matthew calls out as she opens the door. I don't love how my name sounds when she says it. *Air-ee-anna.* I prefer the hard *r.* I get up and walk into her office. She gestures to the seat in front of her desk without looking up from her computer, where she's typing away. Finally, she adjusts to face me and sighs.

"You can't just go around slapping people, Ariana."

I reach for my phone so I can tell her what happened, but she stops me.

"No phones, you know this."

I try not to roll my eyes at her. It's not her fault that she has no way of knowing why I need my phone. I point to a cup full of pens on her desk instead. She looks confused, probably because I've never actually made an effort to communicate with her before now. I keep pointing at the pens until it clicks for her. She hands me a blue pen and slides over a piece of paper so I can write.

*He slapped my butt so I slapped him.*

She sighs, then picks up the phone by the computer and dials.

"Please send Emmanuel Roberts to my office right away." After a moment, she hangs up the phone. "Alright, Ariana, will you wait outside for me until this is settled?"

I nod and leave the room to take a seat back in the waiting area. I can't help but smile. Justice will be served. When Manny comes in, it's hard to hide the satisfaction on my face.

"Come on in, Emmanuel." Principal Matthew calls out from her office. Manny glares at me and walks in, closing the door behind him.

I imagine the lecture he's getting right now about sexual harassment and respecting boundaries. I wonder what punishment he'll get. Maybe detention? I'd rather him get suspended so I don't have to see him.

When the door opens again, I stand up in anticipation. Manny walks out, but he doesn't look defeated. He strides past me, chin up.

"Nothing happened, right?" He shakes his head and smirks at me, then leaves the room.

One by one, the rest of his friends start rolling into the office, and Manny leaves. If it's my word against all of theirs, it doesn't matter what I say. It never matters what I say, or don't.

In the end, Manny gets off scot-free, and I have detention after school.

# SEVEN

When I'm walking to my last class of the day, my eyes are peeled. I hate how it's impossible to keep an arm's distance from people in these halls. I don't want anyone touching me, and my muscles are starting to hurt from being so tense. I still have half the school to cross when someone falls into step next to me. I turn my head to see a familiar face, Jasmine, I think her name is, from my physics class last year.

"They only touch you when you're alone." Jasmine gives me a kind smile.

I smile back and mouth the word "thanks," and she nods.

I haven't really seen her since last year, so I start to notice everything about her that's changed. She has braces now, and her tight curls that used to run just above her shoulders are now cut down so her coils are only about an inch or two above her scalp. Her skin is a few shades darker than my medium brown, and she seems to be just as much of an overachiever as she was a year ago. Her backpack looks about as stuffed as it can be, and she's clutching a robotics textbook to her chest.

We never really interacted before, but Jasmine did tell off Jessica and Melanie for making fun of me once, so I've always liked her. She's a bit of a loner, too, but she's nowhere near quiet. She was always the first to raise her hand in class, and she was never afraid to stand up to the bullies. Still, she knows I don't talk, so she doesn't try to start a conversation.

We walk side by side all the way to my next class in companionable silence.

When school is over, I march over to the detention room as fast as I can. I don't have Jasmine to protect me, so I make it quick to avoid any unwanted touching. I'm the first one in the room, besides the teacher, who smiles at me and gestures to one of the desks. The desks in here have blinders up so no one can really see or talk to each other, which is fine by me. The less human interaction I get right now the better. I take a seat, and other kids start slowly trickling in. One of them thumps their binder on the desk so loud it startles me. Someone's mad about being in detention. I can't say I blame them.

I think about the pros of being in here to avoid thinking about how wrong this whole situation is. At least no one minds that I'm quiet here, and I have some time to do homework. I live so close that I walk home from school anyways, so I don't have to worry about arranging a ride. Plus, by the time I get out of here, most of the other students will be gone, so I won't have to worry about getting harassed again.

Still, it is pretty boring. Because of the blinders up on my desk, I can't people watch. I'm only really allowed to do homework or do nothing, so I reluctantly choose homework. I get out my packet from Chemistry and get to work. To my surprise, it really does make the time go by faster.

By the time I finish it, there's only five minutes left before I get to go home. Those five minutes go by slower than the rest of the hour. The second hand on the clock moves with a resounding tick what feels like millions of times before the minute hand finally takes its turn.

I try not to think about how shitty this is while I wait, but I fail. Someone touched me without asking and I'm the one who got in trouble for it. No one listened to me. And I can't even blame them because I can't fucking speak for myself. Why does talking have to be so hard? How does everyone else do it like it's no big deal?

The second we're let out, the rest of the kids grab their bags and storm out of the room before I'm able to process that it's time to go. Since I finished my homework, I don't have to take my bag home, so I go to my locker to put it away. I'm finally able to relax walking down the empty halls. There's no one here to bother me.

I open my locker to find the note I left in there from this morning.

*Me too.*

I look around to make sure no one's here, then quickly grab it and shove it in my pocket.

When I get home, I kick off my shoes by the door and Boo greets me by rubbing herself on my legs.

"Hey, kitty," I say as I head to my room. She follows me onto my bed, where I finally start petting her. I lay on my back and let her rest on my chest while I stroke her soft black fur. I close my eyes, ready for the day to be over even though it's just barely four in the afternoon. But right when I close my eyes, my phone buzzes. There's really only one person who has my number.

Luis: want to come over?

I turn my phone over so I don't have to look at the text anymore. The last thing I want is to be alone with Luis again. Even Boo tried to warn me about him. I think cats have some kind of instinct about what's good for you or something. Like a sixth sense for detecting assholes. At least, Boo does. She is usually the most affectionate thing, but she wouldn't get anywhere near Luis when he came over before the party. When he tried to pet her, she hissed at him. I got mad and scolded her for it, but he told me not to worry. He said she'd warm up to him eventually.

My face gets hot at the memory at how he understood when the cat didn't want to be touched, but when it came to me he was completely clueless.

I continue to ignore the message. I still feel mad, but I also don't feel like I have a good reason to be. It all just feels wrong, and I don't want to talk to him right now. If I could go back, I wonder if I would do anything differently. I wouldn't know what to change. I never really initiated anything with Luis, even though I was head over heels for him.

He approached me. He took my phone and called himself to get my number. He invited himself over to pick me up for the party. He introduced himself to my parents. He knew where I lived because he also invited himself to walk me home once. He initiated everything. The one thing I did was show up to that party. That's what I should have done differently. I should have stayed home.

# EIGHT

I don't have Tumblr, so I spend about an hour debating what name and picture to use for one. Even though the person I'm making a Tumblr to talk to already knows who I am, I don't want to use my real name. I don't think people really use their real names on Tumblr anyway, do they? How do people do this?

"What name should I pick, Boo?" I ask, and Boo stares at me from my desk next to the laptop. She blinks. Since I don't speak cat, I still have no idea what kind of name to pick, so I settle for a key smash: aadfssd. I end up going with one of the generic Tumblr icons.

When I'm finally done, I look up "TLOSC" in the search bar. The account is completely blank. No posts or asks or anything.

Could this be the right account? Did I do this wrong? I check the note to make sure I got the letters right: T-L-O-S-C. I got it right the first time.

I open a message. If I'm wrong and this is a random account, then they probably just won't respond, and what's the harm in that? I start to send a message when I realize I have no idea what to say. Thanks for sending me a cryptic note I don't understand?

Now the note is making me feel guilty. Not guilty enough to confess to the lie, but just enough to feel like shit about it. If I message this person, I'm just digging myself deeper into this lie. Part of me just wants to forget about the whole thing, but how can I pass up an opportunity for a friend when so many people who've tried to talk to me since that party have been so mean about it?

I swallow the guilt and type out a message.

aadfssd: I got your note.

aadfssd: Hi.

I don't have time to overanalyze the messages I sent or even whether or not I sent them to the right person, because the response comes almost instantly.

tlosc: Ariana?

For some reason, I'm nervous to admit it's me. I know they already know it's me, but once I admit it there's really no going back. I take a deep breath and respond.

aadfssd: Yes.

Again, barely any time passes before I get their next message.

tlosc: you okay?

I'm a little thrown off by the question. I don't even know the right answer. Am I okay? Every time someone approaches me lately it's about what happened. Something I wish never happened in the first place.

**aadfssd:** It sucks really bad.

**tlosc:** I know :/ it'll blow over in a couple weeks though, promise

**aadfssd:** What did you mean, "me too?"

This time the response takes a while. I start typing a message telling them they don't have to share when I finally get a response.

**tlosc:** About Luis . . . I know how you feel.

About Luis? Does this person not believe my lie? For some reason, I thought maybe they would be different.

**aadfssd:** You don't believe me either, do you?

I shut my eyes, praying for a response that doesn't make me want to cry.

**tlosc:** I believe you.

But that makes no sense. If they don't think I had sex with Luis, then what are they talking about?

**aadfssd:** Then what are you talking about?

**tlosc:** you know . . .

I don't know what to say to that, because no, I don't know. I have no idea what they're talking about. Just when I'm about to ask, I get another message.

**tlosc:** he . . . mistreated us

**tlosc:** and now our reputations are ruined

**tlosc:** he's a major dick

Oh. I want to deny it, but they're kind of right. Luis might not have started the rumor, but he definitely didn't stop it. He could have set things straight, but he didn't. I don't know why my first instinct is to always defend him. He didn't defend me.

aadfssd: Yeah, he is a dick.

aadfssd: So, who are you?

tlosc: I can't tell you yet, sorry . . .

aadfssd: Yet?

tlosc: yet 😊

I can't help but smile for some reason. I really want to know who I'm talking to. It could be anyone. They must be nice. It would be good to have someone nice to talk to right now. A friend.

aadfssd: Can you give me a hint?

tlosc: sure

tlosc: ummmmmmm . . .

tlosc: we interacted at some point this week

aadfssd: Like in the last seven days or this school week?

tlosc: school week

aadfssd: Today?

tlosc: lol sorry I already gave you your hint

Okay, well if it's someone I interacted with, that eliminates almost the entire school. I automatically cancel out anyone that harassed me, too, since I doubt they would say anything nice or ask if I'm okay. I do talk to Mrs. Jones, but she wouldn't leave a note on my locker. If she had anything to say to me she would just say it outright. So that leaves only a few people.

Jasmine? Everything I know about her I learned in Physics last year, so it's hard to say if she would have any kind of beef with Luis. I guess I don't talk to anyone enough to know what her reputation is like, either. Maybe . . .

It could be Nina. She was nice to me at lunch. Her reputation I have heard of. Come to think of it, it's likely that Luis could have something to do with Nina being number one on the "slut list." I wonder how many girls on that list got there because of him. My stomach twists. If it went around today, I'd probably have landed myself on the number one spot. Nina doesn't really seem like the type of person Luis would mess with, though. Then again, I guess neither do I.

Maybe it's Angel? I don't really know what happened with him and Luis, but he's kind of a loner now that they aren't friends. He stopped doing sports and everything. If anyone has something against Luis, it's that guy. But then, does a simple nod count as an interaction?

It could even be Shawni. But why would she start a rumor and then anonymously comfort me about it? What would be the gain in that? I guess if she felt guilty she might do it. But I have a feeling she doesn't feel very guilty. The thought makes me want to throw up. I do not want to be talking to Shawni about Luis right now.

But then, what if it's *Manny?* Or one of the other guys, just messing with me? The idea makes my stomach turn. No one's *that* mean, are they?

aadfssd: How do I know you're not just messing with me?

Another longish pause. I start to suck on my knuckles in anticipation.

tlosc: I guess you don't

**tlosc:** but I don't want to stress you out, you don't have to talk to me if you don't want to. I just wanted to let you know that you're not alone right now, even if it feels like it. I can go away now if you want me to, though. Just wanted you to know.

I guess that probably crosses Shawni off the list of who I might be talking to, since all she's been doing is trying to get me to talk to her. I don't think Manny or any of the others have enough brain cells to write that convincingly. So it's either Jasmine, Angel, or Nina. I don't know any of them that well, but I don't want to be left alone, either.

**aadfssd:** Don't go away.

**tlosc:** okay, I won't ☺

The door opens before I can respond. Mami closes it behind her softly, like she doesn't want anyone to hear it. Instead of sitting at the foot of my bed, she crawls into the bed and lays down next to me. We both sigh at the same time. Me, because I know I'll have to stop texting my new friend until my mom gets bored of talking to me. She probably had a bad day at work and needs to vent.

"How was your day, mija?" she asks.

My day was such a roller coaster I don't even know where to start. Should I tell her I got detention? That I got sexually harassed? I feel my phone buzz, and I imagine Nina texting me while she waits for her hair be stripped of its color so she can dye it a new one. Maybe blue this time. Or Jasmine, texting me in between homework problems. Or Angel, maybe lying in bed with his phone like me. I think maybe that's where I'll start.

"I made a new friend today." It feels like something a child would say, but it's my first time getting to say it, ever. Sure, I know TLOSC might not actually consider me a friend. I know it's naive to call them a friend after a simple conversation, but it feels right.

"Oh, wow! Mija, that's great!" she says, but I can tell she's using that fake happy voice she and Papi use around each other. What the hell? Why isn't she actually happy for me? I have half a mind to call her out on it, but I feel like that would break the sacred unwritten pact the three of us share in this house. You can't walk too close to the mirage, or you'll find out there's nothing but more desert. I'll take the fake happy for now.

"Thanks," I say, returning her cheery tone.

"So, have you and Luis made up yet?" she asks, this time her voice is cheery for real. God, I wish I'd never brought Luis over. I'll never hear the end of him.

"Have you and Dad?" I snap back. She looks hurt for a moment, and I can't handle it, so I backtrack. "Sorry, I just . . . Why do you always want to know about Luis? I don't want to talk about him."

She chews on her lip for a while before responding. "No, *I'm* sorry. I shouldn't be so caught up in the idea of a boy you clearly don't care for anymore."

My throat tightens, because, even if I want to hate Luis, I can't deny that I still care for him. But that doesn't mean I want to talk about it.

"So, if it's not Luis, is there someone else catching your attention?"

I sigh. "Luis is the only one who will ever want me." I didn't mean to say that part out loud, and I regret it as soon as I do.

"Why would you say that?" My mom looks like I legitimately just slapped her in the face. "You don't need that boy's attention in order to be worthy of love." My eyes get watery at her words, and I can't bring myself to argue, even though it feels so wrong, so I just let her keep going. "You know I love you no matter what. And your papi does, too."

"How are you and Papi, anyway?" I ask. Anything to change the subject.

"You know your dad is still working out his feelings . . ." A flash of sadness flickers across her features before she bounces back into her cheery voice. Only this time, the cheer doesn't sound fake. "But . . . I met someone." She says it like it's a harmless piece of gossip. I'm too shocked to answer right away, so she keeps going. "His name is Tom. He's one of the chefs at the restaurant. He's—"

"Mami, what the hell?" I finally interrupt. She looks surprised, like she was expecting me to be happy for her. But how could I be happy about this?

"What's wrong?" she asks innocently.

"What do you mean what's wrong? Are you cheating on Dad again?" I accuse.

"No, no. Nothing like that. I just thought . . . well, that we were bonding. I thought . . ."

I don't mean to tune her out, but I can't help it. Papi is nothing like Luis. Just because they fell out of love with each other doesn't mean we can bond over my mom finding someone else.

"I think you should get therapy," I say, not meaning to sound harsh. It's a genuine suggestion. She really needs someone to talk to, and as an autistic selectively mute teenager with an increasingly soiled reputation and a million problems of my own, I'm hardly qualified.

She clucks her tongue. "Therapy is for crazy people. Do you think I'm crazy?"

I roll my eyes. I hate how sensationalist she is. And I don't like how she uses the word "crazy."

"I think everyone could use therapy," I say. Me, especially. If my parents weren't so against it, maybe I'd ask them to sign me up.

"Well, I don't need therapy. I have you!" She grins, and I sigh.

"I'm serious, Mami."

"So am I." She looks at me, then chews on her nails a bit. I don't know why she doesn't let me chew on my knuckles when I'm nervous if she gets to do this just as often. It's not fair that her thing happens to be socially acceptable while mine isn't.

I want to cry. Mom must notice because her smile fades. "Hey, I'll work on things with your dad, okay, mija? Things are gonna be okay. We'll figure it out eventually."

I blink away the tears. "Okay, Mami," I say, even though I don't believe her for one second.

"Mija, don't cry . . . Can I?" she asks, and I nod as I let a tiny whimper escape. Then she runs her fingers through my hair. It feels good. Safe. Even though none of this is good.

I don't even know why I'm crying. Maybe because Mom and Dad will probably be splitting up for good when he finds out about Tom. They're already so distant as it is. This will probably be the last straw.

"I'm tired, Mami. I just want to sleep," I say. It's only a half lie. I am tired, but not that kind of tired. I just want to stop dealing with this. She nods and leaves the room. When she closes the door behind her, I get another message, and I'd much rather answer it than sleep.

tlosc: so what are you up to?

tlosc: I'm guessing you went to bed. Good night ☺

aadfssd: No, I'm up. I was just talking to my mom.

tlosc: everything okay?

aadfssd: Not really.

tlosc: do you want to talk about it?

I do. But I don't know who this person is, so I'm not sure I want to put my business out there like that.

aadfssd: I can't.

tlosc: okay, that's fine. I hope you feel better soon

aadfssd: Thank you.

They don't respond for a while, and I'm worried I ruined things somehow. I do want to talk to them, just maybe not about *that*. I need something to distract me from my thoughts. How can I revive the conversation? What are we supposed to talk about? The only thing I know for sure we have in common is Luis, and I'd rather talk about my family drama than *him*. I don't know how to small talk. How do talking people do this all the time?

Before I have to come up with something, they message me back with a sketch of a baby bat hanging upside down. The caption reads "hang in there!"

I hug my phone to my chest. Did they really just draw that for me?

**aadfssd:** Thank you. I will. <3

**tlosc:** any time friend ☺

Friend.

I'm dying to know who my new friend is. I want to know more about TLOSC. Maybe they won't officially give me another hint, but I can get to know them in more subtle ways, by finding out what they're doing, what they like to do, what kind of music they like. Things like that.

We end up texting all night. About our favorite movies, foods, and dream vacations. We talk about everything and nothing. I may not know who this person is, but I know a few things. They want to visit the Bahamas, they're an only child, they like *cleaning* for some reason, and their favorite artist is Lizzo. Every time I get a new message, I find myself smiling, and then way overthinking every response. I want to sound just as interesting as they do. They called me *friend*, and I really don't want to mess that up.

# NINE

The next day, I walk so fast between classes my calves hurt. I don't want anyone touching me, and speed walking is the only way I know to guarantee it won't happen. I can't count on Jasmine to just happen to find me in between every class, can I?

At lunch, I head to Mrs. Jones's classroom instead of my solitary lunch table so I won't get approached by any horny dudes, but the door is locked, and I don't see her through the window. I end up just sitting outside her room in the hall. Luckily there's no one else here. I pull out the ham and cheese sandwich I packed myself today.

A few minutes into sitting down to eat my sandwich, I get a message.

tlosc: here for your regularly scheduled check-in. how are you today?

I smile down at my phone. Someone cares how I'm doing. I wouldn't complain about a regularly scheduled check-in.

**aadfssd:** I'm alright. Hiding so no one bothers me like yesterday.

**aadfssd:** I wish Luis would just stick up for me. Then maybe everyone would leave me alone.

**tlosc:** I'm so sorry

Why do people apologize when they didn't do anything wrong? It doesn't make any sense to me, but I guess it's just one of those social things I'll never understand. Before I get a chance to respond, I have another message.

**tlosc:** do you want to get back at him?

I stare at my phone for a moment, dumbfounded.

**aadfssd:** What do you mean?

**tlosc:** we should get back at Luis. He deserves it.

It's not that he doesn't deserve it, but I don't think I have revenge in me. Not when I feel like I'm drowning whenever I see him. And I guess . . . maybe I'm not sure if he deserves it all that much. If anything, I feel like I'm the one at fault here. Maybe the reason he didn't stand up for me or go along with my lie was because I hurt his feelings? Somehow, I both wish it were true and don't at the same time. If he's hurt by me saying we're friends, that means I didn't make up his feelings for me.

It's not like he hasn't stood up for me in the past.

He used to walk me to my house after school. He said he wanted to make sure I was safe, and that he liked spending the extra time with me. One day, some guy sitting on the bottom steps of his apartment made some crude comment about my ass as we passed him, and Luis went off on him. Like, really chewed him out. They almost got in a fight before I had to pull Luis away.

So if Luis isn't standing up for me this time, it must be because *I* did something wrong. Not him.

And on top of that, even after everything, I don't want to hurt him. I guess I still care about him. He might not be much of a gentleman, but he was my first. Firsts are supposed to be important, aren't they? It might have made me feel like I didn't exist when it was happening. It might have made it even harder to talk than it already was, but it happened. It hasn't even been a week yet, but I'm ready to be over it. I even dream about it. Actually, no. I have nightmares about it. Nightmares where I relive that party, and what happened in that room. And I can't say no. I can't move. I can't breathe.

I can't ignore what happened anymore. But no matter how hard I try, I can't bring myself to hate Luis, or even Shawni. I don't blame anyone but myself.

**aadfssd:** I can't.

**tlosc:** are you sure?

I hesitate because I don't think I am. I don't *think* what I want is to get back at Luis. I do want him to apologize to me. For what, I don't know. Maybe for not asking before taking my clothes off. For not giving me any kind of warning. But how can I blame him when I couldn't even bring myself to tell him to stop?

Selective mutism is the most inconvenient freaking thing. I shut down most of the time, but especially when I'm nervous.

And Luis makes me so nervous. There was no way I could have told him anything, let alone no.

He should have asked.

But I don't want revenge. I want an apology. I want him to feel guilty and tell me he didn't realize what he was doing and that he'll make it up to me somehow. I want him to feel bad on his own about what he did, just because he cares about me. Deep down, I know it's a long shot, but a girl can hope, right?

aadfssd: I'm sure.

tlosc: alright, well if you change your mind, I'll be in room 205 after school on Friday.

I wonder if TLOSC planned to ask me this from the beginning. My throat clenches around a lump as I swallow over it. Did they actually want to be friends with me, or did they just want me to help with some big revenge plot?

aadfssd: Is that the only reason you wanted to talk to me?

tlosc: I told you why I hit you up. Getting revenge is just an idea, something I'm gonna do anyways. Thought you might want in.

aadfssd: I don't, sorry.

tlosc: suit yourself

tlosc: if you change your mind you know where to find me

tlosc: and if you don't, no hard feelings ☺

I let out a sigh of relief at that last text. I needed to know they didn't just want to use me for their revenge plan. I don't want to lose my only friend over something so petty.

✗ ✗ ✗

After lunch, I have to build up courage to go to dance. I can't hide from Shawni forever, and I really do miss dancing in that class. I decide I'll just pretend I don't know it was her who told everyone what happened with Luis.

But dance today is different from the usual. Instead of making up her own choreography and ignoring us after warmups, Ms. M makes an announcement.

"Before you all run off to the gym, I want to talk about another extra credit opportunity!" Some kids leave anyway, since she does this a lot. Extra credit is a little unnecessary when you get an A for showing up for ten minutes. No one ever really listens to Ms. M, and it makes me feel kind of bad.

"What is it?" Shawni asks, even though we all know it's going to be another dance battle. I wouldn't be surprised if Shawni actually did all the extra credit. She probably has a 200 percent in this class. I would do the extra credit if loud music and crowds didn't make me want to crawl out of my own skin. The rest of the kids trickle out of the room while Ms. M goes on, completely ignoring the fact that she's losing everyone but Shawni.

"I was actually thinking about you when I saw this, Shawni. It's a street style dance battle! But trust me, it's so different from *Step Up* or *Stomp the Yard*. In my experience, everyone in the underground dance community is so supportive!" She gives this same spiel every time. We all know by now that Ms. M is a super badass freestyle dancer, and she competes at these dance battles every chance she gets. She's been urging Shawni

× 73 ×

to battle all year. Ms. M smiles and hands a flyer to both of us, and then goes off to do her own thing as usual. I fold up my flyer and put it in my backpack.

Since it's just Shawni and me in the dance room now, I put my headphones in and stare at myself in the mirror that surrounds the room. Maybe if Shawni sees me in my element, she'll leave me alone. I don't turn music on so I can hear if anyone approaches me. I start doing some simple foot exercises to make it look like I'm preoccupied.

No matter how hard I try, I can't get my toe to point how it's supposed to. My foot doesn't look as pretty as Ms. M's, or Shawni's. I glance over at Shawni, watching her from the corner of my eye. To keep guard, I tell myself. Luckily, she's in her own world, too.

Shawni is on another level. She's doing some kind of freeze. I find my head turning to watch her. She drops down to the floor and starts threading her limbs through and around each other. With her headphones in, Shawni is completely absorbed and all I can hear is her measured breath and the patting on the ground from her movement. Her arms and forehead are shining with a layer of sweat. She swings her feet in the air and catches herself with her hands, and I can't help the tiny gasp that escapes my lips.

She's good at the classic stuff like ballet, modern, and jazz, but she's also a b-girl, which I think is the coolest thing ever. But I don't want to think she's cool. I have to remind myself she spread the rumors about me. She's the reason I keep getting harassed. She's *not* cool.

I have to look focused on myself, so I start practicing the single pirouettes we learned last week. I'm determined to get it right, even though spotting is really hard for me. I must look so pathetic doing these sad wobbly pirouettes while Shawni does *that*. I end up getting dizzy after just a couple of tries. The room doesn't stop spinning when I do, and I have to sit down against the mirror. In order to make everything stand still, I focus on something in the room. The first thing that pops out at me is Shawni. I shake my head. Nope.

Instead, I get my phone out of my bag and focus on that. I don't know what else to do, so I message my new friend.

aadfssd: Hi.

No response, not that I expected one. They're in class, and not every class is as easy to text in as dance. I wait a few more minutes, but my phone stays quiet, and I find myself preoccupied with Shawni again. Maybe I could learn to be that good one day.

I can't keep track of how she's doing what she's doing with her limbs, so I have no idea how I would ever attempt to duplicate it. Somehow, she ends up balancing on her head pointing one of her legs at the mirror.

Headstands don't look *too* hard. Maybe I could learn how to do that.

When she gets back to the floor, her feet move more quickly than before. They move faster and faster around her body until she creates the illusion that she has more than two. She stumbles when she sees me staring, and she swings her legs into a criss-cross position facing me. My eyes widen and I snap my head to face the other side of the room, but it's too late.

"Want me to teach you?" she asks, playing innocent. Two can play at this game. I give her an innocent look back. One that says, "I have no idea you told everyone about me and Luis."

She smiles, and I realize what I just got myself into. How am I supposed to learn how to do *that*? I can see in the mirror that she's still facing me. I sigh and turn back toward her. Honestly, I really do want to learn how to do a headstand. But it feels like a trap. Like if I let her teach me, she'll slip in a threat about Luis or something.

For some reason I can't bring myself to shake my head no. Maybe if I just learn the headstand. I sit down and put my hands and head on the floor so she knows what I want to learn.

She puts her hands and head on the floor, too.

"Okay, keep your head on the ground and just . . ." She lets her elbows carry the weight of her thighs, then slowly lifts her legs up in the air and shoots them into a pose. Like it's that easy.

I manage to get the tops of my thighs onto my elbows like she did, and I can kind of see how you can ease into a headstand with this pose. Shawni gets up and puts her hands near my ankles; she asks the question with her eyes, and I let her touch me. I don't fall over from the fear of contact. I still tense up when she grabs my ankles to position them in the air, but she's holding me steady enough that I don't fall. She makes a figure four with my legs, and from my upside-down view in the mirror, I do look pretty cool. She's keeping me from falling, so the touch feels safe. But it's also Shawni. So maybe unsafe?

I feel like my life is in her hands right now. If she wanted, she could drop me to break my neck. Suddenly I regret letting her teach me this. Definitely unsafe.

"Breathe. If you forget to breathe, you'll fall."

If I breathe, I'll hyperventilate, I know it. She slowly lets go of my legs, and I tumble to the floor.

Shawni mocks me with a little smile, then crawls over to where her backpack is against the mirror and pulls out a piece of paper. Great, she still wants to talk. I pull myself up into a sitting position and dust myself off.

"So . . . I know you're avoiding me . . ." There it is. I can't read the look she's giving me. Anger? Pity? Skepticism?

She hands me the paper and a pencil. I suddenly remember how pissed I am at her. She *knows* what happened. But does she know I know she knows what happened? She's the only one who saw me go in the room with him that night. She's kind of a genius. Pulling me in with the promise of a learned headstand only to throw Luis back in my face. Does she really not know I put it together?

I don't want to talk about this, but I don't want to confront Shawni about what she did, either. I just shake my head, smile, and slide the paper back to her. She frowns. Instead of acknowledging her, I stand back up and put my headphones in. I start stretching in the mirror because I don't know what else to do. Shawni takes the hint and goes back to practicing her freezes.

tlosc: checkin in, how was your day?

aadfssd: Better. No one tried to grope me today thanks to my power walk.

tlosc: someone tried to grope you??? who do I have to fight?

aadfssd: I already slapped him, don't worry.

tlosc: a perve can never be slapped too many times

aadfssd: True.

tlosc: who groped you?

I debate whether to tell them for a moment. Then again, it happened pretty publicly, so if I don't tell TLOSC, they could easily find out if they wanted.

aadfssd: It was Manny Roberts . . .

tlosc: that motherfucker

aadfssd: I know . . . and I got detention for slapping him back.

tlosc: jesus

tlosc: he'll get what's coming to him. Just like Luis.

I don't know what they mean by that. Are they going to get revenge on Manny, too? For some reason, I'm more okay with that thought than I am about getting revenge on Luis. Manny means nothing to me, and I could care less if TLOSC got a little payback for me. Still, I'm not thrilled about spending all my time talking about Manny, or Luis. I'd rather just talk to TLOSC.

aadfssd: So, when are you going to tell me who you are?

tlosc: when you're ready. ☺

aadfssd: ????

tlosc: you know where I'll be in two days, so . . .

aadfssd: I told you I don't want to get back at him.

tlosc: I'm just sayin ;)

tlosc: good night! <3

I smile at the heart on my screen despite myself. The heart makes whatever annoyance I had at the suggestion of revenge disappear. No one's ever sent me a heart before. I tuck my phone underneath my pillow and fall asleep with a smile on my face.

The next day, I'm determined to figure out who TLOSC is, and I don't need to show up for their little revenge plot to do it. When Shawni walks into the journalism room just before the second bell, I ignore everyone else in the room to glare at her extra hard as if I can force the secrets to visibly spill from her pores. Even though it's unlikely, she's one of the few people who might be TLOSC, since we interacted in the last week.

Unsurprisingly, staring at her doesn't make the answer any clearer, so I turn to plan B. I sneakily pull my phone out of my romper pocket and slide it under my desk. I type out a "good morning" message to TLOSC, making sure to keep my head up so Mrs. Jones doesn't see me texting. Then I keep Shawni in my peripheral vision to see if she pulls out her phone at the notification.

All she does is take the hair tie off her wrist and start twirling it around her finger. If she felt her phone vibrate from my message, she doesn't show it. And there's no response from TLOSC, so this proves absolutely nothing.

I don't get a response until lunch time. I'm forcing myself to eat in the cafeteria so I can see everyone I've interacted with in the last week in one place, and maybe catch one of them in the act of texting me. I dart my eyes around the room. Nina is talking on her phone, sitting by herself. She must sense me staring because she glances up at me from across the cafeteria and waves, then starts walking over to me.

I have to make the rest of my search quick before she gets here. Angel is standing close to the front of the lunch line, and I catch him waving shyly at Jasmine, who's a few spaces behind him. I didn't realize they were friends, but I guess they are. Maybe that disqualifies both of them from being TLOSC, since I don't see either of them on their phones. Shawni's also in the same line, but a little farther back, standing alone. She glances at her watch, which is basically a phone, right? If she's TLOSC, can she read my message on her watch? She better not be TLOSC. That would mean she's doing all of this just to fuck with me, and I don't know if I'll be able to handle it if that's the truth. Before I get a chance to glare too hard at her, Nina approaches my table and sits across from me, still talking on her phone.

"I already told you I'd participate in the patriarchal overly gendered idea of a coming-of-age ceremony . . . I *know* what it's called! I'm just saying, why do only girls have to have quinces . . . Of course people will show up! I have, like, sooo many friends." She laughs nervously. "Besides, it's not like my quinceañera is next week. We have plenty of time. Anyways, Igottagoloveyoubyeeee!" *Click.* "Ari! Hi!" She lifts a hand in the air. "Five!" Her mouth opens in a huge grin that says she's very proud of her pun. I don't love touching strangers, but she doesn't put her hand down, so I force myself to slap it as quickly as I can. "Is this seat taken?" she asks, and I shake my head.

Nina sits with me the rest of lunch, chatting nonstop about a game of Dungeons and Dragons she's running online. I feel bad tuning her out, but I can't understand a word of what she's saying. She's not exactly trying to make this game sound accessible to new players.

I send TLOSC another message, hoping I get a response while I can see Shawni in the cafeteria, just so I can disprove my theory that it's her and she's just fucking with me to be mean, but I don't get a response the rest of the day.

After I've put my books away in my locker after school, I head out to the parking lot to leave. I can see Manny and his friends walking ahead of me, which oddly makes me feel safer. If I can see them, they can't sneak up on me.

A tan Toyota Camry pulls up against the curb, and a woman gets out of the car and starts marching right over to me.

No. She's marching over to *Manny*.

"Mom?" he says incredulously, already looking smaller than his usual cocky chin-up self. He cowers when she reaches over and yanks on his ear, turning him around. All his friends laugh and back away from her. Then she spanks him, hard, right in front of everyone, pulling an embarrassed yelp from his mouth. "Mom! What are you—"

"So this is what you do to girls now?" she says as she spanks him again. "Sexual assault? Is that how I raised you?"

People are gathering around, laughing. I cover my mouth to stifle a laugh of my own. I don't know how she found out about what he did to me, but I'm glad she did. This is what he deserves. To be humiliated the way he humiliated me.

"I didn't—" Manny starts, but she doesn't let him finish.

"I know what you did, Emmanuel! Where is she? You apologize to her right now!"

I freeze where I stand. Is she really going to make him apologize to me, in front of the whole school?

Manny's apparently less than loyal friends laugh and point in my direction. "She's right over there, Mrs. Roberts!"

My eyes widen as she drags him over to me by the ear, and the crowd follows.

"Well?" she says, letting go of his ear and putting her hands on her hips.

"I didn't do anything!" Manny lies, but his mom isn't having it.

"Oh, he did it . . ." a familiar voice says from behind me. Then there's a squeeze on my shoulder, which I'm sure is meant to be comforting, but it just makes me even more tense. I turn my head to see Luis giving me a reassuring smile. I assumed Luis was friends with Manny, since he's the one who invited me to Manny's party, but I guess they're not that close if Luis is ratting him out like this.

Manny gives Luis a horrified look, like he was expecting anything but that. Honestly, I wasn't expecting Luis to snitch on Manny, either. But it makes me stand taller. He finally stood up for me. I can't help but grin at Manny in satisfaction, waiting in anticipation for the apology I so deserve.

"I . . . I'm sorry, okay?" he says, eyes glued to the floor. And it almost feels like this is Luis's way of apologizing, too.

"Now get your ass in the car," his mom scolds, and Manny doesn't hesitate. He turns around and bolts over to his mom's car.

"Don't worry, he's grounded until he's thirty," she says to me. I want to thank her somehow, but she doesn't wait for me to. She turns on her heel and meets Manny in the car, where her driver's side door was left open. Then they're gone, and the crowd disperses.

And I've never felt so alive.

# TEN

I spend the entire walk home thinking about what TLOSC said to me.

*He'll get what's coming to him. Just like Luis.*

I laugh. TLOSC really knows how to get me to warm up to them. I pull out my phone.

**aadfssd:** How did you do it?

**tlosc:** do what?

**aadfssd:** How did you tell Manny's mom what happened?

**tlosc:** who, me? 😊

**aadfssd:** Wait, that was you, right?

**tlosc:** I'm just messing with you. My dad and his mom go to church together, so we're kind of family friends, even though I can't stand him.

Now *that* is a major hint into TLOSC's identity. I wish it meant anything to me, but unfortunately, I don't know who anyone's parents are, much less which ones go to church with Manny's mom.

**aadfssd:** Well, thank you.

**tlosc:** any time ☺

When Friday rolls around, I have to remind myself over and over again that I've already decided *not* to meet up with TLOSC. Just because I'm grateful to them for solving my Manny problem doesn't mean I have to help them get revenge on Luis. He stood up for me yesterday when no one else did. Well, no one but TLOSC. And Manny's mom. The thought brings a devilish grin to my face again. I can't believe it happened.

So no, I'm not going to join some revenge plot against Luis. The only reason I might want to go to the meeting would be to find out who TLOSC is for sure, but that wouldn't be fair. Besides, I'm already in enough trouble as it is after getting detention, and who knows what kind of trouble a revenge plot would get me into. I might just go to try to convince them not to go through with it. I don't want TLOSC getting in trouble, either. I decide I'm not even mad at Luis anymore. What happened yesterday wasn't as good as a straight-up apology, but it was close enough. I just want to move past this whole thing and forget about it.

I do need to talk to him about Shawni, though. If she's the one spreading the rumors, then he might be able to put a stop to it. Maybe he can convince her to put the rumor to rest, regardless of whether it's true or not. He should know it's his ex that started it, and if anyone can make her stop, it has to be him.

At the end of the day, I go the opposite direction of room

205. I need to find Luis. I know he usually goes to the gym after school to play basketball with his friends, so I start walking over there.

I open the double doors to the foyer and look around in case Luis is out here. One of his friends is standing by the trophy case with some girl, but there is no Luis to be found. I walk past them and into the gym, where I can already hear his voice. I take a deep breath. I can do this. Luis and some other guys are talking on the bleachers. I know I could just text him what I want to say, but I want to hear his response in person, so I wrote a note to give to him. As I'm about to turn the corner around the bleachers to meet him, I hear my name.

Instead of making myself known, I stay where I am and listen. I crouch and peek between the edge of two bleachers.

"She's so hot, dude. It's always the quiet ones, huh? She's really that easy?" says some guy I don't know.

"Yeah, man." Luis doesn't even hesitate. "It's not like she can say no."

What the fuck.

The blood rushing to my ears gets so loud I have to cover them with my hands. He did not just say that. There's no way he just said that.

I thought he just didn't realize I wasn't into it, but no. He *knew* I wouldn't say no. He took advantage of me.

He knew exactly what he was doing.

And *he's* telling people about it.

It was never Shawni who told everyone what happened. It was Luis.

I run out of the gym, making sure to slam the gym door on my way out. Moments later someone is running after me. I don't even make it out of the foyer when Luis grabs at my hand, and I swirl around like I have something to say to him. Even if I could, what words would be enough for someone like him?

"Ariana, come on, you know I didn't mean it like that."

No words, but I can't stay silent either. Everything I've kept inside me since my last outburst rips itself from my mouth in a blood curdling scream. That should be a clear enough message for him.

With water in my eyes and fire in my throat, I can hear his friend and that girl laughing from over by the trophies. Laughing at my outburst. It's funny to them. I want to keep screaming, but I'm humiliated. Luis doesn't even look a little bit sorry. His lip is twitching like he's trying not to laugh, too.

I turn around and run. Not home.

I go straight to room 205.

I swing the door open without preparing myself to meet whoever is behind it. I don't stop to wipe the tears from my eyes, but I can still see TLOSC clearly for the first time. There are no teachers in the room.

Just Angel.

And Nina.

And Jasmine.

And *Shawni*.

# ELEVEN

I immediately pivot on my heel and turn right back around.

"Wait!" Shawni calls out, and despite the way I feel about her, I stop in my tracks. Is she the one I was messaging before? Or was that one of the others? Maybe all four?

She jogs out in front of me, the corners of her eyebrows raised in worry.

"Are you okay?" She reaches her hand for my shoulder, but I flinch away before she can touch it. "Sorry, sorry. I just . . . You're crying."

One of the other classroom doors opens, and a couple of kids saunter out.

"You don't have to come inside if you don't want to, but thanks for coming."

The two kids are staring at me and Shawni now, and I really don't like being stared at while I'm crying. I realize now all my anger toward Shawni before was misdirected. It was Luis who told everyone about what happened, not her. She doesn't deserve my hatred. Still, I was so mad before that it's hard to shake.

I take a deep breath, wipe my eyes, and lead the way back to room 205.

"I told you she'd show up!" Nina jumps up from the chair she was sitting in. She holds her hand out to Angel, who sighs and slaps a dollar into Nina's palm, then he picks up what looks like a lockpicking kit and starts fidgeting with it.

"You sure you're okay?" Shawni asks again, even though I never answered the question in the first place. There's already a piece of paper and a pencil sitting on one of the desks near Angel, Jasmine, and Nina. I try not to overthink the fact that "are you okay" is something TLOSC said to me, which makes me suspect Shawni was the one I was talking to. Even though it's not like it's an uncommon phrase.

I nod, wipe my cheeks dry, and sit down at the desk with the paper and pencil on it.

"Do you want a hug or something?" Angel asks. It's nice to be asked instead of just bombarded with hugs. I appreciate the sentiment, but if anyone were to touch me right now I would probably have to scream again. I shake my head and start writing.

*I'm in.*

I don't want to just let people treat me like shit. I'm tired of it, and I'm ready to do something about it.

"Great." Shawni smiles, then stands up and faces the rest of us like she's about to give a presentation. "So, you're all probably wondering why I've gathered you here today . . ."

I cock my head to the side. That confirms it. It was Shawni I was messaging with. This whole time, Shawni had been trying to reach out to me as a *friend*. Guilt wells up in my chest for how I've been treating her.

Did she leave notes for the rest of them, too? Part of me feels a tiny pang of jealousy at the thought. The idea that it wasn't only me. But then I realize that's a *good* thing. If everyone else went through the same alienation I went through because of Luis, I'm glad Shawni reached out to them, too. It gives me a newfound respect for her, and I already feel terrible for ever having suspected her in the first place.

"Not really. You're trying to get back at Luis. You want me to kick his ass again or something?" Angel asks.

Nina laughs. "I heard you were the one getting your ass kicked."

"Tch." Angel's face scrunches up like he's going to argue, but he just slouches.

I start writing to ease the tension.

*What is TLOSC?*

Shawni glances down at my paper, then stands up straighter. "Luis has hurt a lot of people. Not just me, and not just us." She clenches her jaw, and if I didn't know she was mad at Luis, I'd think she was pissed at *us*. It makes me remember when she tried to talk to me in journalism after the party. Her anger must have been directed at Luis then, too. "Luis is . . . kind of a life ruiner. We need to stick together. Be there for each other, you know? So think of it as a kind of support group. The Luis

Ortega Survival Club." Her anger dissipates, and she grins. "He ruined every one of our reputations and made it so we would have no one else to turn to. But we have each other!"

I look around at everyone. I know he ruined mine, and Angel's and Shawni's. And if he's the reason Nina got on that list before, that makes sense. It makes me wonder what happened to Jasmine.

I thought Shawni was jealous, but she's just trying to be there for everyone. She almost feels like a therapist. But that's not what I need from Shawni right now. I want to get back at Luis. Need to.

Nina claps her hands. "YEEEES! I love it!"

Jasmine and I exchange skeptical looks. I thought we were here for revenge, not a support group.

"Okay, so how are we getting back at Luis?" Jasmine says, asking what I'm thinking.

"Well, we have to be really careful about this," Shawni starts, looking worried. "But I was thinking we could start out with a few pranks. Nothing major. Just to get him a little scared. Luis has gone his whole life without having to look over his shoulder. Let's change that." Shawni sits back down at a desk, and we all angle ourselves to face her.

"We could say he has a weird-looking dick," Nina suggests. "Spread around fake dick pics or something."

Shawni shakes her head. "That wouldn't work. Too many girls have seen it, and he could just take a real picture and clear it up. We all know he has no problem sending that around."

Angel scoffs. "I still think you should just let me kick his ass."

"Yeah, because that worked out so great for you last time. Is your friend coming?" Shawni asks Angel.

Friend?

Angel looks tentatively at Jasmine, and Jasmine nods.

"She's right here." He nods in her direction.

I write down a few question marks on my paper, and Nina says, "What the heck are you guys talking about?"

Angel leans over to look at my paper before answering us both.

"My beef with Luis isn't about me. I'm just here to support a friend." He looks over to Jasmine and offers a shy smile, which she returns.

"I almost didn't come," Jasmine admits. "It's a good thing you invited both of us."

"That's really nice of you, Angel," Nina says. "You're a good friend."

"Not really," Angel says, blushing. "All I did was show up. Anyways, Shawni, go ahead."

"Thanks, Angel. Before I get into it, I want to make sure you're all cool with this. Is everyone good?" Shawni asks.

We all nod. I start daydreaming about what getting revenge on Luis would be like. If it's anything as satisfying as what happened with Manny, I'm in. Then again, I can't picture Luis's judge dad willingly humiliating his son and wrecking his own family reputation in the process.

"Okay. I was thinking . . . Jasmine, can you maybe hack his

grades or something? You're good at that techie stuff, right?" Shawni asks.

"Oh no. No no nonono. That would get me expelled. I am not risking MIT for his ass."

"What if we say he has an STD? That'll ruin his game for sure," Nina suggests.

Angel shakes his head. "He'll turn that around. Remember what happened to Ed?"

Shawni and Nina both give a solemn nod. I don't remember any Ed, so I shake my head.

"He caught Luis roofying someone and tried to snitch on him, but he didn't have any proof. Luis turned it around on him and made Ed look like the bad guy. Then Ed just . . . disappeared. Luis's dad is a judge or something, no? Pretty sure he used his influence to get Ed locked up to protect Luis."

"You're so dramatic. No one heard from Ed because he moved to Colorado," Jasmine says.

"No, he's locked up . . ." Shawni looks down, like she feels guilty. She was dating Luis at the time. "I only ever heard Luis's side of the story, which was that Ed was the one who roofied that girl."

"Which is bullshit. I knew Ed, and I knew Luis, and if one of them was ever going to pull that shit, it's Luis. He was probably just pissed Ed didn't let him finish the job."

Shawni shudders. "But yeah, Ed is definitely the one who went down for it." My eyes widen. Shawni couldn't have known about what Luis did, but I can't imagine how gross it would feel to find out your ex might have roofied someone and framed someone else for it.

"Hey, it's not your fault, Shawni. You didn't know." Jasmine squeezes Shawni's hand in comfort.

"Still, though, this is why we have to be careful. No rumors or anything, it's too messy. I don't want our names getting thrown around. Whatever we do, we can't get caught."

"Does that mean we can't all hang out together?" Nina asks, looking sad.

"Good point," Shawni says. "Probably not all at the same time. If we hang out, we need to be sneaky or have a good excuse. Like, me and Ari have dance together, so we can hang out to 'practice.' Angel and Jasmine are already friends, so y'all are good. Angel, maybe you can join drama club so you have an excuse to hang out with Nina? And Ari, you could join the robotics club, maybe?"

I was never really interested in Robotics, but I wouldn't mind joining just to have some time to hang out with Jasmine and scheme about taking down Luis. Jasmine does seem the most on my page when it comes to that part. I decide I'll go with Jasmine to the robotics meeting next week.

The door opens, making us all jump, and a teacher walks right in.

"What are you all doing in here? Out of my classroom!"

I freeze and look to Shawni, expecting her to give some kind of explanation or plead for us to be able to stay, but she and the others just scatter, giggling as they all run out of the room. I let out a little laugh none of them could hear since they were all practically out the door already.

"You too," the teacher says, gesturing toward the door, and I run out after them, giggling too, if a bit late.

We all go our separate ways once we're out of the classroom. Can't be seen together yet. I'm itching to get back at Luis, but we got broken up before setting a distinct plan of action. At least now I know I have some allies.

# TWELVE

Both my parents' cars are in the parking lot when I get home. Sometimes my mom gets home early when she works mornings, but my dad is always still at work when I get home from school, so I have no idea what's going on. I wonder if Mami might have told Papi about Tom? That's something they would leave work early to sort out. I take my time walking up the stairs so I don't have to deal with them fighting. I brace myself for the yelling as I walk in, but there is none. Dad must be taking the news really well?

"Hi mija." He kisses my forehead, then kisses my mom, which makes my eyes widen. I don't think I've seen them kiss since before The Incident.

Mami gives me a smile, and I squint to try to decode it. Is this one of those "everything is fine, I promise" smiles, or a real one? "Your dad and I are going out on a date!" she says cheerily. Fake? Not fake? She did say she was going to make an effort with Dad. So maybe not fake?

"That's good!" I say, sighing with relief.

"Listen, mija. I know your mami and I have been going through a bit of a rough patch. But we're working things out." Papi gives me a reassuring smile. "I don't want you to worry about us, okay? Your mami and I will be okay. You've been through enough already." His smile disappears when he says that last part.

"Dinner's in the fridge, mija." Mami kisses my cheek, and they leave hand in hand.

For some reason, seeing them almost happy gives me mixed feelings. I'm definitely glad they're trying to work things out, but at the same time, it makes me feel . . . weird. Like, this isn't what I'm used to. I'm not good at change. Never have been. Even if it's good.

I distract myself by checking ExposeTheMierda but quickly realize I don't have the spoons to absorb anything right now, so I bookmark the latest article for later. I sigh and feed Boo, and then I plop myself down on my bed. I'm too pumped up about potentially getting back at Luis to feel too messed up about anything else. Ideas race through my mind for hours while I lay there. Without anything else to do, I pull up Tumblr and send a few messages to TLOSC—Shawni.

aadfssd: We should smear mud on his windshield wipers.

aadfssd: Or let's make a fake Craigslist ad and put his number in it.

aadfssd: That way he'll get lots of calls from weirdos.

aadfssd: Let's poop in his backpack.

aadfssd: What are his weaknesses? We should exploit all of them.

The thirty seconds it takes for Shawni to respond feels like an hour.

tlosc: DED LMAOOOOOOO

tlosc: you are too funny 💀 💀 💀

I frown because I wasn't trying to be funny. Maybe my tactics are a little bit small, but at least it's *something*. I'm a little embarrassed to admit to Shawni that I wasn't joking, so I text back a crying laughing emoji of my own.

tlosc: hmmmm . . . weaknesses . . .

tlosc: he's afraid of spiders?

That brings a smile to my lips. That, I can work with.

tlosc: so do you want to go to that dance battle?

aadfssd: No.

I answer too quickly, then realize maybe I'm being rude. Was Shawni inviting me to go with her? I really don't know how I would feel about that. It would be nice to be invited to something. But a dance battle with loud music and a big crowd? No, thank you. I'm about to send another message to apologize for being rude when she responds.

tlosc: that's fair. I guess it's not really your scene.

tlosc: what is your scene, anyways? ☺

I smile at my phone. She's trying to get to know me, I think. Now that I'm sure it's Shawni, and I trust her, I don't actually mind sharing more about myself. Still, I don't really know how to answer. What *is* my scene? I've never really gone out before, except for that party. I definitely know what my scene *isn't*.

aadfssd: Home, I guess.

**tlosc:** I guess I don't really know what my scene is either. I like watching dance battles, but I always just go alone or with my dad.

**aadfssd:** Not your mom?

It's a while before Shawni answers, and I start to worry I've said something wrong again.

**tlosc:** just my dad 🙂

**tlosc:** anyway, I should get to bed. Good night Ariana <3

The heart makes something flutter in my stomach, and I'm not sure why. I debate if I should send one back, but I feel like it would be forced and weird if I did. I guess I'm not the type of person to send heart emojis to someone I just stopped hating a few hours ago.

**aadfssd:** Good night Shawni.

I tuck my phone under my pillow, call Boo to come cuddle with me, and fall asleep dreaming about pooping in Luis's backpack.

I wake up in the middle of the night. I can't stop thinking about Luis and how much I hate him. He's a terrible person, and I'm ashamed I ever had feelings for him. But when I really think about it, it's not even him that's keeping me from sleeping.

It's Ed.

If he'd been at the party with me and Luis . . . would he have stopped Luis from taking me to the room? Would he have saved me, like he saved that other girl? I know it's not the same. I wasn't roofied, but I was still taken advantage of. That much I know for sure. What Luis did was wrong, even if some part of me can't help but blame myself, too.

I find myself latching onto this idea . . . What if Ed had been there that night?

Without thinking, I get out my notebook and start writing. I don't even realize what I'm doing until I've written a whole letter.

*Dear Ed,*

*You probably don't know me, but I can't stop thinking about you. Not in, like, a romantic way or anything. But I couldn't sleep last night because of what happened to you. I guess you made me ask myself the hard questions.*

*Would you have saved me if you were there that night?*

*If standing up to Luis means we could go to juvie, is it really worth it?*

*That's a rhetorical question. I already know the answer.*

*It's yes.*

*And I've never been more sure of anything in my life.*

I don't know what I'm going to do with the letter. I know I could send it to Ed, but I don't want to put my trauma on him. He's definitely got enough on his plate.

Suddenly, it's clear why I can't stop thinking of Ed.

He didn't just stand up to Luis. He actually saved someone. Someone like me.

# THIRTEEN

On Monday morning, I'm sitting in the journalism room early with a dopey smile on my face reading a text. Even though I know it's Shawni and I have her number now, we still use Tumblr to talk.

**tlosc:** checking in, how you feeling?

It's a simple question but being checked in on makes me feel all light and dainty, like just the question sends the weight of my problems floating away just for a moment. I wonder if she checks in on everyone like this, or if it's just me. I bet she checks in on everyone.

**aadfssd:** I'm good. How are you?

**tlosc:** good! where are you?

**aadfssd:** Mrs. Jones's journalism room.

"What are you all smiley about?" Mrs. Jones asks.

"I made a friend," I mumble quietly.

"That's great! Who is it?" Mrs. Jones asks with real excitement, not the fake cheery tone my mom used when I told her.

Right on cue, Shawni opens the door and walks in, taking the seat right next to me. I look at Mrs. Jones and nod to Shawni.

"Glad to hear it." Mrs. Jones says with a smile. Then the bell rings, and my voice gets sucked away when Luis walks through the door. One day I'll be able to really talk with Shawni, but not today.

"Helloo? Earth to Ari," Shawni says, waving her hand in front of my face. I don't realize I'm glaring daggers at Luis until Shawni calls me out.

I've been waiting for Luis to get here, because I planted a little surprise on his seat for him, courtesy of Walmart. I made a quick stop at the one by my house before school. Not *all* of our revenge plans need to be big. I just want him to stay paranoid.

An added perk of my pit stop is that more people got to see my outfit: an off-the shoulder crop top with high-waisted cuffed jeans. It's not much, but I feel cute today, and if I can show that off outside of school, where I won't get harassed over it, I'll take it. Unfortunately, I had to put on a sweater when I got to school. Not because of the dress code—that hasn't been a problem for me since that article I wrote about it—but because I don't know if I want to be *looked* at anymore. Not like how I get looked at lately.

"I love your sweater!" Shawni says. When she looks at me, on the other hand . . . That I can't say I mind.

I spare another glance back at Luis. I know I shouldn't seem too eager. I don't want to come across as the obvious culprit, but I can't help it. The anticipation is just too much.

Luis is about to sit at his desk when he sees the little gift I left for him on his seat.

He lets out an actual scream. Like, a little girl in a horror movie type of scream. Everyone laughs, but one glare from Luis's reddened face shuts them all up pretty quick.

"There's a huge-ass fucking spider on my chair!" he says, trying to justify his scream, but his voice is still higher pitched than normal.

"Language . . ." Mrs. Jones says, though she seems pretty uninterested since the second bell hasn't rung yet.

"Relax, bro, it's fake." The guy in the seat next to him laughs as he picks up the fake tarantula from the seat. "BAH!" he shouts as he shoves the spider into Luis's face.

Luis jumps back and falls on his ass, knocking over one of the other desks on his way down, and the other guy bursts out laughing. "That's not *fucking* funny, dude! Did you put that there?" His eyes pierce through the other guy, wiping the smile clean off his face.

"No! I don't play like that," the guy says, all nervous. Ugh. Why does everyone have to be so afraid of Luis? Can't we all just bask in his misery?

Well, I can. I turn to see Shawni trying not to crack up. She looks at me with a question in her eyes, and I grin back. She winks, and it makes my cheeks go hot.

Unfortunately, the hilarity of the situation fades pretty quickly as Mrs. Jones directs everyone's attention back to her.

Scaring Luis with a spider was nice, but I want more than a few laughs. Luis gets over the scare, and the rest of class goes by uneventfully, until Mrs. Jones eventually does a cell phone purge. Apparently, a lot of kids were texting in class.

Including Luis.

"You can get your phones back after school," she says sternly. I've always been glad to be on her good side.

I don't know what comes over me, but when class is over, I can't help it. I want Luis's phone. I don't know what I'm going to do with it, but there has to be something useful on there, right?

I pass Shawni a quick note before she walks out of the classroom.

*Distract Mrs. Jones.*

It doesn't take much convincing.

"Mrs. Jones, can you help me with something really quick?"

"Sure thing, Shanaya," Mrs. Jones takes the bait and walks over to Shawni's desk. I pretend to walk toward the door and slyly slip my hand in Mrs. Jones's phone bucket and pull out the one with the blue case and the PopSocket. Luis's phone.

About twenty minutes into dance class, Nina, Angel, and Jasmine sneak into the room. They come one by one after the other kids leave so it's just me and Shawni. That way no one knows we're all hanging out together.

Ms. M pulls out one of her ear buds. "Can I help you guys?"

"Just visiting. We have free period," Nina says. They can't *all* have free period right now, can they?

Ms. M puts her ear bud back in and keeps dancing. I let out a breath. Shawni was right. I knew Ms. M was lax, but I wasn't sure if she'd let them all spend the hour hanging out in here with us.

Shawni stands up and waves at Angel, Jasmine, and Nina, so I follow suit. I catch a glimpse of my full body in the mirror that covers the entire front of the room, and a lump forms in my throat. I don't know what it is about my reflection that's been making me so uncomfortable lately. I think it's because now I know what my body looks like to the Luises and the Mannys of the world. Now I know the things my body makes guys like them want to do. I look away before I burst out crying in front of my friends.

We all sit down in a circle near the opposite corner of the room from Ms. M, and I make sure to face away from the mirror. I'm not sure if we're supposed to be planning or just hanging out. Shawni reaches in her backpack and pulls out a notebook and a pencil and hands them over to me for whenever I want to add to the conversation. I could really just use my phone, but I think it's kind of sweet that she makes a conscious effort to include me, so I decide I'll use the notebook if I have anything to say.

I subconsciously start folding and unfolding the flyer Ms. M gave us for the battle yesterday as I debate whether or not to tell them about the stunt I pulled. Angel catches a glimpse of the flyer while it's open flat and squints. Then he nudges Shawni's shoulder. "You doing that? The battle?"

Shawni glances at the paper, which I promptly begin folding up again to self-stimulate.

"I've never battled before. I'll probably get out in my first round."

"So? At least you can say you did it!" Jasmine says.

"I didn't say I wasn't gonna do it," Shawni says, biting back a smile. "I think I want to."

"We should all go to support!" Jasmine says, "Can I see that?" she asks, and I begrudgingly unfold it and hand it over to her. Jasmine frowns. "Oh . . . that's the same day as my robotics tournament."

"Damn." Angel sighs. "I promised Jasmine I'd go to that, so I'll have to miss out. Sorry, Shawni."

"Robotics tournament? Is that like where the robots you built have to fight to the death?" Nina asks, fists clenched and arms raised.

Jasmine laughs. "Yeah, pretty much. And I'm definitely gonna win."

"I wanna go!" Nina exclaims.

Shawni frowns down at the floor, and I feel really bad no one wants to go watch her. Maybe I should give crowds and loud music a chance? I start writing on the paper in front of me.

*I'll go to the battle.*

"Really?" Shawni asks me. "But didn't you just join Robotics?"

I shrug and smile. I haven't even gone to my first meeting

yet, and I'm only going to be in robotics because Shawni suggested it. Besides, *someone* has to go with Shawni. It's not like it's mandatory for people in robotics to compete, and if I were to try, mine would be the first robot destroyed.

"Thanks, Ari." Shawni smiles back at me, and for a second when our eyes meet I feel something light flutter in my stomach again. I'm not really good at the whole "looking deeply into someone's eyes" thing, so I look down and ruin the moment almost as soon as it began.

"So, let's talk revenge," Jasmine says, and everyone leans in a little closer.

"Yes, *please*. Can Luis just get struck by lightning, already?" Nina says.

Jasmine giggles. "Maybe God will be good to us and he'll get really bad food poisoning or something."

"Ari put a fake spider in his desk! Maybe he'll get bit by a tarantula." Shawni laughs.

"Or a brown recluse. Something real painful," Nina says, and I bite down my frustration. It's almost like they don't *want* to do anything. I look to Jasmine, who seems just as annoyed as I am. I won't lie, imagining Luis's throat and asshole burning from a bad lunch coming out of both ends is a pleasant thought, but I'm glad I got in some direct action. It makes me wonder what everyone else is doing.

Everyone here seems to hate Luis more than I do, but I'm the only one who's done anything about it. I wonder if they can tell I'm a fraud. That I lied about not having sex with him, and the whole reason I'm supposed to hate him is that he lied on me, but he didn't. All he did was tell the truth, but I hate him for it anyway. The guilty thoughts make me feel antsy, and I feel the need to stim—self-stimulate—by sucking on my knuckles or flapping my hands, but my mom's voice rings in my head: *manos*. Nina and Shawni are stimming, though, and no one is looking at them all weird like they always look at me when I do it. Shawni is twirling her hair tie around her finger, Nina is bouncing her leg, and Angel keeps picking and relocking his lock. Those are more socially acceptable stims, though. Angel's might even be considered cool. I just want to suck on my knuckles.

The need to stim grows the longer I'm sitting here, like an itch I can't scratch. Jasmine took my paper, and I feel weird using the notebook paper and pencil just to ask for it back so I can scrunch it up and unfold it over and over again. But I know if I don't stim soon I might not be able to avoid an outburst, and I'm too embarrassed to make a scene. Then I have the most genius idea of my life. I start fanning myself, pretending like the room is hot. It's a socially acceptable way to hand flap. I immediately feel a sense of relief and let out a breath. I need to use this trick more often.

"You okay, Ari?" Shawni asks, looking all concerned. Am I flapping too hard?

I nod my head, but stop waving my hands, glad I at least got a little out of my system. I still want to flap, but I don't want to draw attention, so I look around to distract myself. That solution didn't last very long at all.

Angel reaches into his pocket, pulls out a fidget spinner, and holds it out for me nonchalantly. I just stare at it for a second. It's like he saw right through my attempt at stimming like a "normal" person. He gives me a reassuring nod, and I finally take the fidget spinner and start whirling it around to my heart's content.

Then we're back to fantasizing about Luis spontaneously combusting. I'm tired of fantasizing, so I break the fantasy by pulling out Luis's phone.

Recognition flashes across Shawni's face. "Why do you have Luis's phone?" she asks.

Jasmine laughs. "Gimme that," she says, and I hand it to her, hoping she'll be able to do something with it that I can't.

"How are you gonna get into it without the passcode?" Nina asks.

"Just watch me," Jasmine says. From the corner of my eye, I can see her turning on Luis's camera, then messing with the camera settings, and after a while she's in his phone.

"Whoa," Nina says, a grin plastered on her face, which I then mirror.

"Uh, no offense, but what are we gonna do with Luis's phone? Isn't he gonna notice it's missing?" Angel asks.

*It got taken away in class, and I stole it. I'll put it back before he notices,* I write.

Everyone looks at me, stunned.

"We're not doing anything with his phone. I just want to

get a liiittle bit of information real quick," Jasmine says as she tinkers with the phone for a few more moments, then hands it back to me.

I grin. I don't know what Jasmine has planned, but I know at least she and I are on the same page.

Jasmine just laughs. "Who knew you were such a badass, Ariana?"

I join her laughing, my pride swelling at the compliment.

"Just be careful, okay? Make sure you wipe your fingerprints off and everything." Shawni looks concerned but impressed.

I nod, but I can't wipe the smile off my face.

By the end of class, we've scheduled a time to plan some actual revenge shit on Sunday. I started something for once, and it feels damn good.

# FOURTEEN

I make sure to sneak Luis's phone back in Mrs. Jones's phone bucket before the last class of the day, so when I get home from school I'm armed with extra adrenaline. I make a beeline for my room with Boo following me.

"He's gonna pay for what he did, Boo," I say. She meows her approval.

I pull my laptop onto my lap from the nightstand and open up my Tumblr messages to find a text from TLOSC aka Shawni.

**tlosc:** how are you?

Since I'm not used to it, I'm automatically skeptical whenever Shawni asks me how I'm doing. Does she really want to know? Does she really care? I kick myself for those thoughts, because Shawni doesn't deserve my skepticism. She's never given me a reason to believe she doesn't care. It makes me feel bad all over again for how horribly I misjudged her before. If anything, I'm the one who doesn't deserve *her* trust since I lied about this whole thing in the first place. I have to say something. I can't bring myself to admit to the lie, but I open up a message to Shawni anyway.

**aadfssd:** I owe you an apology.

**tlosc:** for what?

**aadfssd:** I thought you were the one who started the rumor about me and Luis having sex. I was really mad at you before I found out it was actually Luis.

The pause before Shawni responds is grueling. What if I just ruined everything? What if she wants nothing to do with me now? What if she realizes it wasn't a rumor at all, but the truth? Before I spiral too much, she finally responds.

**tlosc:** that explains a lot lol

**aadfssd:** So you're not mad?

**tlosc:** nah, you didn't want to believe he would betray you like that. I get it.

I let out a sigh of relief.

**aadfssd:** Thanks.

**tlosc:** <3

In my dreams—my nightmares—I'm back at that party. I'm watching Luis and me on that bed like I'm outside of my own body. The whole time, I hear his snide voice ringing in my ears.

*It's not like she can say no.*

*It's not like she can say no.*

*It's not like she can say no.*

I wake up in the middle of the night in a cold sweat. I can't stop thinking about Luis and how much I hate him. He's a terrible person, and I'm ashamed I ever had feelings for him. But this whole "survival club" thing isn't getting anything done. I know it just started, but I can't help the impatient urge inside of me. I want Luis to suffer. *Now.*

And not even just for what he's done to me. He hurt Jasmine, Nina, Angel, and Shawni, too. And Ed, who I for some reason can't bring myself to forget.

If what Angel and Shawni said was true . . . that means Ed caught Luis *roofying* someone. And Luis somehow managed to frame Ed for it. Bile rises in my throat. Luis is more than a terrible person. He's straight-up evil.

I don't know why this Ed thing has me so fixated, but I can't get my mind off it, no matter how long I lay there trying to fall back asleep.

I decide to write another letter. This time, I go off writing out my righteous anger at how unjust Ed's circumstances are. How he doesn't deserve what happened to him. In fact, he deserves everything good in this life for what he did. At the very least, he deserves better.

Then I get an idea.

Even if I can't make Luis take the fall for what he did, I can at least scare him. I can let him know someone out there knows the truth. That he didn't get away with the perfect crime.

I push my blanket off me and get out of bed, kneeling on the ground in front of my bookcase looking for last year's yearbook. When I find it, I plop it on the floor and pull it open, searching for Ed. After a while of flipping through pages, I realize I need more information than just a nickname. I pull out my phone and shoot Angel a quick text, since I know he and Ed were friends.

**Me:** What is Ed's last name?

I'm surprised when I get a text almost right away, since I wasn't expecting him to be awake at two in the morning.

**Angel:** Aguirre, why?

I immediately start scanning every page of the yearbook until I find an Edgar Aguirre. A quick Google search confirms that he was found guilty of drugging a classmate over a year ago and sent to juvie. I search "Ed Aguirre" in Instagram, and the face in the first profile matches his mugshot. I click his profile and scroll a bit, as if his Instagram would provide me with any answers about what happened, but of course there's nothing. I instinctively hit the follow button, even though there's no way he'll be able to see it now.

Then I go back to my Google search. His mugshot is plastered on the front page of the first article about him.

I screenshot it and type the word "INNOCENT" in big letters over the picture, then print out copies until I run out of paper and send one final text.

**Me:** I need your help with something.

# FIFTEEN

I make sure to keep my knife in my pocket as I sneak out of the house. I tiptoe across the living room past my snoring mother and open the door as quietly as I can. The second I close it behind me, I bolt down the stairs and over to the leasing office, where Angel is already waiting for me.

"You ready?" he asks, letting out a nervous breath. I nod, and we start walking.

On our way, I reach for the fidget spinner in my pocket and hand it back to him.

"Oh, you can keep that," he says, waving me away. "I have way too many."

I tilt my head at him as the gears turn in my brain. I pull out my phone once it clicks.

*Are you neurodivergent, too?* I type, then show Angel my screen.

"ADHD," he says with a shy smile. "Is it that obvious?"

*It was just a hunch,* I type. *You're always stimming.*

"I am?" he asks, and I laugh.

*Just because picking locks makes you look cool doesn't mean it's not a stim.*

He chews on the inside of his cheek. "That's true."

*I'm neurodivergent, too.*

He chuckles. "Yeah, kind of figured that."

I laugh too. I guess I'm not quite as subtle as I thought. Then again, being the only mostly nonverbal person at school does make me stand out quite a bit.

Before I know it, we're right in front of the school gate.

I pull out the copies of the "INNOCENT" Ed mugshots in my backpack, Angel gets out his lockpicking kit, and we share a grin.

"Let's do this."

Before school starts, I sit at my desk early in anticipation.

Once the bell rings, I listen hard.

"I knew Ed was innocent," Melanie says as she and Jessica walk into the room and take their seats.

"No, he did that shit for sure," one of Luis's friends says as he sits down next to Jessica.

"How can you be so sure?" Melanie asks, but before he can answer, my attention is yanked away from them.

Luis comes in.

And he looks like he's seen a ghost. His face is paler than usual, and he's almost more green than brown right now.

"What do you think, Luis?" Jessica asks, and Luis practically jumps out of his skin, like he forgot there were other people in the room. "Do you think someone framed Ed?"

Then his paled face turns red, and his fists are clenched. "Can you not hear?" Luis snaps. "Ed did that shit. And why aren't we more concerned about who's defacing school property and trying to scare everyone with some rumor?"

I roll my eyes. Putting up a few fliers is hardly defacing school property.

"Why are you so pressed about it?" Melanie asks accusingly. Yes. *Yes.* Now we're getting somewhere.

"Do you have something you want to say, Melanie?" Luis steps toward Melanie aggressively, and she shrinks into her desk. "I know you're not trying to start rumors about *me* with all the shit I could say about your skank ass."

Melanie's eyes go wide. "No, of course not! I didn't mean it like that. I'm just kind of freaked out about this whole thing, you know?"

I sigh. That was so close, but once again, no one is actually willing to stand up to Luis. At least I got them thinking about Ed, though.

Then Shawni walks in and sits down next to me. She turns to me with a curious look on her face, and whispers, "Did you . . . ?"

I nod, knowing she must have seen the fliers too. We both have to hold back our smiles.

Shawni and I turn our heads so we can eavesdrop on Luis's conversation. Seems like they're back to gossiping about other things now.

Melanie must have made some kind of joke, because she playfully touches Luis's arm, and he jumps again.

"The fuck do you want?" he snaps. She just looks at him, stunned.

"What is your problem today?" Jessica says. But Luis just shakes his head and sits down at his desk without saying a word.

I can't help but grin. He's starting to crack.

The second bell rings, and Mrs. Jones interrupts my view of his scared shitless face to start teaching class. Luis is a little jumpy the rest of class whenever he gets called on or when someone talks to him—probably paranoid and wondering who could be messing with him. Wondering who knows what he did.

Success.

At lunch, I go to sit at my usual table alone, and Shawni is already there waiting for me. There's a paper and pencil laying on the table, presumably for me so we can talk.

"Hi," she says shyly as I sit down across from her, and then she cracks a smile. "You are so bad."

I smile proudly and get out my lunch. When I notice she doesn't have anything to eat, I grab for the pencil and start writing.

*No lunch today?*

"I forgot my money at home." Shawni shrugs. I take one half of my peanut butter and jelly sandwich and hand it over. She glances down at it, then back at me. "Are you sure? I feel bad taking your food."

I keep holding out the half sandwich to indicate that yes, I'm sure.

"Thanks!" She finally takes it out of my hand. "I didn't want to say anything, but I'm starving," she says as she takes a big bite of her half, and I take a smaller bite of my own. I can't help the voice in the back of my head that says if I'm extra nice to her, maybe she'll forgive me for lying about having sex with Luis if she finds out. I'm in too deep to admit anything. I know if I do, I'll lose all my new friends, and I don't want to give that up right when someone's finally talking to me without expecting anything in return.

No boys dare to approach me today. It's like Jasmine said: they only touch you when you're alone. And Shawni made sure I wouldn't get left alone today. I don't feel like writing out a conversation right now, but I'm more than happy to be in Shawni's company in silence. I find myself staring at her while she eats. She chews her food on one side of her mouth, so her lips lean to the side, which I think is so cute. Her brown eyes wander the cafeteria as she chews and they settle somewhere across the room. She doesn't seem to notice I'm staring at her, since she's preoccupied with the food and whatever she's looking at. Her eyes are all soft, and I can't help but wish that longing look was directed at me. An unexpected flicker of jealousy rushes over me and I turn my head to see what she's looking at. What the hell am I jealous of? I try to snap myself out of it. We barely know each other.

I follow her gaze to find Luis standing across the room,

laughing with one of his friends as he waits in line for food, dimple and pretty gray eyes on full display. So much for his little meltdown earlier. It almost feels like his friends are surrounding him like a little army, and he's their king. They make it seem like going after Luis means war.

I want to throw up. I look back at Shawni, who's looking down now. Does she still like Luis? No, that wouldn't make any sense. *She's* the one who started the whole revenge thing! Whatever she's thinking, she must not want me to bring up her staring, since she immediately clears her throat and changes the subject.

"We should have another meeting soon. I want us to follow your lead and bring us one step closer to making this thing happen."

I look back over to Luis, and he glances over to our table. But he's not looking at me. He's looking at Shawni. He waves, and I shoot my head back over to Shawni, who, thank the Lord, does not wave back.

The next day, all I can think about is Robotics. I'm actually a little nervous to go with Jasmine. I know nothing about tech of any kind. But Jasmine assured me that newbies come and go all the time, so I won't stand out too much.

For once, all my classes are going by way too quickly. I'm so nervous I think about ditching Jasmine, but I know I can't do that. If we're going to get back at Luis, I need to be seen hanging out with her, so this has to work. From what I understand, after-school clubs are supposed to be really social, and being social isn't exactly my forte.

Jasmine meets me after my last class, and we walk to the robotics room together. It's a good thing, too, because if she hadn't met me, I might have gotten cold feet.

There are already about fifteen kids in the room when we get there, all off in their own worlds working on something or other. Some kids are by themselves, while others are working in groups. They're all pretty concentrated on doing their thing, tinkering with their respective robots. I let out a breath of relief, and all the tension I felt from before fades away. No one is whispering about me. No one stares. It's all much less intimidating than I was expecting.

"We're making robots for a tournament—to the death." Jasmine grins at me, and she must catch my eyes widening. "Of the robots, of course."

Jasmine leads me to the back of the room, where there are cabinets full of what I assume is material to make robots? I don't know. There are some little robots already made with wheels and remote controls, and others that look like they're still in the early design stages. Jasmine takes a quick look before picking hers out from the bunch. Hers looks almost finished. It's slightly smaller than the rest, in a disc shape with six wheels instead of the usual four, with wires peeking through the metal skin of the robot. I follow her to the corner, where she sits on the floor and sets her robot and some materials gingerly in front of her. I maneuver myself onto the floor with her and watch her work.

Part of me wants to take this time to do something useful. Something that will further our get-back-at-Luis plan. Really, I feel like I should be doing more, but I'm kind of stumped about what else to do. It seems like everything I've done so far is small enough that Luis forgets about it within a couple of hours. But I don't want him to forget me. Not even me, Ari—but me, the person who knows what he did. I want him to always remember, no matter what he does, that someone out there knows what he did. That he didn't just get away with it. I want him to be afraid. I start typing a message for Jasmine in my phone.

*Do you feel like we could be doing more?*

She stops what she's working on when I turn my phone for her to see.

"What do you mean?"

*Like to get back at Luis.*

"What, like telling people what he did?" It's like she's reading my mind. Her lips push to the side like they do when she's thinking. "I don't want to talk about my Luis story. Do you?"

My eyes fall to the floor as I shake my head no. I definitely don't want to talk about my Luis story. There's a moment of silence before she says anything else.

"This sucks!" she whispers frustratedly, which kind of startles me. I didn't realize she was upset. "Can I tell you something personal?" she asks.

I nod.

She looks around to make sure no one's listening, then leans in closer to me. "I'm used to being the one in control of everything in my life. I control my grades, my extracurriculars, what I put into my body . . . pretty much everything. I know some people don't like that about me. People say I'm too bossy or too controlling, but I just . . . I don't like being out of control. But then Luis . . ." Jasmine's voice cracks at his name. "He took that control from me." She wipes her eyes and averts her gaze to the ground.

I wish I could tell her how much I can relate. Luis took control from me, too.

Jasmine clears her throat. "So, I guess what I'm saying is that I really want to take back that control. That's why I'm doing this in the first place. I want to make him feel how I felt. And I hate sitting here on the sidelines while everyone else makes that happen. So yeah. I feel like we could be doing more. I want to *do something*."

I grin as I type in my phone for her, then force myself to meet her eyes after she reads it.

Come over after school tomorrow. I have an idea.

# SIXTEEN

After school the next day, Jasmine meets me outside my last class, and we walk to my house together. I feel so much safer walking home with someone. I know we're both pretty small, so we're still vulnerable, but not being alone gives me a sense of security. I don't feel the need to keep my hand on the pocket-knife in my jean pocket, at least.

When we walk in, my mom is already lying on the couch eating Takis. When she sees I've brought a friend over for the first time in my life, she springs up from the couch. Luis came over once right before the party, but my mom and dad definitely didn't see him as a "friend" kind of friend. It was like they were expecting us to be dating right from the get-go.

"Who's this?" Mami asks. I think she's trying to hide how excited she is, but she's not doing a great job.

"I'm Jasmine." Jasmine holds her hand out to my mom, and my mom takes it with her pinky and ring finger, aka her two non-Taki-dusted fingers. "We're working on a project together."

I like how it's not a lie and somehow makes us sound responsible.

"Fun! Okay, I won't get in your way, then!" Mom winks at me and shoos us away. I think she wants *us* to get out of *her* way, since she's watching her favorite telenovela. Jasmine and I go to my room.

"Alright, what's your big plan?"

I grin and start typing on my phone. I knew Jasmine was on the same page as me when she took Luis's phone and started doing her thing with it. I have a feeling she already has an idea of what I want to do.

"Want to dig for some dirt in his social media? I got all his passwords from his phone!" she says with an evil smile. And while it wasn't *exactly* what I had in mind, it's not a bad idea.

Once I show Jasmine the message, she grins.

"I like you," she says, and I hide my blush by reaching under my bed for my laptop, then hand it to her.

"Oh, I don't need that," she says, and pulls out her phone. I don't know anything about hacking since I've only ever seen it in movies or TV shows, but I always assumed you needed a computer. I guess not, since Jasmine already has his passwords. She sits down at the edge of my bed and gets to work on her phone. I'm almost attached to the back of her shoulder, watching carefully.

It's not long before she has Luis's Instagram opened up on her screen. My jaw drops. She's *fast*.

Looking through Luis's messages is fun at first. Most of his messages are just him blatantly asking every damn girl at school for sex.

"Holy shit, he's so desperate!" Jasmine laughs, and I giggle and nod. Then we slowly go deleting the messages, following my plan carefully.

But after a bit of scrolling, there's Shawni's name.

Before even reading the messages, my stomach drops. I can't tell if I'm jealous or disappointed or just nervous, but I don't like it.

Jasmine and I share a look. Is Shawni still talking to Luis? The last message between them was a few weeks ago, before any of this happened. But way after they broke up. It feels like such an invasion of privacy to look through Shawni's messages, but we're here to look for dirt. Plus, I hate to admit it, but we need to make sure she can be trusted. Jasmine looks at me as if asking for permission to open the messages. I rub my belly with both hands, trying to smooth out the knots in my stomach, then nod.

Luis: you up?

Luis: I miss talking to you . . .

Luis: do you miss me?

Shawni: please don't ask me that

Luis: why not?

Shawni: because you already know the answer. Don't make me say it.

Luis: if you say it, I'll leave you alone . . .

Shawni: fine.

Shawni: I miss you too . . .

Luis: thought so ☺

We both stare way longer than it takes us to read, as if looking at the words longer will somehow change them. Does she really miss Luis?

"Do you think she still likes him?" Jasmine finally asks.

I shrug. It's possible Shawni has feelings she doesn't want to have. Like I did. Maybe still do? I don't know . . .

Jasmine gets up from the bed and starts pacing. "If she likes him, she's gonna ruin this whole thing. She could change her mind and end up telling him everything!"

The knots in my stomach tangle themselves right back up. That's true. I think back to when I caught Shawni staring at Luis at lunch. She didn't look angry, she looked . . . kind of sad? Like, exactly the kind of look you'd give someone you really missed. We're all relying on Shawni here, and if she's not all in, who knows what could happen to us? The image of Ed's mug-shot pops into my head, and I gulp down my anxiety.

I pull out my phone to answer and show Jasmine my screen.

Maybe we should talk to her.

"Yeah . . . I think we have to."

We glance at the message one last time before deleting it, and every other message on Luis's Instagram besides the ones between him and Ed. Despite the Shawni complication, I smile. This might just be enough to tip Luis over the edge.

Jasmine, Shawni, and I meet at the park closest to the school. School let out over an hour ago, so we're not worried about anyone seeing us together, and Shawni's been practicing in the dance room this whole time.

"What's up?" Shawni says.

"We were looking through Luis's messages on Instagram, trying to prank him . . ." Jasmine starts. She pauses for a while, as if giving Shawni the opportunity to confess. When she doesn't say anything, Jasmine goes on. "We saw your messages with him."

Shawni's quiet for a second before she crosses her arms and frowns. "So what is this, like, an intervention or something?"

"Well, do you still like him?" Jasmine accuses.

"No! If I still liked him, why would I start a fucking support group? I *hate* him."

"That's not what it seemed like in your messages. You said you *missed* him."

Shawni looks down, awkwardly not saying anything, so Jasmine continues.

"How can we trust you if you're still pining over the guy we're trying to ruin?" Jasmine's voice is increasingly frustrated, and I really do get why she's mad, but I don't know. I just want to know what's going on. If Shawni's really okay with all of this. If we're similar in more ways than we think. If she really does still have feelings for Luis. I fight the pang of jealousy eating at my gut, and it kills me that I'm not even sure which one of them I'm jealous *of.*

"You *really* don't trust me, do you?" Shawni says. "Did you even read the messages? I said that so he'd leave me alone!" Shawni is shaking now, and she sits down on the bench, hugging herself.

"So you lied about missing him?" Jasmine asks.

"I don't know . . ." Tears start falling from her eyes. "I don't want to miss him! I don't want anything to do with him, but it's

like he snaked his way into my head and I can't get him out."
She's full-on crying now. I wasn't expecting the confrontation
to hit her so hard, and now I feel really bad.

I sit down next to her and start texting.

I trust you.

She gives me a firm side hug, and I tense up.

"Sorry, sorry! Natural reaction. You okay?" she asks. I guess
I wouldn't mind hugging Shawni if I knew a hug was coming.

Ask first please.

Jasmine sits down on the other side of me and softens up a
bit. "Okay, I believe you, Shawni. Sorry I flipped out. I just
really want this to work out. What happened with you two,
anyway?"

Shawni shakes her head rubs her arm.

"He's just really not a good guy. He was so manipulative,
constantly made me feel like shit, and he was so emotionally
abusive. I don't know what the hell is wrong with me . . . Why
would I ever miss someone like that?"

I hate how relatable that is. Seriously, what is wrong with us?
I type out another text.

*I miss him too . . .*

*I miss how he made me feel. Important. Seen.*

Jasmine sees my text and blows out a deep breath, pinching
the bridge of her nose.

"Okay, I'm not gonna judge, but y'all better not let your
feelings get us caught."

# SEVENTEEN

**tlosc:** have you ever been to pride?

The question is a little random, but I appreciate that we're not talking about Luis.

**aadfssd:** No, I haven't. Have you?

**tlosc:** I've always wanted to, but never had anyone to go with before . . .

I have to admit there's always been a part of me that's wanted to go to Pride. I don't really have a label for myself yet. But I know I would belong there. I'm pretty sure those are my people. Part of me wants to ask Shawni if she wants to go together this year, but my nerves get the best of me, so I say goodnight and put my phone away.

I spend the rest of the week excited about meeting up with the survival club on Sunday. We decided to try a meeting at Shawni's house so we wouldn't have to worry about being seen together at school.

When Sunday finally comes around, my parents are gone for work by the time I wake up, which I could have predicted. I know it's just the survival club, but I still straighten my hair and try on a few different outfits before pocketing my knife and heading to the bus stop. I ended up deciding on a knitted cropped sweater paired with some mom jeans that make my butt look really nice. I might not really understand why, but I want to look cute today. It's important to me.

My effort pays off when I get to Shawni's, and she actually *looks* at me when she opens the door. And I mean really looks at me.

"I love your sweater!" she says, and I feel myself blushing as blood heats up my cheeks.

Her dad comes up behind her. "You must be Ariana! Mucho gusto." He holds out his hand to shake, and when I take it, he kisses the air next to my cheek.

I smile, forcing myself not to flinch at his nearness, hoping he won't ask too many questions, because there's no way I'll be able to make words happen in a house I've never been in with a man I've never met.

"*Papi.* I told you Ari doesn't like touching."

He holds up his hands innocently. "Ah, I forgot." He looks apologetic, but I still can't help but feel judged. As a Latina, I should be used to the hello hugs and cheek kisses, but I don't have a big extended family who expects that of me. It's really just my parents, and occasionally my grandpa, who lives like an hour away, so we never see him.

Shawni's dad opens the door wider for me to come in, and then I follow Shawni to the kitchen, where Nina, Angel, and Jasmine are all sitting at bar stools around the island. I guess I was the last one here, since the bus was running a little late and I took my time getting ready.

There's a paper and pencil waiting for me on the island counter in front of one of the bar stools, so I take my seat there. Shawni sits down in the stool next to me, folding her arms across her chest and listening into the second half of the conversation.

Shawni's phone rings, and her face lights up when she looks at the screen. "I have to take this! I'll be right back!" she says, then answers her phone and runs over to her room. "Hi Mom!" she says just before shutting her door. Everyone continues talking about Jasmine's robotics tournament until Shawni comes back.

I glance around at everyone, and I can't help but notice how random our little group is. We have a girl who never talks, a b-girl with no friends, a laid-back ex jock, a freshman drama kid, and a robotics nerd. Luis is the only link that bonds us. I start laughing. Nina laughs with me, like she doesn't want to be left out of the nonexistent joke, but the rest of them just look at me for an explanation.

I pick up the pencil in front of me and start writing on the piece of paper.

*The only thing we have in common is that none of us have any friends.*

Nina stops laughing.

"That's not true," Jasmine says.

"Yeah, it is," Angel argues. "Besides me, who's your friend, Jas? Besides you, who's mine?"

"It's not true!" Nina frowns and crosses her arms. She and Jasmine look like I just told them their puppy died.

"Don't you guys get it?" Shawni says. "That's the *point*. Luis goes after people with no support system. It's *intentional*. If you don't have any friends, you have no one to believe you. He even *told* me. No one wants to be friends with the slutty bi girl that supposedly sleeps with anyone. Which makes no sense, since Luis is the only person I ever . . . ugh, whatever. Even Ed didn't really have any friends besides Luis and their little group. But once Luis turns on you, the rest of them do, too. The point is, no one really talks to any of us. That's why I started this group. We can't let him get away with it. And we're not easy targets anymore. We have each other now."

We all sit in silence for a few moments. Nina has tears in her eyes, so Angel and Jasmine hold her hands. It's a hard truth to hear, but Shawni's right. Luis chose us for a reason.

"So what do we do?" Jasmine asks.

"Maybe we just tell the truth?" Shawni says.

"That never ends well, does it?" Jasmine says. "Then it's just our word against his, and anyone else that takes his side."

I sigh. If ExposeTheMierda ever caught wind of this, Luis would be on the front page of their website.

That's when the idea comes to me. Starting rumors won't work. We can't say anything about him without undeniable proof. Sure, his shitty friends might still take his side, but if the rest of the school turns against him? He won't have the same kind of power anymore. I start writing and feel all their eyes on me until I put the pencil down on the counter.

*Then we expose him.*

# EIGHTEEN

I find myself scribbling notes in my notebook throughout the next day, taking notes on different angles we could use to expose Luis. We already know he's a horrible person, but we need *proof*. Ed's mugshot pops into my brain once again, and I shoo it away. We are not going to end up like Ed.

So, it's probably best to leave the whole roofying someone thing out of the equation, especially since none of us were there. What we can do, though, is go after the parts of him he doesn't try to cover up. He's cheated on Shawni so many times and bragged about it. Maybe we can start there . . .

Our next survival club meeting is on Tuesday, and since Jasmine's last period and mine are right next to each other, we walk together to room 205 for an incognito meetup. We walk about five feet apart, so we know we're together, but other people won't catch on. When we get to room 205, I pull on the handle, but the door's locked.

"Shawni has to let us in. Give it a minute," Jasmine says under her breath as she casually walks right past me. She leans against the wall on the other side of the door to room 205, and I make sure to linger a good distance away from her. Eventually, I catch a glimpse of Angel across the hall, and Nina loitering by the bathrooms.

After a few minutes, the door peeks open, and Shawni sticks her head out.

"Hurry before anyone sees," she says softly enough for only me and Jasmine to hear. I nod to Angel and Nina as covertly as I can, and we all file inside. The hallway is still crowded enough that no one would notice a few people sneaking into an empty classroom.

There are five desks set up in a circle for us when we get inside. I take the one that has a piece of paper and pencil set down on it. I'm starting to like writing things down instead of using my phone. I don't know, it just feels kind of old school and a little more intimate for some reason. And it's nice to be included, even if it takes me longer to write something down than it does for anyone else to say what they want.

Jasmine's laugh cuts through the room, and I look up to see Angel tickling her side.

"Stop!" she laughs, but there's no anger in her tone. Still, Angel retracts his hands from her waist with a smile.

For some reason, the little gesture surprises me. I *know* you're supposed to stop touching someone when they tell you to stop, but I guess I just didn't think it was something most guys respected, especially when the person they're touching is smiling and laughing. So Angel's small display of respecting consent makes me like him that much more.

"So, tomorrow is drama club and robotics. How has that been going for y'all?" Shawni asks me and Angel. I give a thumbs up since the last robotics meeting went well.

"Going great. I'm about to be the next Lin-Manuel." Angel grins with his chin up. I can't help but snicker picturing Angel rapping on Broadway.

"Great, so let's get serious. I want to make a plan," Jasmine says, leaning forward in her seat.

"I thought we were getting dirt, right? I already got some!" Nina enthusiastically gets out her phone and plays a recording where we can hear her talking to some girl.

"Can I have you say that for the recording?" Nina says.

"Yeah, Luis cheated on Shawni with me. I was drunk and I feel really bad about it."

"How was the sex?" Nina blurts out. Jeez, she is really not shy, to say the least.

There's a bit of a pause, then, "I don't know . . . It was kind of like I wasn't even there, like he was just using me to get off, and as soon as he did he put his clothes back on and left. What a fucking asshole, right?"

The recording ends there. Nina's smile is contagious as she looks around at all of us. "Eh? Eh? Good, right? We got proof he cheated on Shawni, *and* that he's horrible to the people he has sex with. Double whammy. I can get more."

"How'd you get her to admit that? Do you guys know each other?" Shawni asks.

"Not really. We bonded over our hatred for Luis first." Nina shrugs like it's no big deal. I can believe it, considering how friendly she was to me when we first met. I could see how she could get someone to open up.

"We can get a whole bunch of people to talk about why they hate Luis. And we should participate, too! Then maybe Ariana can put a piece together in like a post or something." Nina leans forward, elbows on the table with her head in her hands, looking eager for our thoughts.

"We can make an anonymous 'fuck Luis' Instagram or something!" Jasmine offers. "We can spread that around school."

"Should we really call it that? Maybe we should be a little more subtle, get people to open the account and then hit them with the 'fuck Luis' content?" Shawni asks.

"I'm all for naming and shaming upfront!" Nina says. "There's definitely power in naming abusers."

"Good point. Okay, I'm down for that," Shawni says. "Can we just record our pieces right now? Ari, you can write yours down."

Something sinks in my belly. I don't want to tell my story. Thinking about what happened with me and Luis is the last thing I want to do. And that isn't even what they want me to talk about. I'm supposed to lie. Say Luis and I went in the room to talk, and that Luis made up the rumor about us having sex. Lying on Instagram was one thing, but can I lie to my new friends right to their faces? Nina already has her phone out, ready to record. She presses the Record button and starts talking first before I can write anything down to protest.

"My name is Nina De La Cruz. Luis Ortega told me he really liked me, and said he wanted to break up with his girlfriend Shawni so he could date me." Her shoulders slump and she pauses her recording. "Sorry, Shawni . . ." She presses Play again. "But yeah, anyways. He wanted me to send some . . . you know. Nudes. And I did. I thought it was just between us, you know? But apparently he sent them to all his friends, and now practically every dude at school knows what my boobs look like. He also lied about having sex with me. I already didn't have any friends, but after that, it was like everyone kept their distance. That's like, child pornography or something, right? I mean, I'm not a child, but I haven't even had a quince yet. Luis is an adult boy who distributed my nudes." She ends her recording and looks to Shawni. "Your turn?"

"Nina, I had no idea . . ." Shawni's eyes look shiny, and she reaches out for Nina's hand and squeezes.

Nina gives her a reassuring smile, as if this doesn't faze her at all. "It's okay! I'm fine, really."

"I'm gonna fucking kill him," Angel says, fists balled.

"I said it's okay," Nina says, still smiling.

"It's not okay, Nina," Jasmine says.

"I have you guys now! Everything is good. Let's just move on, okay?" Nina says, a slight edge to her tone, like a warning.

Nina hands Shawni her phone.

"Okay." Shawni takes a deep breath, then presses Record. "I'm Shawni Rodriguez. Luis and I dated on and off since eighth grade, so I know him pretty well. He was extremely overprotective, and he didn't let me have any friends besides him. He was really emotionally and verbally abusive. Always calling me a slut, but also a tease and a bitch if I ever didn't want to have sex. He made me feel like he was the only person I could rely on, since I didn't have anyone else, and that's why I stayed with him for so long. When we finally did break up, he made sure my reputation was completely ruined so I would be alone . . ." Shawni stops the recording and wipes her eyes. "I'm sorry, I don't think I can say more without crying. I don't want to cry right now."

Nina returns Shawni's gesture from before and reaches her hand out to Shawni, who takes it. I want to reach mine out, too, to offer some sort of comfort. Isn't that what you're supposed to do when someone cries? I feel completely useless, unable to offer any words of support. Since I'm sitting next to her, I awkwardly extend my arm and pat her back a few times. That is supposed to be comforting, right?

"Anyway, who wants to go next?" Shawni asks, and I want to disappear in my seat.

"I don't want to do it," Jasmine says without explanation.

"Why not?" Nina asks.

"It's okay, Nina. No one has to put themselves out there if they don't want to. What about you, Ari? You can write about how Luis lied about having sex with you, like he did with Nina. That establishes a pattern."

I look at my hands on my desk. I really don't want to lie about this anymore, but what else can I do? I end up just shaking my head, grateful for the out Jasmine just gave me. If she can opt out, so can I.

"Okay, that's fine. We're doing great, though. Nina and I can do lots of interviews like this, since we can share our stories with anyone who Luis fucked over. That way they'll be more likely to talk to us. Obviously we won't pressure anyone to state who they are unless they want to."

"I can help, too," Angel offers. "I have PE with Luis. You'd be surprised at some of the shit he just openly says to the guys in the locker room. I'm not part of his group anymore, but I can probably sneak a recording if I hear something worth taking down."

"That's perfect!" Shawni grins widely. "This is really going to work, you guys! We might even get Luis himself or one of his friends to admit something incriminating!"

I can't help but smile, too. Angel, Shawni, and Nina have the best chances of getting Luis or one of his friends to actually admit to the shit he did. Out of all of us, I'm pretty sure Shawni is the only one Luis actually had feelings for. We can use that. And because Nina's already known for having no filter, people won't think twice about her approaching them asking questions. Angel's in the background all the time around Luis and his friends. In the boys' locker rooms, in gym class, at lunch.

Hopefully between the three of them, they can get him to admit to *something*.

I don't have to tell my story in order for us to take down Luis. All I need to do is help everyone else tell theirs.

# NINETEEN

After school, I find Shawni sitting at a bench in the courtyard alone. I walk over and join her, so we're both sitting together in silence. I like how Shawni doesn't always press me to talk. She's not like how Luis was. With Luis, he didn't mind me not talking, but the whole time we were together he'd be looking me up and down, like he was imagining himself devouring me like a piece of steak. With Shawni, we're just . . . together, appreciating each other's company. I'm not in a huge rush to go home, since I have to admit I'm enjoying this. I feel closer to Shawni now that I know we both have complicated feelings for Luis. Not that it's a good thing, it's just nice to not be alone.

Don't get me wrong, I'm still one hundred percent on board with ruining him, and I'm sure Shawni is, too, since she's the one who *started* this whole thing. But it's hard to get him out of my head. He was the first person to notice me, and even though I know now it was only to get me in bed, my heart still betrays me sometimes when I think about him. I have a hunch Shawni might feel the exact same way.

We're sitting really close, Shawni and I, and even though I could move since there's an empty spot on the other side of me, I stay. We're about as close as we can be without touching, which I like. Shawni checks a text on her smartwatch, then finally breaks the silence.

"Want me to walk you home? My dad doesn't get off work until six, so I don't really have anything else to do before he picks me up."

I have to think about it for a minute. I'd rather just hang out with Shawni than go back home by myself. I start typing.

*Want to come over?*

She smiles as she reads. "I'd like that."

By the time we get back to the apartment, my parents are already home. I take a deep breath before walking inside, expecting them to embarrass me in front of Shawni by either being all cold to each other or weirdly fake and happy. At least I'll have Shawni as an excuse to run to my room and hang out with her as a distraction.

But when we get inside, Mom and Dad are sitting together on the couch.

"Oh!" My dad sounds all surprised when I walk in with Shawni, and he and my mom stop whatever conversation they were just having. "We weren't expecting company, but we're happy to have it!" Papi waves at Shawni, looking all happy that

I already brought home someone else.

I'm thrown. If they were willingly spending time together when I wasn't even home, it can't be fake, can it?

"Who's this, mija?" Mami asks with a smile.

"I'm Shawni. Ari and I have dance together." Shawni waves shyly, and it catches me off guard. It's not often I see Shawni looking shy.

I give my parents a curious look, wondering what they were just talking about so secretively. My dad must catch on because he answers the nonverbal question.

"We were just about to watch a movie! Why don't you two join us for Estar Güars?" he says. I'm about to grab Shawni and pull her into my room to avoid them when she ruins that plan.

"Sure! I've never seen any of the Star Wars movies, actually." Part of me is surprised Shawni understood my dad's heavily accented version of the title, but Shawni's dad has an accent, too, so she must be used to it.

My dad gives Shawni a wide-eyed look like she just grew a second head. "You've never seen *any* of them? We have to start it from the beginning of the prequel trilogy." Without hesitating, Mami picks up the remote and puts on *The Phantom Menace*, and Papi nods enthusiastically. "There. Wouldn't want you to miss anything important!"

I sigh and follow Shawni onto the couch to join my parents. It's supposed to be a three-person couch, so it's impossible to sit the four of us down without touching and squeezing together. I sit next to my mom, and Shawni sits at the edge of the couch next to me. I'm about to retreat and sit on the floor to give them all more room, but Shawni's shoulder against mine does something unexpected, and I feel all warm and tingly. In a good way.

Touch always has a huge impact on me, good or bad. Usually it makes me want to shrivel up and disappear, but sometimes it fills my body with a warmth I can't get from anything else, and I can't get enough. I've only ever felt that with my parents before, like when my dad rubs my back or my mom plays with my hair, but Shawni's touch right now is like that. Our shoulders are barely touching, and I find myself giddy from the feeling it gives me.

When I look down at my arm I'm horrified to see that I have very obvious goose bumps. Luckily Shawni's too into the movie to notice.

I turn my attention to my parents. Have they noticed my reaction? But they're completely immersed in the movie. They're even holding hands! The warm fuzzy feeling from touching Shawni blends into the warmth of this whole moment. My mom must have been serious when she told me she was going to work on their marriage.

I bask in that feeling until Shawni eventually checks her smartwatch and realizes the time.

"My dad's here. Thanks so much for having me over, Mr. and Mrs. Ruiz!" Shawni stands up from the couch and stretches out, the bottom of her shirt lifting just enough to reveal a sliver of the skin underneath. I blush.

"The pleasure is all ours!" Mami gets up and pulls Shawni into a hug, and Papi follows. Then Shawni turns to me and brushes a couple of braids behind her ear.

"Bye, Ari. I had a great time." There's that shy voice again. "Can I . . . do you want a hug?" she asks, and I nod my head eagerly, standing up as she wraps her arms around me. I lean into the embrace, kind of forgetting to hug her back in my nervousness until the last minute. Just when I reach my arms up to return the embrace, she devastatingly lets me go and rushes out the door.

Once she's gone, my parents both turn to me and raise their eyebrows.

"So tell us about Shawni," my dad says with a grin he's trying to hide.

"I . . . she's a friend. She . . . dances?" Suddenly I don't know what to say. I don't know why I'm all nervous about talking about Shawni. I guess I don't know what to tell them. Do I tell them about how fuzzy she makes me feel? How I don't mind her little touches? "She's a good hugger," I say with a childlike smile. "I like her."

"You like her? Like, like, or *like* like?" Mami asks.

"What?" I ask.

"Mija, I'm just gonna put this out there," Papi adds, "but it's okay if you don't end up with Luis. It's okay if you don't end up with a boy at all, okay?" He winks and kisses my forehead, but I'm not really sure what either of them are implying.

Then my parents say goodnight and go to their room

together. I smile to myself. I can't remember the last time they slept in the same bed.

On Friday at lunch, Shawni arranges for us all to meet up in the journalism room in secret again. By now, we've had a little bit of time to gather some dirt. When I get there, Shawni is already inside sitting in her usual seat, and there's a paper and pencil sitting on the desk I'm always at. When she sees me open the door, she smiles all big, and it makes my tummy do a happy little flip. Just as I take the seat next to her, Jasmine, Nina, and Angel come in and sit around us.

"So, what are we meeting for?" Angel asks.

"I just wanted to check in with everyone on how we're doing. What kind of dirt everyone has. All that."

"Well . . ." Nina says with a mischievous grin. I tilt my head in curiosity, and she shrugs. "Telling my story about Luis made me really remember why I hate him so much. So, me and my brother TPed his car. I wanted to do his whole house, but Luis's dad scares me, so . . ."

"Nice!" Shawni laughs. "Yeah, his dad would have been pissed, so that's probably for the best," she says. I forget she was with him so long that she not only knows Luis but his parents, too.

I couldn't be more thrilled at this development. That explains why Luis seemed so pissed in journalism today. He must be walking on eggshells, looking over his shoulder everywhere he goes now. As he should.

Nina blows out a breath of air. "Whew. Glad I didn't do the whole house, then."

"Well, that is amazing. But maybe we should lay off the pranks until we expose him in a bigger way. That way we let him get comfortable before it all explodes in his face. Jasmine and Ari already messed with his Instagram messages, and Ari and Angel put Ed's mugshot everywhere. He's gotta have his guard up right now, and that might be dangerous."

I slouch in my seat. Pranking Luis is fun, but I have to admit Shawni is probably right. The main event will be much more satisfying if he doesn't see it coming.

"True," Nina says. "Speaking of exposing him, though, I got sound clips of two more girls talking about what an asshole he is."

"That's awesome! I had a little bit of trouble getting anyone to talk to me," Shawni says. "Some of the girls I talked to were a little shy." She hangs her head. "Sorry, I should be better at this. Maybe they just don't like me very much."

"No!" Nina says. "I talked to a bunch of people who didn't want to say anything, too. I just asked, like, a *lot* of people." She shrugs like it's no big deal.

"Oh, well that makes me feel a little better, but it's also not great. Why doesn't anyone want to help us?"

If they're anything like me, I know why. Talking about Luis is hard. Even if I hadn't lied, I wouldn't want to tell my story in a million years. Jasmine doesn't want to tell hers, either. Is it that hard to believe that others would feel the same way?

"Don't force it." Jasmine says what I'm thinking, as usual.

"Not everyone's going to want to open up to someone they don't know. That's fine. We did what we could."

"You're right." Shawni sighs. "We did what we could. Angel, did you get anything?"

Angel's leg is bouncing up and down, and he keeps fidgeting with his lock. Is he nervous?

"I . . . I got a video today, but I don't know if we should use it," he finally says.

"What'd you get?" Jasmine asks.

His face pales when he meets Jasmine's eyes. "You know what, just forget I said anything. I didn't get shit."

Jasmine pushes Angel's shoulder playfully. "No, tell us!"

"It's really not that important."

"Seriously, quit playing around. Just tell us and we can judge if it's important or not." Jasmine rolls her eyes. I have to resist rolling mine, too. I wish Angel would just come out and say what he got.

"It's . . . it's about you," he says to Jasmine. "I don't want to say it in front of everyone."

"Let me see." Jasmine grabs Angel's phone and presses Play on the video.

"Wait, maybe we should—" he starts, but the video's already playing, and it's showing an odd angle of Luis's back. Angel must have had to hold his phone low so Luis wouldn't notice him recording.

"Jasmine Mendez, too? Was she as prude as she acts?" some guy asks.

"Nah, man," Luis says. "I'm telling you, you gotta get 'em drunk or high and they'll do anything. Bitch let me smoke her out, and her legs opened up quicker than—"

Jasmine stops the video, her eyes all shiny. She puts the phone down on the desk. "Yeah, we don't need to use that."

Something sinks inside of me. He talks about Jasmine the way he talked about me. Like he's bragging about the fact that he doesn't care if we're actually willing.

"Are you okay?" Shawni asks tentatively.

"Fine," Jasmine says curtly and hands the phone back to Angel.

"Can I hug you, Jas?" Angel asks, and Jasmine shakes her head and wipes her eyes. Angel takes his phone back without touching her. "I'm sorry, I shouldn't have said anything. We all know Luis is a fucking liar. Obviously we don't need to use that video."

"It's fine, I'm fine. I have to go to the bathroom." Without another word, Jasmine stands up and leaves. She takes her backpack with her, which means she has no intention of coming back. Angel runs a hand over his face.

"I fucked up, didn't I?"

Since Angel is sitting in front of me, I awkwardly pat his back. I feel like I'm getting good at this whole neurotypically comforting my friends thing.

"No, it's not your fault Luis is a fucking asshole," Nina says.

"We'll give her some space and check on her later, yeah?" says Shawni, and I nod in agreement. Jasmine doesn't seem like the type of person who wants anyone around her when she's crying, and she's most definitely crying right now. "Anyway, I think we have enough here to go off of, so Ari, can we send everything to you and leave you to put it all together, like you do in your articles?"

I nod, even though I'm scared. I need to make this all convincing enough to actually make a difference, and I don't know if I can.

Before I can freak out about it too much, the door opens, and Mrs. Jones walks in, arms full of notebooks.

"Having a secret party in here without me?" She smiles as she sets the books down on her desk. But the bell rings before we have to explain ourselves, and we're forced to all go our separate ways.

Well, Shawni and I don't go our separate ways since we're both walking to dance class. It's nice walking with someone. My anxiety always skyrockets when I walk alone now, because of what Manny did. But I feel much safer now.

That is, until I catch a glimpse of Luis. He's walking in our direction, and I can't tell if he's looking at me or Shawni, but he grins as he gets closer. His dimple deepens on one side, and I feel my own cheeks get hot with nerves. I have to remind myself that I hate him. He was cruel to me. He took advantage of me. He is a horrible person. So why do I have this feeling in my stomach when he smiles at me? Why did he have to be so nice to me before he was so horrible? The nervous tingle in my gut immediately turns to slush when he gets close enough for me to realize he's actually smiling at Shawni. I kick myself for the tiny pang of disappointment I feel. I look to Shawni, whose face is just as flushed as mine.

God, why the hell are we like this?

Shawni catches my eye and then averts her gaze quickly, looking embarrassed. She knows I saw her, but she doesn't know I felt . . . *something* when I thought he was looking at me. We walk the rest of the way to dance avoiding each other's gaze.

When we get there, there's a guest teacher standing in the middle of the room with Ms. M. When the rest of class tries to leave for the gym, Ms. M stops them, for once.

"I have an exercise I want to work on today! Partner up and then take a seat against the mirror!"

A few students groan and reluctantly partner up. Shawni chooses me, and even though I knew she was going to, it makes my insides light up with excitement. I think it's the first time in a partner activity that I wasn't the last one to get paired up.

"We're doing something called contact improvisation today, or as I like to call it, vibe-offs. This is my boyfriend, Greg. He doesn't really dance, but since he stopped by, I'm making him help us out. Your skill level doesn't matter in a vibe-off. You listen to your partner's body language and react. It's a conversation. Use each other's energy, your intuition, and the music instead of your dance vocabulary," Ms. M explains, then plays an instrumental track on the speakers. I watch intently since I have no idea what she means.

Greg looks a little stiff at first. Ms. M takes a full-body deep breath, stretching her arms out with her inhale and relaxing her body with the exhale. Greg doesn't do the whole movement, but he doesn't seem as stiff anymore. It looks like Ms. M relaxed his body with her breath. She closes her eyes, and he follows suit. How are they supposed to know what the other person is doing if they can't see?

Neither of them moves for a few moments. Then at the exact same time, they start swaying in tandem, eyes still closed. Maybe it was a musical cue I missed? She reaches out and puts a hand on his shoulder, and he opens his eyes and kisses it. Everyone "awws" at that. The entire time they're dancing, they don't do a single move that we've learned in class. They gracefully move around each other, he starts to lift her, she rolls out of it and runs back to him. They dance like this until the song is over.

Then she asks for volunteers. Of course the only hand that goes up is Shawni's.

"Go ahead, Shawni." Ms. M and her boyfriend join the rest of the class by the mirror, and Shawni takes their place. I've never danced in front of a crowd before, so I hesitate.

"Come on, Ari." Shawni smiles and holds her hand out for me, and despite all my instincts telling me to run away, I take it and let her pull me to the center of the room.

As soon as the music comes back on, I feel my body tense. The quick drumbeat matches the pounding in my heart. Is it possible to do a vibe-off without touching? The music makes me feel too nervous for touching. If Shawni were to touch me, there's no telling whether my reaction would be good or bad. Luckily, she doesn't try to get too close. She motions her arms to her chest as she inhales, silently telling me to breathe. I mirror her breath, then let my arms float into the air and sway with the whistle of the flute. Shawni mirrors me this time. The flute moves us for a while, and I'm not sure which one of us is leading and which is mirroring, but our movements are the same. It feels like there's an invisible wall separating us, and in order to reach each other, our bodies have to be synced. The space between the walls gets smaller with each movement, each beat.

When the drum kicks in again, I realize how close we are, and it shakes the anxiety back into my body. Shawni leaps forward with the beat as if she knew it was going to speed up, and runs full speed past me, breaking the invisible wall. I find myself running after her. Her energy was more calming than the music, and I need to get back to it in order to relax right now. When I catch up, we're on the other side of the room. The drum is a soft patter now, and the soft winds of the flute are back. This time we stand still. We're much closer to each other than before, but that's okay. The wall is barely there. She reaches a hand across the invisible boundary. A question.

I prepare myself, then take it. The touch feels safe, and I'm immediately filled with relief. She twirls me around, and I laugh as I spin. It's not a fancy twirl, more like how you would twirl a child, and I feel comfortable with this. Safe. The flute quiets and the only sound we're left with is a soft wind.

Maybe it's because I'm dizzy from spinning, or because the

wind is pushing me toward Shawni, but our bodies kind of clash into each other in a sort of hug, and we just sway. It doesn't feel so bad touching right now, though. It feels like Shawni is protecting me from the anxiety that was bubbling up a minute ago. I don't know how to explain it, but her energy is just . . . good. I want more of it. Instead of jerking away when we crash together, I let myself melt into her.

It's amazing how different wanted touches are from unwanted ones. I don't feel like I'm sinking or being tangled up in seaweed while I'm drowning. I don't feel any phantom hands on me burning my skin long after they're gone. I feel light again, untainted by any complicated feelings of anger or fear. Just light.

Shawni walks home with me after school to help me with the article. When we get inside, my mom doesn't look too happy to see us for some reason.

"Oh, you brought your friend . . . again. That's great!" she says, using her fake cheery voice that I hate so much. Why would she have a problem with Shawni coming over? I thought she liked Shawni.

"It's nice to see you again, Mrs. Ruiz," Shawni says happily despite my mom's rude greeting. Well, maybe Shawni didn't catch the fakeness in her tone, but I know her well enough to be able to tell the difference.

"Yeah, you too," Mami says. "Well, you ladies have fun. Don't mind me, I'll just stay out of your way out here . . ." She lets out a small sigh as she sits on the couch.

"'Kay, Mami," I say softly as I lean over the couch to hug her before leading Shawni over to my room. Boo sneaks into my room with us before I can close the door.

"Are you sure it's okay for me to be here?" Shawni asks as she sits on my bedroom floor to stroke Boo.

I nod and sit on the floor with her. Why wouldn't it be okay for her to be here? I open up my laptop and pull up all the notes, screenshots, and recordings everyone has sent me about Luis. I haven't really looked at all this yet because thinking about Luis makes me sick.

I've been dreading this part all day. I know I was the one all eager to make something happen, but now that I have the opportunity to do something, I feel like I'm stuck in quicksand, and I'm not sure if I want to fight my way out just yet. I wonder if we'll all still be friends when this is over. I'd like to think we would still hang out afterward, but I'm not convinced. I'm sure we'll have to be even more careful about hanging out after than we are now if we want to avoid getting caught.

To make matters worse, my usual inspiration is reading stories from ExposeTheMierda, but with all the pressure to write something good enough to go on their blog, all the stories just give me imposter syndrome. I close my laptop.

I do want to expose Luis for the asshole he is, but I don't want to lose my friends. Plus, I don't love thinking about him, and that's something I have to do if I'm going to write this article. It was one thing pulling pranks and sticking Ed's mugshot in the halls, but writing a personal essay would require really, truly thinking about Luis and what he did. Maybe if I just stall for a few days, I'll be able to handle it?

But Shawni is here *now*. I don't know how to put it off any longer when she's looking to me so hopefully. I put on a brave face for her.

"Okay, I think we have a pretty good case here. When people find out everything he did, they'll hate him worse than they hate us. But I think . . . what?" Shawni has been smiling so hard since we got in here.

"You're talking," she says.

"Oh . . ." My mouth drops for a second before I let out a shy giggle. I guess Shawni's never heard me talk before. Maybe I can do it here because we're in my house, my safe space. When I open my mouth again, there's no sea witch keeping my voice hostage. Instead: *words*.

"I do talk sometimes. Just, only when I feel really comfortable. Can't really talk at school, you know?"

She nods like it makes total sense. "So, are you just really shy then?"

"I don't think shy is the word for it. I don't have a formal diagnosis, but I think it's called selective mutism. And autism, probably. I can't really talk to most people, or in most places." I expected to feel nervous admitting this out loud to anyone, but all I feel is relief. I'm so relieved at sharing with Shawni that I can't stop info dumping. "It's not that I don't *want* to talk at school, either. I want to. It's actually really freaking inconvenient that I can't. Like, I love that you always think of me and leave out papers for me to write on, but everyone talks so much faster than I can write, and the conversation sometimes just moves on without me. If I could make myself talk all the time, I totally would. But I really can't control when my voice decides to come out. It only happens when I feel super safe and comfortable . . ." I trail off, laughing awkwardly. It seems like I either don't talk at all or talk way too much.

Shawni smiles all big and dorky again. "You must really like me, then."

I'm blushing so hard I can feel it in my chest, but even though I'm nervous now, the sea witch can't touch me.

"I do," I say, and Shawni smiles, then looks down at her smartwatch thoughtfully. "Did you get a text?" I ask.

She shakes her head, then unsnaps the watch from around her wrist and holds it out to me. "Maybe this could help?" she says tentatively. I must be giving her a confused look because she elaborates. "Since you can talk sometimes but not others, maybe you can have some pre-recorded messages that are common things you find yourself writing down. Like, yes, no, can I use the restroom, I need to leave—that kind of thing. Do you want it?"

"But you love your smartwatch." I stare at the watch she's holding out for me.

"I want you to have it," she says earnestly. "Can I?" she asks, gesturing to my wrist. I stifle a nervous giggle and hold my hand out to her. She takes it and straps the watch to my wrist, then takes a few minutes teaching me how to use it. "Oh, and Ari?" she says, looking up at me.

"Yeah?"

She holds my gaze, the corners of her lips tugging upward just slightly. "I really like you too."

# TWENTY

Without expecting much, I check ExposeTheMierda one more time before going back to trying to compile everyone's stories myself. The most recent story is about a girl who got expelled because of a freaking school dress code. I bite back some bitterness at the fact that *my* dress code article wasn't good enough for the blog, but this one is.

Whatever. Maybe ExposeTheMierda is open to more stories like this now than they were when I submitted mine. This is a *good* thing. That means when I write my Luis story, I'll be practically guaranteed a spot on the front page. Now all there is to do is write it.

But . . . something's just not clicking. Aside from what I was able to get done with Shawni the other day, I haven't been able to make any progress on the story. Everyone's counting on me, and I need to make this good. Better than good. It has to be perfect. It's a lot of pressure. Especially since I'm not even sure if I'll still have my friends once I do my job.

Out of everyone in our group, Jasmine seems to be the only one who understands. In Robotics, we're definitely on the same page.

"It's okay if you take your time with the posts. We don't really have a deadline. I know it freakin' sucks thinking about him. No one will blame you if you're not done yet."

I smile in response, but she doesn't see me. She's too busy smiling down at her phone. I'm curious, so I type something out on mine and hold it out to her. She's too preoccupied to notice, so I decide to finally make use of one of the prerecorded messages I took on Shawni's—my—new watch.

"Hey," the watch says.

Jasmine's eyes shoot up. "Did you just—"

"Hey," I play the recording again so she sees it was just that, then I hold my phone out to her, showing her the message I'd typed.

*What are you all smiley about?*

Jasmine glances up from the phone and blushes. "Oh, I was just texting Angel."

I grin. I wonder if they like each other. I would be willing to bet money they do.

*You like him, don't you?*

"What? *No!* We're best friends!" She lets out an awkward giggle. "He would never go for someone like me, anyway."

*What does that even mean?*

"You know, like, a nerd? A loner? He can do better." Her smile disappears.

*He's those things too though lol,* I type. I happen to know Angel has a full-ride scholarship to ASU's honors college, Barrett. I guess that doesn't make someone a nerd by itself, but he's definitely in Jasmine's league, is what I mean.

Jasmine laughs. "True."

*I bet he likes you too,* I type, hoping I'm not crossing a line. It's just so much more fun to talk about crushes than it is to think about Luis or this goddamn story.

"Really?" She blushes again, then coughs and goes back to tinkering with her robot. "*Anyways.* Like I said. We're best friends." Then she looks up at me with a mischievous grin. "What about you?"

*What about me?* I write.

"Who do you like?"

Now it's my turn to blush. If I'd been asked before that party, I would have said Luis definitively. But now? Definitely not.

"Is it Shawni?" Jasmine asks, and my eyes widen.

*Why would you think that?*

She shrugs. "Just a guess."

*We're friends.*

Jasmine laughs. "Right. You're friends with Shawni the way I'm friends with Angel." She winks at me, and I can't help but laugh. Maybe I do like Shawni. If I do, I like her in a different way from how I liked Luis, though. I don't feel like I need her approval or her praise or compliments. I just like being around her. Looking at her. Touching her shoulder with mine.

I nod and wink back. We'll keep these crushes as our little secret.

✕ ✕ ✕

When I get home, I'm mindlessly scrolling through Instagram to get out of my own head when I get a notification. I click it and see the last thing I would have expected.

Ed followed me back.

Is he out of juvie? It did all happen a couple of years ago, when I was still in middle school. I guess it's totally possible he could have gotten out early on good behavior. I immediately go to his profile to see if he's posted anything new. Nothing.

I glance at my notebook full of the unsent letters to him, and I'm filled with an irrepressible urge to talk to him. Now's my chance. I don't know why I feel it so strongly. Maybe because he's the only one before the survival club who tried to stand up to Luis. Really, I guess it's because he's one of us.

I take a deep breath and send a message.

Ariana Ruiz: Hey. You probably don't know me

I don't know what I'm supposed to say. "I know you're innocent"? No, that would just freak him out.

Ed Aguirre: I remember you. We were in the CMS newspaper club together. I think you were a couple years younger. But yeah, I remember you. The quiet girl, right?

Ariana Ruiz: That's me.

I can't help but feel a little guilty that he remembers me and I don't remember him. Sixth grade was a long time ago, and my memory isn't that great.

Ed Aguirre: what's up?

Maybe this was a bad idea, but I'm already in too deep. I

want Ed to know he has allies. I'm not about to expose the rest of the club like that, but I can expose myself. Knowing what Ed went down for, I trust him.

**Ariana Ruiz:** I want to help make things right.

There's no response for a while, and the wait is excruciating. Did I cross a line?

My mom knocks on my door, pulling me out of my almost-spiral. She opens the door before I respond.

"Hi, mija. What are you up to today?" she asks as she walks over and sits on the edge of my bed.

"Nothing, really," I say without looking from checking my phone again. Still no response from Ed. Sigh.

"Want to hang out with your mami?" she asks.

Then I feel my phone buzz, and my eyes snap down to it again. He responded!

**Ed Aguirre:** what do you mean?

"Uh . . . maybe later," I say as I start to type out a message in response.

"Alright, honey. I'll be here. All day." Mami sighs but doesn't leave my room, which I'm fine with. She can sit here on my bed if she wants to, but I'm way too distracted to make conversation.

I'm typing a message about getting revenge on Luis before I realize that would be pretty incriminating. Using my notes app and deleting the messages seems much safer.

**Ariana Ruiz:** Can we meet up somewhere?

It turns out Ed only lives a ten-minute walk from school, so we decide to meet at the park outside campus. I was half expecting to have to meet him at his house, since he's on probation and I didn't really know if he'd be allowed to go anywhere, but he said it was fine. I'm relieved, because I didn't want to have to go to the house of a guy I've never met.

I get to the park first and sit at one of the tables, waiting impatiently. I start typing a message up in my notes app for him, detailing how I'm going to expose Luis (I didn't want to put the club on the line, so I'm only mentioning myself), how Luis is going to pay for what he did, etc.

I'm just finishing up when I'm startled by someone sitting down across from me at the table.

"Hey, Ari." I look up to see Ed smiling at me. I give a polite smile back, play a "hey" from my new watch, then hand him my phone so he can see my message.

I wait for him to read, anticipating his response. I expect his smile to grow bigger when he realizes someone is going to finally get revenge on Luis. Maybe he'll offer to help.

But instead, his smile drops, and he hands me back my phone.

"I don't think this is a good idea." His face is solemn as he looks at me. I start typing again.

*Why not?*

He runs a hand through his hair. "Not to be blunt, but look what happened to me. I lost two years of my life for trying to stand up to him." I don't say or type anything then, so he goes on. "If you want my advice, I say don't do it."

I frown as I text.

*I'm doing it.*

"Why?"

*He deserves it*, is all I type.

He shakes his head. "*You* don't deserve whatever happens after that, though."

*I'll be careful.*

"Why are you so set on this? It's not worth it."

But it *is* worth it. I don't know how to explain it to him. I don't know how to tell him that, even if I get caught, it'll be worth it if Luis gets a fraction of the suffering he caused me or anyone else. And if it stops him from hurting anyone else.

"Why'd you want to meet up with *me* anyway? Why involve me in this after what happened to me?" He looks hurt, and for some reason, my eyes start to get misty at the question. I don't even know why I wanted to talk to Ed, but I know it was important to me.

Maybe I feel like I owe him. I type for a while, deleting and rewriting several times before I have something I'm ready to show him.

*You saved someone like me. I had to say thank you.*

"Oh." His face softens. "I'm sorry. Listen, I get it. Well, I don't get it exactly since that's never happened to me, but like, I understand why you're so set on this. But please, leave me out of it, okay? I don't want to have anything to do with that asshole ever again. I just can't—I have to go."

He shakes his head, and tears fill my eyes as he gets up to walk away. He turns around but stops walking before he gets too far. He types something in his phone, then turns back around.

"Here," he says, showing me his screen, where he has his phone number typed out. "I still don't want to be involved, but I know how Luis works. And, I don't know, maybe you need a friend right now. Hell, I need one, too. I'm just saying, you can call me if you need anything, okay?"

I wipe my tears and quickly save his number into my phone, then play one more voice message from my watch.

"Thank you."

When I get back home, I go straight to my room. I don't know what I was expecting by meeting up with Ed, but it wasn't that. And I can't even blame him. Of course he wants nothing to do with Luis. Of course he's afraid. I just wish I could fix what happened to him. Or what happened to me.

But the only way I know how to do that is by getting back at Luis. So that's what I'm going to do. With or without Ed's blessing.

# TWENTY-ONE

When dance class on Monday comes around, Angel, Nina, and Jasmine sneak in after everyone but Shawni and I leave the room. By now, Ms. M doesn't ask any questions when they come in. She just assumes they all have free period and lets us do what we want.

Today Shawni is so focused on training for the battle that she barely acknowledges the rest of us. And I'm so emotionally drained I couldn't be bothered to text or write any responses to anyone, so Nina, Angel, and Jasmine just talk among themselves while I half listen, making sure to sit against the mirror so I don't have to look at myself. Just being in their presence is good enough for me, since I don't have a lot of interacting energy today.

"I feel bad we can't make it to Shawni's battle," Angel says softly enough so Shawni can't hear. I doubt she'd hear anyway, since the music in her headphones is loud enough I can hear the beat from where I'm sitting against the mirror. "Do you think

Shawni's upset about us not showing up to support?"

"I don't know, I feel a little bad that it's because of me." Jasmine hangs her head.

"No, don't feel bad! At least Ari will be there, so Shawni won't have to go alone," Nina says.

"True. I still just feel like we should make it up to her, you know?" Angel says.

"How?"

An idea forms in the back of my mind, and I start writing on the piece of paper Shawni set down for me before she got to practicing.

*Maybe we can all go to Pride?*

"Oooh! I've never been to Pride before!" Nina exclaims.

Pride here happens in March instead of June since the summers in Arizona are hotter than Rihanna in that one see-through dress, so it'll be happening next weekend.

"Would Shawni even want to go?" Angel asks.

I'm already regretting bringing it up. I don't even know if *I* want to go . . . the big crowds, the loud noises, the heat . . . I don't think I'd have a very good time. Then again, maybe I could give it a try if it would make Shawni happy. I look over at her. She's practicing some kind of freeze. It's like a headstand, but her back is arched instead of straight, and one of her legs hangs behind her. Her shirt falls down a bit when she freezes, and I can see the lines of her abs. I think back to what she told me before. That she's never been to Pride because she didn't have anyone to go with. But does that mean it has to be *Pride*

Pride? Maybe everyone will decide to have just a friends-only Pride celebration. A quiet little kickback or something. I somehow don't think that's going to happen, though.

"We can ask her," Jasmine suggests. "I'm definitely down to go. We could go to show support for Shawni . . . and, maybe for uh . . . someone else in this group. If you know what I mean." There's something weird to Jasmine's voice, but I can't really place it. It's just like she changed the normal rhythm of her words for some reason. Everyone is staring at me now. I guess I have to say something? I get out my phone to text.

*I'll go if Shawni wants to go.*

I don't mention that I'm kind of hoping she won't want to go. But I think it might hurt Shawni's feelings if she thinks I'd rather stay home than go with her.

Jasmine waves Shawni over, so she takes out her headphones and comes to sit with us. It takes a moment for the rise and fall of her chest to slow down to a relaxed rhythm, and I find my own chest following her breathing pattern. By the time I realize I spaced out a little, the group has apparently decided on going to Pride. Part of me regrets agreeing to go, but the other part of me is surprisingly excited? I've never been to Pride, and I can't think of any better people to spend it with than my new friends.

"So," Jasmine starts with a smile on her face. "I made a website. It's just like a landing page where Ari can put the piece she writes about Luis. We can link to it on the 'Fuck Luis Ortega' Instagram bio when we make that, and post screenshots and stuff on the Instagram. Now all we need is the story!" She looks at me, and I can't help but return her grin. The only thing standing in between me and Luis getting what he deserves is this story. I can do this.

Maybe I can't do this. I've been staring at my computer every day after school trying to make the words happen, but nothing does. Finally, on Saturday, I stare at my phone instead.

More specifically, I stare at Ed's contact. I know the last thing he probably wants to hear is me complaining about how hard writing this Luis article is, since he doesn't want me even going through with it. But maybe that's a good thing. Maybe I need a friend who doesn't want to talk about Luis. I decide to text him.

    **Me:** What are you up to today?

    It's not long before he responds.

    **Ed:** absolutely nothing. Want to hang out?

    **Me:** Sure. ☺

Instead of meeting Ed at the park like last time, I take the plunge and meet him at his house, since the park was full of people and I don't have the spoons for being around crowds. He reassured me that his mom would be home, and that if I wanted to meet somewhere public we could just meet up another time. The small reassurances made me feel safe enough to go, only bringing my knife with me for the walk there.

When I get to Ed's first-floor apartment, he opens the door for me, greeting me with a genuine smile when he sees me.

"Hey, Ari," he says, then opens the door wider and gestures for me to come in.

When I do, I immediately smell the caldo his mom is cooking.

"Welcome, Ari!" she calls out from the kitchen with a wave, and I wave back and smile.

Instead of leading me to his room like I half expected, Ed leads me into the living room behind the kitchen, where his mom can hear every exchange between us. Even though I don't know Ed's mom, this gesture makes me feel safe.

We sit on separate sides of the couch, and Ed doesn't try to sit too close, which also helps me relax. I know I'm the one who sought him out, but I'm glad he isn't reading too much into it, thinking I like him or want to do anything, you know, like *that*, the way Manny and Jesus did.

"So how are you, Ari?" he asks, and I get my phone out to respond to him.

*Not good . . .* I type, and show it to him, only remembering the social rules against what I've just done after he takes my phone from my hand to look at the message. When people ask you how you're doing, you're supposed to say you're good. Why, I don't know, but that's the rule my mom drilled into me. Apparently, I need more practice. It's not my fault people only started talking to me a few weeks ago.

"Do you want to talk about it?" he asks as he hands me back my phone, looking genuinely concerned, which makes me feel relieved. I haven't ruined the day by breaking the rule.

He seems to actually want to know. But I know he doesn't. He doesn't want to talk about Luis stuff, and that's what's bothering me. I shake my head and type out, *How are you?*

Ed looks at the message and gives me a sad smile. "Same as you."

*Do you want to talk about it?* I type.

After glancing down at my message, his eyes flick up to meet mine. "Yeah, actually. If you don't mind."

I give him a smile that hopefully says, "I don't mind at all."

He must get the message because he goes on. "I feel like I have no life anymore. Like, literally. Everything I used to have is gone. All my friends, my clean record, I lost my job. I know it was just a summer lifeguard job, but what else do I have now? No one will hire me. None of my old friends want anything to do with me. And don't get me wrong, I'm glad we're hanging out now, but we barely know each other, and you're the only one who will give me the time of day besides, like, my mom."

Then I get an idea.

*What are you doing next weekend?*

"I . . . nothing?" He laughs, but it sounds bitter. "I don't ever do anything anymore."

*Want to come to a dance battle?*

# TWENTY-TWO

After robotics on Wednesday, everyone is supposed to come over to review any final details before I post the story on Instagram, which I really should be working on but have been procrastinating. When everyone comes over, my dad's still not home yet. Mom's car is here, but she's not home either for some reason, so we have the house to ourselves. We're all basically just waiting on me to finish the story now, which I'm still putting off. We all sit in a circle on the floor in my room, and Boo hides under my bed. It's like she wants to be close to me, but she's intimidated by all the people. I'm expecting them all to grill me on why I'm not finished yet, but no one does.

Instead, Shawni asks, "Does it bother you guys that the only reason we ever hang out is because of Luis?"

"What? That's not true," Jasmine says.

"It's kind of true." Shawni frowns.

"No it's not! Angel joined drama with me. Ari joined robotics with Jasmine!"

"Well, sure, but the only reason we did that is because of Luis," Shawni says.

I start picking at the ripped fabric on the knee of my jeans. Shawni's right. Even in robotics, Jasmine and I were talking about the piece. But it's not like we didn't also talk about . . . other things.

"You're right," Angel says. "And yeah, it bothers me too."

"No, we're friends!" Nina insists.

"Okay, name one thing you know about me that doesn't have to do with Luis," Angel says. "Besides Jasmine, anyone?"

No one says anything for a while. He's right. I can't think of a single thing I know about him.

"Can I be blunt?" Everyone looks at Shawni. "I'm really tired of always talking about Luis. I know he deserves to get what's coming to him. He really does, but can we take a break and just . . . hang out? I thought we were supposed to be friends, you know? I don't think I can do this if all we do is talk about *him*."

Jasmine squints at Shawni. "You sure this has nothing to do with . . . um, you know, what we talked about at the park?"

"No!" Shawni answers quickly. "It has to do with us. I want to be friends. I don't want this all to be about him, you know?"

I type my answer on my phone, then show everyone.

*I agree with Shawni.*

I hate to admit I'm relieved about this development. Everyone else has pretty much done their part, and if we're not talking about Luis, we're not talking about how I haven't done mine yet. I tried, hard. But the words haven't been coming, and I don't know if I even want them to. Maybe I need a break from thinking about Luis, too. All thinking about him does is piss me off and make me feel guilty for lying to my friends.

"You're right. We need to change that," Nina says. "Let's make a new rule. Every time we meet up for project smear campaign, we have to hang out once without mentioning him at all. Deal?"

"What would we even do?" Angel asks.

"I don't know, we can do like a sleepover or something maybe?" Jasmine says.

"I don't think my mom will let me sleep over with a bunch of girls," Angel says. "But you guys go for it."

"Well you can hang out with us and then just go home for the sleeping part," Shawni suggests, and Angel shrugs.

"Sure."

"And Nina, isn't your quinceañera coming up?" Jasmine asks.

"Um, not really." Nina shrinks into herself. "It's not for another few months. You guys don't have to come . . ."

"Of course we'll be there!" Shawni says with a supportive smile.

"What about Dungeons and Dragons?" Nina asks, not so sneakily changing the subject. "I've always wanted to play with people in real life. It's fun online and stuff, but it's just not the same. I mean, probably not, I wouldn't know."

"Yeeeees!" Angel balls his fists and does two little pumps, and I'm pretty sure it surprises all of us. I never would have thought Angel would like tabletop role-playing games.

I don't really know how I would fit into a game of D&D. Isn't it a really interactive game? It seems like a lot of pressure to talk. My friends feel pretty safe though. Maybe I'm getting there with them.

"You'll all have to make character sheets before we play. We can do it next week?" Nina claps her hands in excitement.

"I might need some help with the character sheet," I mumble, and I swear I hear a record scratch. Everyone stares at me.

"You can TALK???" Nina and Angel say at the same time.

I feel my face flush.

"Don't make a big deal about it or she won't!" Shawni says, and then Nina swoops in and brings the conversation back on track with a smile.

"I can definitely help you with the character sheet."

"What's on your mind, Ariana?" Mrs. Jones asks me when I get to her class early the next morning.

I sigh. I can't exactly tell her what's on my mind—Luis and the article I have to write—without getting myself and the rest of our group into trouble. Still, maybe she can help? I just need to be careful.

"What do you do if you need to write an article, but you might be too biased to pull it off?" I ask.

"Well, I think that depends on what makes you 'biased,' as you say." She puts finger quotes around "biased."

"What do you mean?" I ask.

"For example, some people might have called you biased for the article you wrote about this school's dress code. It was an issue that directly affected you, and you clearly went in with the opinion that the dress code was sexist, correct?" Oh no. Did I mess up *that* article too? "As a journalist, it's true that you're meant to be completely unbiased. But don't confuse being unbiased with being neutral. Some issues are just right or wrong, and it's okay to report on them as such. Having a moral compass does not make you biased. In fact, I'd say those who purposefully ignore the ethics of a situation to appear neutral are actually far more biased than you are. That's my opinion." She winks at me, then goes back to writing something down at her desk.

"Thank you, Mrs. Jones," I say, almost speechless. Just because I know Luis is a horrible person doesn't mean I'm the wrong person to write this article. In fact, who better to shine a light on it than someone who knows firsthand?

The door opens, and Shawni walks in.

"Hey, Ari!" She smiles at me, then takes the seat next to mine.

"Hi, Shawni." I say, the words coming easily around her now. Then I go over to my desk next to her.

Mrs. Jones looks up from the papers she's grading with curiosity. She's never heard me talk to anyone besides her. She shoots me a supportive smile and gets back to her work.

I whisper the next bit so Mrs. Jones doesn't hear me.

"I'm almost done with my story," I lie. It's true that I finally started working on it last night, but it felt all wrong. I felt like I was trying too hard to seem fair and presenting everything as speculation instead of the facts that they were. I'm definitely going to have to rewrite it without being afraid of my own "bias," like Mrs. Jones said. Still, I don't know why I felt the need to give Shawni an update on my progress. I want to kick myself. I know I'm supposed to come up with other things to talk about with Shawni.

"Awesome!" Shawni says, thankfully not annoyed by my talking about Luis.

Mrs. Jones doesn't interrupt as Shawni and I discuss our secret "project." We whisper and use code terms so she doesn't know what we're talking about. But I know neither me or Shawni actually *wants* to be talking about Luis right now, so I hate that I brought it up. Why am I like this? I don't know how to change the subject, so instead of doing so, I leave to go to the bathroom before class starts.

The bell rings while I'm gone, and when I get back, my chest sinks in at the sight of Luis trying to take my spot and sit next to Shawni.

"That's Ari's spot," Shawni says.

"You don't mind, do you Ariana?" Luis winks at me.

I mind.

"Seriously, Luis, *move*." Shawni's voice is stern and a little scary, but Luis doesn't budge.

"I just want to talk to you, baby."

Shawni's face flushes. "No, I . . . that's . . . that's Ari's seat."

The next bell rings, and Luis still hasn't moved, so I take the seat behind Shawni instead of next to her like I usually would. Luis pulls out his phone and *pssts* at Shawni. She rolls her eyes before looking at him. He points to his phone.

"Check yours."

"It's off," Shawni says. Pretty sure that's a lie.

Luis folds up a piece of paper and puts it on Shawni's desk when Mrs. Jones has her back turned. He really doesn't know how to quit. Shawni opens the note. I picture myself throwing a spitball at Luis. I don't like this.

I lean forward, trying to get a view of what Luis wrote in the note. Shawni is writing back now. When she's done, instead of giving the note back to Luis, she slips her hand behind her back to give it to *me*.

Luis rolls his eyes and mouths the word "seriously?" at Shawni. He looks pissed.

On top of the paper is Luis's original message.

*come over after school. I wanna talk*

And Shawni's response, to me.

*can you believe this guy? pretend to laugh a little so he gets mad.*

I don't have to pretend.

Mrs. Jones turns around, and I put my hand on the note so she can't see it.

"Would you like to share what's so funny with the rest of the class?" Mrs. Jones asks, and I can't help but feel a little betrayed. I thought Mrs. Jones and I were friends. She knows I won't be able to answer her here in the middle of class, so why would she call me out like that? Just because I was talking to Shawni earlier doesn't mean I can do it in front of the whole class. She looks disappointed, too, and it makes me feel even worse. Face hot, I look down until she keeps teaching.

I shake it off and write back to Shawni when Mrs. Jones's focus moves to someone else. We end up passing notes throughout the class, saying random things that don't mean anything, just to piss off Luis. Without anything real to talk about, I end up admitting to Shawni that I'm feeling really nervous to play Dungeons and Dragons with the group. I can't really predict if I'll feel comfortable enough to talk to them. I might be fine, but I also might be silent. And I'm afraid of making the game less fun if I'm not able to talk.

Shawni says not to worry about it, and that I can write things instead of talk if I need to, and that it will still be just as fun either way. To make me feel better, we start planning out our characters and their backstories. I'm a human ranger, and she's a half-elf rogue, and we're on a mission to avenge our fallen friend. After a while, I forget about pissing off Luis, and I'm just having fun making up this story with Shawni. It's the little things.

# TWENTY-THREE

When I get home after school, I sit down at the desk in my room and absentmindedly type in the ExposeTheMierda URL, like I do every day. Boo walks right in front of the laptop, purring and rubbing herself against it. I humor her for a second and give her a few pets before I pick her up and put her on the floor, then look at the screen.

*CALL FOR SUBMISSIONS:*

*Hi friends and foes! This is just a reminder to all of you that we are open for submissions! ExposeTheMierda is dedicated to publishing stories by anonymous (or not!) folks from all walks of life who have mierda to expose. Got a story to tell? Please fill out the submission form below with the details, and I'll get back to you with an acceptance or a rejection as soon as I'm able. These stories will not be exclusively told on ETM, so feel free to post them on your own mediums while you wait for a response.*

*Speak truth,*

*ETM*

I was right! They must really be looking for new stories to post now if they're putting out a call for submissions. Over the years, they've only posted calls for submissions "once in a blue moon," as the neurotypicals say. Our timing couldn't be more perfect.

Filled with a sudden burst of inspiration, I fill out the form, then get to writing the story. I don't worry about sounding "biased" this time, I just write. And I feel damn good about it.

I stay up practically the entire night reading and rereading my new and improved takedown of Luis. Everything is perfect, but I somehow still feel like I'm missing something. Some big piece of this puzzle that will really drill the nail into Luis's coffin. But I have everything we need and more. There's video footage of Luis talking shit about girls he's had sex with and captioned audio of Shawni, Nina, and a few other girls talking about how Luis screwed them over. I very intentionally left my lie out of it, though. If we're going to take down Luis, I want it to be for what he actually did, not for "lying" about us having sex when it wasn't a lie at all.

Maybe that's what feels wrong about this. That I'm missing from it. But I can't put myself in this article without lying again or admitting I lied in the past, and I'm not ready to do either just yet.

So, I send the group what I wrote in the middle of the night, and I wake up the next morning to a text from Jasmine with a link to the FUCK LUIS ORTEGA Instagram account, which has a single post with screenshots of what I wrote, and the link to the full story in the bio.

I get to school early in the morning to find Shawni already in the journalism room waiting for me.

"We did it!" she whisper-sings when I sit down next to her.

I smile. We did it. Luis is finally going down.

We practically count down the seconds until the bell rings. Most of the class is already in the room before Luis finally saunters in with his friends, seemingly completely unfazed. But he can't be, right? Can he?

He almost looks . . . proud? And his friends are extra groupie-like today. Like they're literally worshipping this asshole.

Have none of them been on Instagram yet?

Then Melanie comes rushing in. She shoves her phone in Luis's face.

"Is it true?" she asks.

Yes. Yes, it's all true! I want to scream it at the top of my lungs.

"Of course it's true," Jessica says without looking up from her own phone. But . . . if she knows it's true, why is she still sitting next to Luis? Then she looks up, her gaze falling directly on Shawni. "True that most sluts are hypocrites who can't handle when a guy breaks up with them . . ."

Luis laughs, but Shawni just pretends she didn't hear it. The only indication that she did hear is that she stopped spinning her hair tie around her fingers. I feel my face heating up, and not in the good way, like it sometimes does around Shawni.

"Jess, are you seriously defending him?" Melanie asks incredulously. Luis raises an eyebrow and crosses his arms, like he's amused.

"You have something to say?" he says, locking eyes with Melanie. There's a warning in his piercing gray eyes.

Melanie just shakes her head and walks to the other side of the room, sitting somewhere in the back, away from her usual spot by Jessica, Luis, and the other guys, who are all nudging Luis and snickering.

I can't believe I'm seeing this. Sure, Luis might have just lost a friend over this, but was that . . . it? And *Melanie* is the one who was just treated like an outcast for having a moral compass, not Luis. What the fuck? I turn to Shawni, catching a glimpse of her clenched jaw and shiny eyes before she quickly gets up and runs out of the room.

"Shanaya, where do you think you're—" Mrs. Jones starts, but before she finishes, I find myself running out of the room after Shawni.

I chase after her all the way to the bathroom, where she slides her back down against the wall, falling into a sitting position with her face covered. She's not crying out loud, but I can tell by the movement of her shoulders that she's sobbing. I feel like a hole has just been ripped out of my chest at the sight of her. This is all my fault.

I failed.

I sit down cross-legged in front of Shawni and wait for her to move her hands from in front of her face. I reach for my phone, but I left it in my bag in Mrs. Jones's room, so I use the watch.

"Hey."

"It didn't work . . ." Shawni says from behind her hands.

I don't know what to do. I can't talk right now to comfort her. I can't make any of this better. I wrote the damn article the best I could, and still nothing happened to Luis. This was our whole master plan. We have nothing left.

Just then, my smartwatch dings with an unexpectedly quick email response from ExposeTheMierda!

Hi Ariana,

Thank you so much for submitting your story to ExposeTheMierda! I really appreciate your dedication to speaking truth. Unfortunately, I'm unable to post your story at this time. I can only post so many, and I'm afraid I'm lacking the specific pull to this story that I need in order to move forward.

All the best,

ETM

My heart sinks in my chest. It's the same form rejection I've gotten every other time. If ExposeTheMierda doesn't think I have what it takes, of course the story didn't land. A lump forms in my throat, and I let out an involuntary whimper.

Shawni finally moves her hands from over her face, and I reach out both of mine. She takes my hands in hers and squeezes.

"What do we do now?" she practically whispers.

I shake my head. I have no idea. Do we give up? That thought feels so hopeless, but I don't know what else there is to do.

Shawni seems to realize then that I don't have my phone, so she takes hers out of her pocket and hands it to me. I just shake my head and hand it back to her. I have no idea what to say. There's nothing *to* say.

Shawni bursts out crying again, and she falls into my arms. I rub her back like my mom does for me when I'm upset, hoping that will help.

I hold Shawni while she cries, numb to the tears myself. I'm more angry than sad.

We failed.

*I* failed.

# TWENTY-FOUR

I storm into the apartment after school, walking right passed my stunned mom.

"Mija, what's wrong—"

But I slam my door before she gets a chance to pry into what happened. I can't talk about it anyway.

I spend the next week sulking in my room after school, crying and reeling from having to see Luis happy and popular and thriving during the day. My mom occasionally tries to comfort me by asking to hang out, but I can't bring myself to talk to her. I don't know how to lie to her, and I don't know how to tell her the truth.

So, I ignore her.

When Friday comes around, Shawni's battle presents a nice distraction from my failure with Luis. Her dad pulls up to the school in a blue minivan to pick us up. Shawni wanted me to go home with her so I could help her pick out an outfit for the battle, since she likes my style. It's kind of a lot of pressure, but it did give me a bit of a big ego that she trusts me for something like that.

"So nice to see the famous Ari again!" Shawni's dad says with a warm smile as I file into the backseat of the car while Shawni takes the front. He glances at me from the rearview mirror, and Shawni puts on some music to save me from the conversation since she probably figured I wouldn't be able to talk, thank God.

When we get to her house, her dad doesn't get out of the car.

"God bless you girls, be safe!" he calls as we get out of the car, and drives off.

"He's going to church." Shawni answers the question I was thinking as she leads me inside. It's not until we're in the house, away from the open danger of the front yard, that I'm able to speak.

"On a Friday?" I ask.

"Yeah, he leads the youth group." Shawni doesn't look too happy about it.

"How come you don't go with him?"

"I'm not Catholic." She shrugs.

"Oh, cool." I guess the only reason I consider myself Catholic is because that's what my parents call us. We're not devout and barely ever go to church, but I never really questioned the label.

We both take off our shoes and kick them over by the front door before making our way further into the house. It's so freaking clean compared to mine. I remember that Shawni told me she likes cleaning back when she was only TLOSC to me. She must *really* like cleaning, because the floors and counters are spotless, and I don't see a single thing out of place. This house was clean the last time I was here, but not like *this*. I wonder if she did this to impress me. It worked.

Shawni doesn't waste any time. She leads me right to her room to pick out an outfit. We don't have very long to decide, since the battle starts at six, and it'll take us about two hours to get there on the bus.

There are already two outfits neatly laid out on Shawni's bed. Her room is just as clean as the rest of the house. There's nothing on the floor except for a blue and white boho rug by her perfectly made bed.

"Which one?" she asks me. I carefully weigh the options. One of them is a pair of high-waisted jeans, a crop top, and a maroon beanie. The other is a pair of workout leggings with a mesh design on the outside of the thighs, a flannel wrapped around the waist of the leggings, a tank top, and a black beanie.

"You don't even need me. These are both good outfits," I say.

"Okay, but which one is *better?*"

I take a second to look over the options again. She would probably have an easier time dancing in the leggings than the jeans, so I point to that outfit.

"That's what I was thinking, too." She grabs the clothes and heads to the bathroom to change. I hadn't really thought of what to wear, but I guess the outfit I'm in now is fine. Jeans and a cropped halter top. It's not like I'm battling like Shawni.

"Wanna go get food first?" Shawni asks.

"Aren't you worried about being late?"

"We'll be fine. The first hour is just cyphers."

"What are cyphers?" I ask.

She chews on her bottom lip. "It's like dancing for fun in a circle. No competition, just getting down and vibing with the music."

"And you don't want to be there for that?" I ask, shocked. That sounds incredible.

Shawni laughs softly. "Okay, if you're worried about missing the cyphers, we can just eat on the bus. I'll make sandwiches."

"Okay!"

We'll be taking the bus back, too, which is a little intimidating since it'll be dark by then. But I have my pocketknife with me like always, just in case, so I feel a bit better about it.

Shawni must know I'm useless for conversations on a public bus, so she doesn't try to engage me. Or maybe it's because she's nervous herself. It is her first battle, so she has to be.

I nibble on my sandwich until it's gone, and I realize she hasn't even touched hers. She's bouncing her leg and fidgeting with the sleeves of the flannel tied around her waist. Since I can't talk here, I text her.

Ari: You're going to do great. ☺

When Shawni looks down at her phone, her eyes get a little shy, and she gives me a reluctant smile. Then she blows out a measured breath of air. "I'm really nervous . . ."

Shawni's hands are shaking a little, so maybe I should hold her hand? But what if Shawni is like me and doesn't like touching without warning? I should ask permission.

Ari: Can I hold your hand?

I hold my phone in front of her lap so she can see the text on the screen. She looks into my eyes eagerly, less shy than before, and she turns her palm up. Is that an answer? Is she saying yes? I hesitate. She's probably saying yes, but I don't want to hold her hand unless I'm sure.

"Of course," she says when I take too long to analyze what she meant by an upturned palm. It would be nice if I could read minds, or at least just body language with more certainty. I take her hand and squeeze it. Her hand stops shaking, and we ride the rest of the way in silence.

We don't stop holding hands once we get to our stop, and we walk to the venue hand in hand. Our friendly silence is broken the second we get to the parking lot of the battle venue. The music is louder than I expected, and the venue is already packed. Shawni reaches for my hand again, but stops before making contact.

"Can I?" she asks, and I answer by taking her hand. I think she wants to hold hands because she's nervous, but I step closer and hold onto it like a clingy toddler. She's the only thing familiar in here, the only thing that's safe.

I feel my phone buzz, and I check it with my free hand to see a group text from Angel, and a text from Ed.

**Angel:** good luck Shawni!! We're cheering you on from the robotics tournament!

**Ed:** running late, but I'll be there ☺

I smile at my phone, excited to introduce Ed to Shawni. When I first told her he was coming, she was a little confused, but I explained his situation and how he'd been having a hard time, and she got it.

When we get inside, the first thing we do is take a selfie by the entrance, wrist bands on. That way we have proof to show Ms. M so we can get our extra credit, just in case she doesn't show up to battle for some reason. There are two separate cyphers on the dance floor. One cypher has way more people crowded around than the other, so Shawni and I go to the smaller circle. Someone is bugging out in the middle. All the people on the sides are bobbing with the music and cheering their support, shouting yeses and ayyyys whenever something cool happens. Some people are even full-on dancing along on the sides. When the guy in the middle is done, he joins the outside of the circle again, and another guy takes his place almost immediately. He walks around the circle a few times, to get a feeling for the music, I guess. Then he starts doing this super-fast footwork, and it looks really awesome until he stumbles and falls on his ass.

No one laughs at him. They *cheer*.

They're encouraging him to get back up.

Instead of getting embarrassed, he starts threading on the floor. It's like the fall was a sign that the floor was his medium for movement now. The crowd goes wild. When he's done,

Shawni takes the opportunity and hops in. She steps closer to the center with each offbeat in the music. She top rocks for a minute before swinging a leg around and dropping to the floor, completely in her element now.

Shawni doesn't always move to the obvious part of the music, and it makes me hear things I wouldn't have noticed if I hadn't been watching her. I don't know how she hears all of this when she's breaking. The bass, the lyrics, the background singing. There's a little tinkering beat that I probably wouldn't have even heard if it hadn't been for Shawni repetitively kicking out on that beat. The song fades away, and Shawni fades into the sidelines. I feel the emptiness of the cypher calling to me. It's pulling me forward like a magnet, and I'm helpless to stop it. Before I know it, and before anyone else gets a chance, I'm in the middle. Frozen stiff and waiting for the next song, with no idea what I'm doing here.

I close my eyes to block out the people staring. When the music plays, the encouraging cheers of the cypher become a part of the song. I imagine myself alone in my room after school or in the dance room with Shawni. I start bouncing with the beat. I don't know how to freestyle dance, at least not the way these people do, so I do some of the across-the-floor footwork we learned in class. It doesn't fit with the music, but it's fun for me. Fun, but unsatisfying.

I decide to let loose a little bit. I let my torso sway wherever it wants, and my shoulders twitch to the beat. Who says I can't freestyle?

I open my eyes, expecting the worst, but no one is pointing or laughing at me. Everyone is just as into the music as they were when Shawni or one of the other guys was in the cypher. It's like it doesn't matter what happens in the circle. We're all just here sharing the space with whoever is brave enough to take it. And I was brave.

The emcee breaks up the cyphers over the loudspeakers to announce the lineup for the battles, and Shawni is up first. The crowd widens to form a larger circle around the dance floor, leaving just enough room for the battle. The emcee introduces the judges, and Shawni takes her position on one side of the floor, opposite her opponent. I stand behind Shawni to support her, but I don't have enough standing room to be comfortable. I'm only inches away from another human in any direction of my body, and I don't have Shawni to cling to for safety right now. They flip a coin for who gets to go first. The other guy.

This time, when the music starts, the sound gets mixed up with my other senses, and my vision blurs. The base shakes the blood in my veins. I swear it was dark in here a minute ago, but suddenly all the lights make it hard to breathe. My throat closes up, and I can't focus on anything to ground me. When it's Shawni's turn to dance, I can't even focus on her. I can't breathe if I can't focus. I look around, trying to find a spot on the wall, anything to focus on to loosen the grip that all the noise has on my throat. I find the doorknob at the entrance. It's tempting.

Then the door opens, and the light that comes from the outside amplifies the music. I can't see, hear, *breathe*.

Breathe!

The door closes again, and my eyes adjust to see the person who walks in.

Luis.

I close my eyes and open them again to make sure I'm not seeing things. He's still there, accompanied by two of his football friends, and they're making their way over to us. To Shawni.

I can't be here. I can't see him.

The way he's watching her makes me sick. He looks all starstruck, like he's proud of her or something. Like he has any right to be here for her.

I push through the crowd and make my way to the back where the bathrooms are. There's a back door I can escape from. I run for it.

There's no one outside, thank God. I run to the first trash can I see and throw up into it. I sit down on the curb for a minute, head between my knees, trying to breathe life back into my brain.

What the hell is Luis doing here? Is he here for Shawni? Did she invite him? She couldn't have invited him.

I am so tired of Luis ruining my good days. I wish I could get back at him without having to play everything he did to me on repeat in my mind.

Then I see his car.

I take a quick survey of the area. Nothing's out here but cars. No cameras, no people. Without taking the time to second guess anything, I march right over to his car, gripping my pocketknife in my jeans. Direct action.

I go for the tires.

# TWENTY-FIVE

I don't just stop at the tires. Luis doesn't have the nicest car in the world, but he'll still be pissed if it's scratched up. I run the knife along the driver's side door. Who knew the sound of metal scraping against metal could be so satisfying?

"What the *hell* are you doing?"

I jump to my feet, instinctively pointing the knife at . . . fuck. Ed looks pissed.

"Why the fuck would you invite me here if you were gonna pull this shit?"

I open my mouth to answer, but no words come. I want to explain myself, but I can't. Not here. Still, I don't get why he's upset. Luis needed to pay somehow. I finally feel like I've done *something*, and Ed is mad about it?

He doesn't stop there, though. "Who did you think was gonna go down for this, Ari?" he snaps.

I just stare at him, wide-eyed.

"If anyone sees me here, I'm the one they'll blame, not you.

Goddammit! I have to fucking go!" he says before storming off without another word.

I stand there frozen for a few moments before my body kicks into high gear when I hear someone else coming. I flip the knife closed, shove it in my pocket, and run to the door before anyone can see me, heart pounding along the way.

Guilt wraps its fingers around my pounding heart and squeezes as I hear Ed's car peel off the road. I slip back inside before anyone else can see me. I really fucked up. I could have gotten Ed sent right back to jail. Dammit. The one time I was able to do something that would actually hurt Luis, and I can't even enjoy it.

Still, picturing how mad Luis will be when he sees his car fills me with a mixture of guilt and catharsis. Guilt over Ed, of course, not Luis's feelings.

Then I realize I effectively ditched Shawni to deal with Luis on her own. How could I be such a horrible friend? I scan the area looking for her.

I find her dancing again, but with a different opponent. Looks like she got past the first round! But even more interestingly, her opponent is Ms. M! I run over to get a better look. I try not to look at anything but Shawni and Ms. M. I don't want to accidentally see Luis. The adrenaline rush from slashing his tires is enough to dull the sensory overload I was feeling before.

I've only ever seen Ms. M dance ballet or contemporary, but here, she's a popper. Each time her body locks into place with the beat, it's like her whole body vibrates in time. When she starts waving, her arms, body, and legs look like there are no bones as she directs the invisible wave through her body.

Then the round is over, and the judges unanimously point to Ms. M, who then moves on to the next round. Which would be great, if it didn't mean Shawni was out of the battle now. I'm a little bummed I missed her first round and didn't get to see her win, but at least I got to see her dance in the cypher. Shawni and Ms. M share a quick hug, and then Shawni finds me.

"Where were you?" She frowns, and it kills me that she knows I missed seeing her dance. I feel terrible.

Before I can answer, someone else finds us.

"Hey, Shawni." Luis has his hands in his pockets like he's shy. Looks like he ditched his friends to come talk to us. To Shawni.

I grab Shawni's hand on a reflex. She squeezes back so tight my hand cramps, but I don't mind, because it's grounding me. I think we're each other's safety right now.

"You did great out there," Luis says. His eyes flicker down to our hands, but he doesn't comment on it.

"Thanks," Shawni says. She gives him a polite smile like he's a normal guy and not the horrible toe scum he is. Why is she being so nice to him?

"Hey, Ari. How you been?" He grins like our last confrontation never happened.

*It's not like she can say no.*

I flip him off.

"Okay, then . . . well, we just came to see Shawni dance, so I don't really have a reason to stay. You guys want a ride?" I try to keep a straight face. He's not going to be giving anyone a ride, including himself.

"No thanks. I think I want to stay and watch the rest of the battles," Shawni says.

"Alright, then. See you around."

I text Shawni as soon as he's out of sight.

Ari: Why are you being so nice to him?

I point to Shawni's phone, then wait patiently for her to pull it out and read my text.

"Don't want him getting suspicious. If he suspects us at all, he's gonna know we made that website, and I don't want to get caught."

Shit. I hope he doesn't put the tire thing together. I'm pretty sure I was careful enough. No one saw me other than Ed, and I wasn't out there for that long. Besides, Shawni has an alibi of being in the battle, and I could just say I was watching her. We should be in the clear. Still, I don't think I can just leave Shawni in the dark about it.

Ari: I should probably tell you something . . .

"What . . ."

Instead of typing it out, I lead Shawni to the back door. I put my index finger to my lip and crack the door open so we can peek out of it without showing too much of our faces. Since Shawni is taller than me, her chin is resting on the top of my head in order for her to get a view outside. Luis's car is in view, but he isn't. Where is he? It's hard to get a good view without opening the door more, but I don't want him to see us.

"What am I looking at exactly?"

Before I can answer, Luis walks into view, pacing back and forth and yelling at someone on his phone.

"It's not my fault!" A pause. Hopefully he's getting yelled at. "I don't know who slashed my fucking tires! Someone's been fucking with me, I swear!" His face is a deep red and I can see his neck veins bulging out all the way from here. One of his friends laughs and he turns on them in an instant. "Shut the fuck up or I'm leaving you here!"

"Uh, I don't think you're gonna be able to take us home either way . . ." one of his friends says.

"Oh . . . oh my God." Shawni pulls me back in and shuts the door.

I brace myself for the lecture I'm sure she's about to give me, but Shawni just bursts out laughing.

"You did that?" She wheezes and wipes a tear from her eye. I nod, then lift my chin. *I* did that.

Shawni cracks the door open again to get another look. I peek out with her. Luis is still pacing, still shouting.

"Dad, it's not my fault!" Luis pleads, and his friends look increasingly bored.

"You can figure that shit out Luis. We're gonna go watch the rest of the battles," one of them says, and they both start heading toward the door.

"Run!" Shawni shouts, the music loud enough to mask it more than a few feet away. We run.

We weave through the crowd, giggling so hard we're making a scene. Luis didn't see us, though. He doesn't come back inside. Probably too embarrassed.

We run into the bathroom, where we finally burst out laughing together. With the music blaring outside the bathroom doors, no one can hear us in here.

"Oh my God! Ari, oh my God!" is all Shawni manages to say through fits of laughter. I'm surprised she's not mad, but I'm not complaining. I need *some* kind of celebration for ruining Luis's day. "You little badass! Who fucking knew!"

She keeps laughing, and I laugh with her through my guilt.

"It's kind of perfect, actually. He'll never suspect quiet little you. And I was battling, so it couldn't be me. Genius!"

Just then, both of our phones buzz, and we share a deer in the headlights look. I'm sure we're both thinking the absolute worst right now. Maybe Shawni's wrong, and Luis did suspect me, and we're both getting served with court orders or something. I don't know.

But no, when I get out my phone, it's a group text from Angel.

**Angel:** JASMINE WON!!!!!!!!!!!!!!!

I let out a squeal of excitement, and Shawni fist pumps.

"Yes!" she shouts. "This is seriously the best day."

The look she gives me makes me want to crash into her and kiss her right here and now, but I don't. Instead, we go back out to watch the rest of the battles. I'd rather be home where it's quiet, but being able to have Shawni as a lifeline definitely makes it a lot easier than when she was battling.

I try to enjoy the battles, but every time someone comes too close to us—which is often—I find myself squeezing Shawni's hand or her arm. I wouldn't be surprised if I accidentally left a bruise.

"You okay?" she eventually asks.

I get out my phone.

Ari: Too loud. Too many people.

"Oh . . . If it's really bothering you we can leave."

Ari: What about the rest of the battles?

"I think you want to leave more than I want to stay. It's fine." She gives me a soft smile, and I melt, softening my grip on her arm as I let out my breath.

Ari: Can I hug you?

Shawni laughs, then pulls me into a hug. "Of course."

# TWENTY-SIX

Even though we left early, it's too late for me to go home on my own, so I stay the night at Shawni's house. I'm happy to be with her, but I think I'll need a while to recharge before I can talk again, since the battle took a lot out of me.

The nice thing about being with Shawni is that even though she knows I can talk sometimes, she doesn't try to force it. She just communicates with me however I'm comfortable, and we never have to be talking. With the night we just had, I don't have the energy to make words happen, and she seems to understand that just fine. Instead, we sit on Shawni's bed to watch a movie.

I'm so exhausted from the day that I feel my eyes getting heavy only thirty minutes into it. Just when I'm about to fall asleep, I feel added weight on my shoulder from Shawni's head, and I stiffen. She doesn't react to me tensing up and doesn't move her head. She didn't ask to touch me this time, or warn me at all, so I wasn't prepared. Then I hear her snore.

Oh my gosh, she actually just fell asleep on me.

I guess it makes sense that she'd be more tired than me, since she was the one actually dancing. Still, I am very tired . . .

I reach for the remote without moving the rest of my body so I don't wake Shawni up. The movement makes her stir, but she keeps sleeping. When the TV is off, my eyes shut, and I let myself fall asleep next to her.

When I wake up, I'm spooning Shawni with my whole body like I'm a baby koala. She must have woken up at some point while I slept because she's wearing spanks, a tank top, and a bonnet now. My eyes widen and I freeze up. Does she realize we slept like this, or is she still sleeping? Her eyes are closed, and she has a faint hint of a smile on her lips, like she's having a good dream. I carefully slip my limbs away from her so I can get up to brush my teeth, but she stirs before I can separate my body from hers.

Instead of freaking out at our closeness, she smiles.

"Good morning," she says groggily as she shifts to stretch.

"Good morning," I say back, slightly disappointed at the loss of contact.

But before I get a chance to embarrass myself further, I rush out of bed and into the bathroom, where I quickly brush my teeth and wash my face, wondering if splashing water on my cheeks will wake me up from what was surely just a really good dream.

I smooth out my hair and my clothes, which I'm still wearing from the battle. Once I'm semihappy with how I look, I go back to Shawni's room to find Shawni on her phone. But when she sees me, she quickly puts it away, like she's afraid I caught her committing a crime or something.

"What's wrong?" I ask, not really sure what else to say.

"Nothing," Shawni says at first. Then she lets out a sigh and slumps her shoulders. "Okay, okay, please don't be mad though."

"Um, okay?"

"I made plans to hang out with Jasmine later."

"Oh, okay," I say, confused as to why I would be mad about that. "Have fun!"

"Wait, you're not mad?" Shawni asks, her eyebrows knitting together in confusion.

"Why would I be mad?" I ask.

"Well, it was just going to be the two of us," Shawni says.

"So?"

"So . . . I don't know. When Luis and I were together, he used to get really mad at me if I tried to hang out with anyone one-on-one without him."

"But we're not together," I blurt out.

And I must have said or done something wrong somewhere along the way, because Shawni looks like I just punched her in the chest. Dammit. Between Shawni and Ed, I can't seem to do the right thing.

"Oh. Okay, then. I guess we're not," she says softly.

"Are you okay?" I ask. She's hugging herself like she does sometimes when she's upset.

"Yeah, I'm fine. Why wouldn't I be okay?" Shawni says, letting go of herself and standing up straighter. "I'll get my dad to take you home now."

"Okay, thanks," I say, but I still feel like I did something wrong.

Ed still hasn't responded to any of my texts telling him I'm sorry. I don't know what else to do, so as soon as I get dropped off at home and change into clean clothes, I leave the apartment again and head over to Ed's. I need to apologize to him somehow. If he slams the door in my face, then so be it. But I have to try.

I knock on the door to Ed's apartment and wait in excruciating silence for well over a minute. Finally, instead of the door opening, I hear a resigned Ed speaking from the other side.

"What are you doing here?"

I clear my throat, hoping words might come out so I can explain myself, but unfortunately, the sea witch isn't ready to release her grip on my throat just yet. I get out my phone to send him a text, but before I get a chance, the door finally opens.

"No one else is here, just so you know," he says, and it feels more like a consideration for me feeling safe than anything else. My chest sinks even deeper. Even after what I did to him, he's still putting my comfort first. "Are you gonna come in, or should I step out?"

He doesn't sound happy with me exactly, but he's still being nice enough that I feel safe. I take a step forward, and he walks back inside, leaving the door open for me to follow.

I close the door behind me and kick off my shoes, then meet Ed on his living room couch and get to typing.

*I'm really, really sorry.*

Ed reads my text and sighs. "I don't know what you want me to say, Ari. What you did was fucked up. I could have lost everything, *again*. You didn't even think about that, did you?"

I feel tears well up in my eyes. When I slashed Luis's tires, I have to admit that Ed was the last thing on my mind.

"I . . ." I start, and, shockingly enough, the words come out. "I'm sorry," I say. "I just . . . I didn't know what else to do!" I feel a lump forming in my throat and tears blurring my vision. "I went through with the original plan. I exposed Luis for everything! Everyone knows he spread around Nina's nudes, that he cheated on Shawni, and that he brags and talks shit about all the girls he has sex with! I exposed him! But . . . nothing happened!" I can't help it. Before I can finish my thought, I just break down crying. I say the rest through a blubbering sob fest. "No one cared! He's still *Luis*. He didn't lose a damn thing. I was desperate. So yeah, I wasn't thinking, and I slashed his tires. I just wanted to do *something* to make him hurt. I didn't know what else to do!"

Ed is quiet for a moment. He doesn't try to comfort me, which I'm grateful for, because that might make me feel even guiltier. I deserve to sit in this feeling. When he finally talks, he doesn't sound mad, though.

"You know why no one cares?" he asks, and I shake my head in response. "Because they all already *knew* that stuff. He talked shit about girls to everyone. No one cares about that. He didn't really hide the fact that he cheated on Shawni from anyone but her. Everyone knew he spread someone's nudes around because, well, he's the one who sent them. They don't care that he's a shit person. Everyone lies and cheats and makes bad decisions, so no one cares about those things. What they don't know is what he's really capable of . . ." he trails off like he's waiting for me to put it together.

Then Luis's words flood through my head one more time.

*It's not like she can say no.*

Luis didn't just take advantage of me.

He raped me.

I look up at Ed through teary eyes, and he nods his understanding.

"I know what I have to do," I say.

"What do you mean?" he asks.

I pause a moment before going on. If I'm really going to do this, I need to be sure.

But I don't think I've ever been more sure of anything in my life.

"You saved someone like me, Ed. Let me save you back."

"What are you talking about?"

"I'm going to get you your life back." I let out a shaky breath. I'm doing this. "I'm going to tell *my* story."

# TWENTY-SEVEN

I can't think of anything but Luis for the rest of the night. I know I need to tell my story now, but how? How am I supposed to admit to my friends that I was lying to them this whole time? That something *did* happen between me and Luis, no matter how nonconsensual it was.

*It's not like she can say no.*

I shudder, feeling cold in my chest even though I'm snuggled up between my pillows and Boo on my bed. I just lie in bed and blank out for a while. I just feel . . . weird now. I don't know how to explain it. Empty, almost. Like I want to cry about what Luis did now that I've come to the realization of how severe it really was, but I can't. And even though I sort of came clean about it to Ed, I still feel like a fraud.

My mom knocks on my semi-open door and peeks her head inside. I left it open specifically because I was hoping she or my dad would come check on me.

"Dinner's in the fridge for you, okay mija? If you need

anything while your papi and I are gone, just call me."

"Wait, you're leaving?" I ask, sitting up in bed. My mom's been wanting to hang out so much the last few weeks, and I haven't been able to because of survival club things, but I could really use her support right now.

Her brows scrunch in concern for a moment. "Do you want me to stay here? I can cancel our date."

"Oh, you're going on a date?" I ask, and she nods.

"I know I upset you by talking about Tom before, and I want to make things right. I really need to make an effort with your papi. But only if you'll be okay here. I really don't mind cancelling . . ." she says, but I can tell she's lying. Besides, I would feel bad making them cancel for me, since my mom's putting in so much of an effort to work things out with Papi. And by the looks of it, things seem to be getting much better.

"No, that's okay. You guys have fun!" I say in that fake cheery tone I'm so used to from her. "I'm sleepy anyway. Think I'll go to bed early," I lie. I'm not sleepy, just tired. Tired of existing in this moment. Drained from the realization I came to today and scared of what it means for my relationship with my friends. I just want a break. I want to sulk in my room.

Mami blows me a kiss before closing my door and meeting my dad outside, leaving me alone to sulk.

I pull the covers over me, hugging my extra pillow to my chest.

At least Ed isn't mad at me anymore.

But Shawni might be.

I'm not really sure what I did wrong, but it seemed like I hurt her feelings earlier. She hasn't texted me for my "regularly scheduled check-in," which makes me worry. I get out my phone and shoot her a text, hoping to patch things up to the best of my ability.

Me: Hey. Are you okay?

There's a moment before Shawni responds.

Shawni: I'm great! Why wouldn't I be okay?

And that just makes my head hurt. Like, did I make up that she seemed sad earlier? I truly don't know why she'd be sad, and her asking right now confuses me even more.

Shawni: are you?

I'm relieved she asked. At least she's not too mad to care how I'm doing. And I'm tired of lying to her. I know I need to tell her the truth about Luis. Maybe not yet, but I'm not going to start with another lie.

Me: No, not really.

Shawni: What's wrong?

Me: I'll tell you another time. Right now I just want to talk to you, if that's okay.

Shawni: Of course <3

Shawni proceeds to do the greatest job of getting my mind off Luis. We talk about everything and nothing for the next couple of hours until I finally close my eyes and let the world fade away, with only thoughts of Shawni lulling me to sleep.

# TWENTY-EIGHT

A knock on my door takes me out of the deepest sleep I've had in a while. I check my phone with heavy eyes to see that it's already afternoon. I must have been in bed all morning.

My dad walks in and sits at the edge of my bed, and puts a hand to my forehead.

"You feeling sick, mija?"

Unsurprisingly, I'm unable to form the words to respond, so I shake my head no. Dad frowns.

"You were locked in here when your mami and I got home after dinner last night. I'm worried about you being in bed so long. ¿Tienes hambre?"

I don't realize how hungry I am until he asks. I nod, and he helps me out of bed. Mami must have told him I seemed a little off yesterday. It's tradition that when I have my extra bad days, Papi takes me to lunch in our pajamas. We usually go to In-N-Out and eat on top of his hood in the parking lot if it's not too hot. Or inside the car if it is. I already feel better knowing what we're about to do.

Mami and I have our own separate traditions. Like both of us telling each other our every problem and pretending we have the emotional capacity to be each other's therapists, since my parents don't believe in those. Usually, Dad has to buy Mom a massage or something when we go to In-N-Out so she doesn't feel bad about being left out, but when he offers today, she waves him off.

"I haven't had the house to myself in a while. I'll just stay home and take a good long nap. Here, mija . . ." She reaches into her purse and pulls out a twenty, then hands it to me. "Why don't you two see a movie after you eat?"

"Thanks, Mami!" I pocket the money, then head outside with my dad.

We spend the car ride blasting oldies like "Atomic Dog" and "Got To Be Real." I've grown to associate dad's music with a good time, since he always blasts it when we go for lunch, and has ever since I was little. It's nostalgic, and I can't get enough.

We always get the same thing from In-N-Out: a double cheeseburger, animal-style fries, and a milkshake. No matter how upset I am, my appetite always comes right back when we go here. He used to race me on who could eat the cheeseburger faster, but now that I'm older I actually like to enjoy my food more.

It's warm even in March here, at ninety degrees, so we sit in the car to eat instead of on top of it. I slowly pick at my fries, enjoying each one individually, stalling so this meal doesn't have to be over.

"How was your date last night?" I finally ask.

"I don't know . . ." He lets out a frustrated sigh. That's not a good sign.

"What happened?" I ask.

"We don't have to talk about it, okay? We're working things through. Let's just leave it at that. So what else is on your mind, mijita?" he asks. He really is the worst at talking about his own feelings but always wants to talk about mine. I wouldn't be surprised if that's why the date didn't go well. If I know anything about my mom, it's that she needs constant validation and affirmation. She needs to be reminded that she's loved, or she won't believe it. And I *know* she means a lot to my dad, but he can't share his own feelings to save his life. Or their marriage, apparently.

Sure, he can express his worry or love in a way that puts all the focus on the other person, but anything that requires him to open up is a no go, and I know Mami's always hated that.

If he can deflect, so can I. "I think this is what heaven is gonna be like." I take a slow sip of my chocolate milkshake, letting the cold, sweet slush coat my esophagus.

"You're doing alright then? I'll be honest, you had me worried for a minute there. I feel like we haven't caught up in ages."

I can't even argue with that. He's right. Besides the time Shawni came over to watch *Star Wars*, my dad's either not home when I'm there, or I'm too depressed to leave my room when he is. But we're together now, and I might as well enjoy it while I can.

"Right now, I'm great," I say, doing my best to fake that happy tone without him noticing. When I get home, who knows how I'll feel. But this is a great distraction.

"Talk to me, mija. Let it out," he says.

"Because you're so good at letting it out," I snap, but he's unfazed, still looking concerned. As always, he expertly keeps the attention away from himself.

"What's gotten into you lately? You know you can always talk to me."

I want to just pretend I'm fine and keep eating, but Papi doesn't allow it. What am I supposed to say? *I just realized I got raped by the guy I really liked?* Somehow, I feel like he'd be mad at me. For what, I don't know. Maybe for letting it happen. For being weak. Then again, that is so not my dad. He's never given me a reason to think he would react that way. So why am I so afraid to tell him?

"I don't know how to talk about it," I finally say truthfully.

"Did something happen?"

"Yes."

"Was it with a boy?"

"Yes."

He pauses for a moment, a look of anger flashing across his face for only a split second before he goes back to his jokey self. "Do I need to whoop somebody's ass?"

"Yes." I sniffle and laugh. I wish I had the strength to tell my dad exactly what happened, if only so he could scare the crap out of Luis. But if I did that, I'm afraid my dad would actually kill him, and with Luis's dad being a judge, I'm not too keen on the outcome. I have my own revenge coming for him anyway.

"You okay?"

"Yes." I smile. Right now, I am.

"Good." He puts a hand on my shoulder and squeezes, and I flinch.

"*Dad!*" I'm suddenly tense. I *know* dad's touches are safe, but unless I get a warning, my body doesn't know how to differentiate.

"Ay ay ay, I was just trying to—okay, mija, I'm sorry. Sometimes I forget."

"It's okay." It's not okay. I hate that I'm like this. One little shoulder touch from my own dad and I'm not hungry anymore. Dad's already finished with his food. "Can we go to the movies now?" I ask. I'd still much rather hang out with my dad than go home to sulk. And at the movies, he won't be able to interrogate me.

"Sure, mija." He turns on the car.

I sift through my bag for the money Mom gave me, and I realize I forgot my student ID at home. We have to stop by the house on the way to the movies to get it if we want a discounted price for my ticket, which we do. I have a major food coma right now, so I'm basically useless to the world, and when we get to the apartment, I *really* don't want to walk up the stairs.

"Papi, can you carry me?" I whine dramatically.

He pinches his belly. "Mija, I don't think I got it anymore. You're way too heavy for me."

I pinch his bicep. "No, there's definitely some muscle there. I think you can do it."

"Really?" He laughs and jiggles his hand so the fat under his arm wags back and forth. "I guess I still got it." He winks and gets out of the car, doing high knees as he makes his way over to my side. When he opens my door, I hop on his back, and he actually carries me!

I didn't think he would (or even could), since I'm practically an adult now. But Dad's always treated me like I'm much younger than I am. Usually, I don't like being treated like a child, but I milk it in times like this. He's panting the whole way and making a scene. By the time we get to our apartment door, he topples face down on the floor with me on top of him.

"No me puedo levantar . . ." he chokes out softly. He pretends to try to get up, his arms quivering hard, and he falls back on the ground. He closes his eyes with his tongue sticking out like he's dead. I roll over onto my back, laughing so hard my stomach hurts. It is not a good idea to laugh this hard after eating a double cheeseburger and animal-style fries. *Ow.*

He finally helps me up and we go inside for my ID. I start running to my room, but trip over something in the living room and fall flat on my face. My vision turns white and it feels like my nose just slammed through to the back of my brain. I grab my nose, and my fingers feel hot and wet. It's bleeding.

I sit up and tilt my head back, plugging my nose. When I look back at my foot, I see it's tangled in a pair of pants. They look like men's pants, but they weren't here before we left . . .

"You okay mi—" Dad starts. Then he sees the pants. His face does something I've never seen before. "*Ariana.*" He's using his "you're in trouble" voice. "Go to your room, please."

"What did I do?" My voice is all nasally from my pinched nose.

"I said go to your room!" he shouts, pointing at my bedroom door. He didn't even check to make sure my nose was okay. Why am I in trouble?

Before I'm off the floor, my mom stumbles out of their room wearing something different from before. Some white guy in just his boxers comes out after her. Then it hits me. The guy she told me about before she promised to work on her marriage with Dad.

"Tom?" I ask.

Dad looks at me and back at the guy. "How the fuck does Ariana know this person?"

"Emiliano, I can exp—"

"GET OUT OF MY HOUSE!" Dad yells at Tom, louder than I've ever heard him. Tom throws on his shirt and runs over to me. He snatches his pants from under my foot and fumbles around trying to put them on and make his way out at the same time.

"NOW!" Dad shouts again. Tom's out the door in seconds. "Ariana, I won't tell you again. Go to your room."

"But I—"

"Listen to your papi, Ariana," Mom cuts in.

I let go of my nose and ball my fists at my sides, letting the blood drip. "So *now* you don't want me in the middle of your drama? Why now?" I say as tears and blood start streaming down my face.

"GO!" my dad shouts again. He never shouts at me, so I run to my room and slam the door. I yank a tissue for my bloody nose out of the box by my bed so hard the box falls to the ground. Even with my door closed, I can still hear everything.

"Why the fuck does Ariana know him?" he shouts louder than the first time he asked.

"I was going to tell you! I can explain everything, please!"

I pull my pillow over my ears. I hate when they fight, but this is worse. It's worse because I knew about Tom, and dad knows I knew about him. How can he forgive me? How can he forgive my mom? How can I?

I cry into the tissue, knowing that Mom and Dad can't hear me over them screaming at each other.

"I'll come back for my things later," Papi says. Then I hear the front door slam. Then nothing but the sounds of my mom bawling. And me. I cry and cry, until I finally sob myself to sleep.

# TWENTY-NINE

My dad is gone and it's all my fault.

I should have known my mom's attempts at getting closer to him were just to ease her own guilt. I should have told Dad about Tom myself. But I took her at her word, even though she rarely gives me a reason to. I've always been taught that hate is a really strong word, and I shouldn't ever use it on family, but god-fucking-dammit, I really hate her right now.

As if on cue, there's a knock on my door, and it slides open with my mom peeking in tentatively.

"Hi, mija," she mumbles, like she knows I'm pissed at her.

Just then, I get a text.

Nina: We good to go for D&D tomorrow?

I send a quick thumbs up in response before my mom inevitably interrupts.

"Can I come in?" Mami asks.

"Sure," I say, deciding to bottle up my anger since I don't want to deal with a fight right now. She comes and sits down next to me on my bed. Heat rises in my ears at the proximity to someone I'm so mad at, but I ignore it.

"Your papi will come home soon, okay? He just needs some time away from me."

"Okay, I understand," I say, making a point to put on that fake cheery voice, even though she *has* to know it's fake right now.

"What are you up to tomorrow? Maybe we can hang out when you get home from school? Go see a movie or something?" Mami asks.

"I can't," I say. "I'm supposed to go over to Nina's to play D&D."

She frowns. "Aren't your friends sleeping over next weekend? You never hang out with your mami anymore."

"We're hanging out now," I say, probably sounding more sarcastic than I mean to.

She grunts.

"Please, Mami?"

"I'll think about it."

"So, when is Dad coming home?" I ask, since the information about him coming back soon took a second to sink in. Sometimes when I hear something, it takes a while to absorb the words.

"I'm not sure. He went to stay with your grandpa in Glendale. Hopefully just for a few days?" She doesn't sound convinced.

For some reason, even just the thought of Dad being away for a few days brings a small whimper out of my mouth. I don't mean to cry, but I can't help it.

"I'm so sorry, mija. I know I really messed up this time, didn't I?" she asks, her voice catching.

I know what she wants me to say. That it's going to be okay. That I forgive her. That she's not a bad person. But I'm done playing therapist with her. I just shrug my shoulders. I don't have the energy to give her anything more than that.

She gives me a sad look but brushes it off quickly. "So, let's do something tonight. What do you say?" she asks as if everything is totally fine.

"I'm tired," I say, using the same excuse twice in a row. "Just want to go to bed."

"Okay," Mami says, a sad twinge to her voice, but I could care less. "If you need anything, let me know, okay?"

"Kay."

And then she leaves.

After school on Monday, I find Shawni sitting at a table outside the cafeteria, and she stands and waves at me when we meet eyes. She's supposed to come over before we go to Nina's for D&D, and Nina's older brother is supposed to pick us all up to go to their house when Nina and Angel are done with Drama at four. Shawni holds her arm out for me, and after I decide I'm okay with this, I link mine in hers, and we walk to my house arm in arm. Even though it's pretty damn hot outside, I don't mind the closeness. I never do, really. Not with Shawni.

The sound of someone's car horn honking makes me jump

and yank my arm from Shawni's. We turn our heads to see Luis with one hand on the wheel and the other resting on the open window.

"Y'all need a ride?" he asks. I have to resist the urge to throw my shoe at him or something. If I could talk to him, I'd answer with a "fuck you," but instead I let Shawni answer.

"No, we're good, thanks," she says as we continue walking, Luis following slowly with his car. Luis being Luis, he doesn't immediately take no for an answer.

"Come on, Shawni, I know you hate walking."

Shawni gives him a smile that makes me dig my nails into my palm. "I like walking with Ari, actually," she says, then turns that sweet smile onto me, and the tension in my hand melts away.

"Whatever, suit yourself." Luis rolls his eyes and drives away.

It takes a moment for the butterflies in my stomach to calm themselves at the simple compliment Shawni just gave me. I like walking with her, too. I let the butterflies dance in my gut as we walk arm in arm all the way to my house.

"I think I'm gonna be able to play tonight!" I say aloud the second we're inside. I don't feel the usual pressure on my throat that keeps me from talking, even though I've been nervous about playing. I think since it's just going to be our little group and Nina's brother at Nina's house, I should be able to talk.

"What do you mean? Were you not going to play?" Shawni asks.

"I've never been to Nina's house, so I thought I wouldn't be able to talk, but I don't feel that nervous anymore, and I think it'll be fine," I say.

"You could still play without talking. Like I said, I brought a notebook, just in case. But I'm glad you're not nervous anymore!" I feel myself blushing a little. Shawni is always so nice to me.

We spend the next hour or so watching *Queer Eye*, until my mom gets home *right* before four o'clock. We're in the middle of packing up our stuff to take to Nina's when she walks through the door. I really wanted to leave before she got here, since she's been acting all clingy lately and I just don't have the bandwidth or desire to hang out with her after what she did to Dad.

"Where do you think you're going?" she asks.

"To Nina's house," I remind her.

"No, you're not."

"What?" I open my mouth to say something disrespectful, but I stop myself. She *knew* about this. "But I told you about this yesterday! Mami, we've been *planning* this!"

"Well, you need to *plan* to spend some time with family." What the hell? My mom never cares what I do, and now she wants to be all controlling?

Anger bubbles up in my chest, and I surprise myself at the harshness of my words, not even caring that Shawni's right there watching. "Dad would let me go. He actually wants me to have friends besides my mom."

"*Don't* talk to me about your dad right now!" She slams her palm on the counter and I flinch.

Shawni takes a small step back, like she wants to disappear from this conversation, but I keep going.

"But I *told* you about D&D!"

"And I never said you could go!"

Nina's brother honks his horn from outside.

"I said no Ariana, that's final. You're out too much. It won't kill you to stay home for one night."

The horn honks again.

"We won't be out that long, Mrs. Ruiz, just a couple of hours," Shawni tries to offer, but she's not budging.

"This does not concern you. Please get out of my house so I can talk with my daughter."

"Mami, are you serious? *Why?*" I'm yelling now, and tears are starting to fall. If Papi were here he'd stand up for me and let me go.

Another honk.

"Get out!" she yells to Shawni.

"Sorry, Ari . . . I'll text you," Shawni says, and rushes out before my mom can escalate the situation even more.

"What is wrong with you?" I shout.

"Do not raise your voice at me! You can't just leave the house to be with your *friends* whenever you damn well please." She says the word "friends" like it's poison. "You need to spend more time with your *family*. What happened to spending time with me, huh?" She's tearing up a little, too, but I don't care. She has no right. Except that technically I'm the one with no rights, and she can one hundred percent do whatever the hell she wants.

"You can't just pick and choose when you want to be my mom! You never care what happens to me unless I'm not here to help you with all your problems! I'm not your *friend,* Mami. I'm not your therapist. I'm your daughter!" I'm full-on crying now.

"Don't talk to me like that." Her words are firm, but her lip is shaking. "Give me your phone. You're grounded."

"But I didn't do anything!"

"You *never* talk back to me. I won't accept that. Give me your phone, and go to your room."

"But Mami—"

"Now!" She stomps her foot and points down the hall. I storm off to my room, throwing my phone on the couch on the way. I slam my door and throw myself on my bed. Then I burst out bawling.

# THIRTY

I feel like such a baby. I hate how sorry I'm feeling for myself, but I can't help it. It's not just that my mom won't let me play D&D when she already said I could. It's that D&D was supposed to help make me feel better after everything. It's that my dad left. It's that he's mad at me. It's that I almost got Ed in trouble again. Maybe it's even a little that I feel bad about hurting my mom's feelings. It's that Luis raped me. And yes, it's that I can't play D&D. That I can't have one night of reprieve from thinking about everything else.

I don't even try to muffle my crying with my pillow like I normally would. I don't care if my mom can hear me. I don't care if it makes her feel bad. She *should* feel bad. And she must, because she softly knocks on my door after a couple of hours.

"¿Tienes hambre, mija?" she asks, as if I would want anything to do with her right now. I don't answer. She can eat alone for all I care. It's her own damn fault.

I'm too mad to talk to my mom. I'm too mad to dance by

myself in my room. Too mad to do anything but lie here and cry.

I bury my face into my pillow and scream into it until my throat is so dry it hurts. Why can't I just have a normal mom who asks about my day without wanting to use me as her therapist?

I so badly wish I'd told my dad about what happened with Luis. Maybe he wouldn't have left if he knew what I'm going through.

If Mami knew what I'm going through, would she have grounded me? Would she still not want me to hang out with my friends knowing that they're my lifeline right now?

I clench my jaw, knowing the answer. Of course she still wouldn't want me hanging out with them. If anything, she'd probably just be mad that *she* isn't my lifeline. I shake my head. Why do I even care? Why does it matter what she thinks?

Why does it matter that I'm grounded?

I get out my computer and send a quick message to Shawni.

Me: Send me the address. I'm coming.


I make sure to lock my door before leaving so my mom thinks I'm still mad about being grounded if she tries to come in. But I know she won't, since she usually goes to sleep after dinner. I should be safe for tonight.

When I get to Nina's house, I can hardly hear myself knocking on the door over the music and commotion inside.

"Just try it on! For me, please?" a voice rings out from the other side of the door.

"Hell! No!" Nina shouts as the door swings open, letting Olivia Rodrigo's "Brutal" blow out of the house past my eardrums. "Oh, hi Ari! Come in!"

I laugh awkwardly as Nina steps aside, and she echoes my uncomfortable giggle, cheeks matching her freshly dyed cherry red hair. I point at it and give her a thumbs up with a smile so she knows I like the new color.

"Aw, thanks, Ari!" Nina says with a grin, though her reddened cheeks haven't faded yet. Shawni, Jasmine, and Angel are sitting at the dining room table with their D&D character sheets out and ready to go, but they all look stiff as hell, which immediately puts me on edge. What did I just walk into?

A fancy blue dress fit for prom is splayed across the table over everyone's papers.

"*Mami*, drop it, *please!*" Nina groans, head squished between her hands in exasperation.

"Mrs. Lewis, with all due respect," Shawni starts, fiddling nervously with her hair tie on the table as she speaks, "if Nina doesn't want to try on the dress, maybe she could wear something else to her quinceañera?"

Mrs. Lewis crosses her arms and gives Nina a guilt-inducing look. "You really won't even try it on? Just to see if it fits!"

"I don't want to!" Nina shouts. "*Mom*, my friends are kind of waiting on me?"

"But there will be so many people at your quinces! We can't disappoint them!"

Nina's face goes red and I share a look with Jasmine. As far as we know, we're Nina's only friends, so I'm not sure why her mom seems so convinced lots of people will be there.

Then Nina and her mom have the world's most intense stare down for a solid ten seconds before her mom finally huffs and grabs the dress off the table. "We'll talk about this later," she says before storming off to her room.

Nina sighs in relief and slumps into a chair at the dining room table. "Thank God. There is no way I'm wearing a fucking prom dress to my quinces."

"You want it to be more casual or something?" Angel asks.

"Not exactly." Nina hesitates as she chews on the inside of her cheek. "I guess part of me really does want to dress up, but whenever I try to, I just feel so *weird*. I don't like it."

"That makes sense," Jasmine says, nodding in understanding. "Dresses are uncomfortable and itchy and tight."

Nina just shrugs, and I can't help but feel a little confused. Nina doesn't seem like the type to not want to wear something because it's uncomfortable, considering the lengths she goes to bleach her hair and all the bracelets she wears.

"Whatever, let's just play, yeah?" she says, and everyone looks down at their character sheets.

It's then I realize I'm the only one who's not sitting down, so I hurry over to the table and take a seat next to Shawni. I won't lie, I'm looking forward to all those little barely-touches that come with sitting really close to someone. Shoulders, knees, maybe even the tips of our shoes? I can't wait. I pull my character sheet out of my pocket and unfold it on the table.

Since I came after they'd already started playing, it takes me a while to catch up. Apparently, we're just roleplaying right now. Jasmine's character (an eccentric bard named Valia) and Angel's character (a broody druid named Drew—very original) are fighting over some magic book that seems like it belongs to Drew.

"Okay, so if Drew doesn't want to let me see the book, can I cast 'charm person' on him and make him show it to me?" Jasmine asks, pointing her thumb at Angel.

I lean forward and feel my knee brush against Shawni's, sending a giddy shiver up my back. But just as quickly as it happens, she adjusts herself so we're not touching anymore, and the feeling goes cold.

"Hmmm . . . I'll allow it," Nina says, tapping her chin with her multicolored fingernails.

"Hey! Don't I get a say in this?" Angel protests.

Nina shakes her head. "You only get a say if it's something that would deal damage to your character in game. That's my rule. Now, roll a wisdom-saving throw."

Angel makes a face but rolls his dice anyway. Nina sucks in through her teeth.

"Oof. A nat one. You're definitely charmed by Valia. Jasmine, do you want to roleplay how you charm Drew?"

Jasmine turns to Angel and gives him a smirk, which make his cheeks darken.

"Drew . . ." Jasmine leans toward Angel and walks her fingers up to the spot on the table in front of him, then taps the table as if it were the book she was after. She tilts her chin down and looks up at him from under her thick lashes, moving in closer so their faces are just inches apart. Then she speaks in a tone sweet and soft as honey. "I think you want to let me read this, don't you?" she asks, tapping the table-book again.

"I . . . uh . . . yeah. Take it," Angel says breathlessly.

Nina bursts out laughing. "You're supposed to take his book, not give him a boner." She laughs again. I catch Shawni's gaze and let out a little laugh of my own. Angel's cheeks are dark and his eyes are wide, but he doesn't say anything.

But seeing Jasmine so blatantly flirting with Angel makes me happy. It also makes me wonder if I could possibly pull something off like that with Shawni, or if she would even want me to.

I feel the slightest ghost of a touch on my shoulder as Shawni leans forward, but it seems like the moment she feels it, she pulls away.

Did I do something wrong again? She was fine with touching me at the battle. Maybe she's in a bad mood? Suddenly the music feels way too loud, and I'm hyperaware of what every part of my body is doing. And is it just me, or am I breathing really loud right now? Am I having a panic attack? *Why?*

"Shit," I accidentally say out loud, and when Shawni looks at me, I can't bear looking back. I stand up, quickly scooting the chair out behind me, and run out the front door.

I sit on the steps leading up to Nina's porch with my head tucked in between my knees, trying to get my breathing under control. What the hell is wrong with me?

After a while, the front door opens and hesitant footsteps make their way toward me. I can hear someone sitting down next to me, but they don't try to touch me or even say anything until I lift my head up from between my knees.

"Angel?" I ask, trying not to sound disappointed that it wasn't Shawni who followed me out.

"I know exactly how you feel," he says with a sad smile.

"What are you talking about?" I ask, and he chuckles.

"You're not as subtle as you think you are," he says.

"What do you mean?" I shoot back, feeling my stomach tightening.

"Don't worry, I won't tell anyone you like Shawni." He smirks at me, and I don't have it in me to deny it, so I just slump my shoulders.

"Is it that obvious?" I ask.

"Maybe not to everyone else, but, like I said, I know how you feel." He shrugs and looks off into the distance, then sighs. "I'm in love with Jasmine."

"Really?" I say with a wide smile. I mean, I could have guessed he was into her, but hearing the confirmation out loud gives me a giddy sense of pride. I *knew* it.

"Since last year." He nods. "The guys always made fun of me for it. Glad I'm not friends with them anymore. Please don't tell her. Or anyone."

I hold out my pinkie to him and smile. "Promise."

"Good." He lets out a small laugh and takes my pinkie in his.

"What I'm trying to say is, I know it sucks having feelings for someone who doesn't feel the same way, you know?"

I wish I could tell him it's different, because Jasmine *does* have feelings for him, but I can't betray her trust like that, and I can't betray Angel's by telling her. I just have to hope they figure it out for themselves.

"I mean, I was really different before I met Jas. Like, I don't think I was ever as bad as Luis or Manny . . . We kind of always butted heads, actually. The guys would make fun of me and call me a simp and I'd say they're all assholes, but none of us took it seriously until Luis . . ." He trails off. "Anyways, none of that matters anymore. I'm happy with who I am now. It doesn't matter that I don't run with Luis's crowd anymore or that I'm not playing any sports. What matters is that Jasmine's in my life. I'm happy to have her in it, even if it's as my best friend. And you, you're really lucky, too. Shawni's an amazing girl. And she's in your life, one way or another. That's enough, right?"

I pause for a while as I think about it. I hadn't actually considered the possibility of being anything other than a friend to Shawni. I've always been her friend, and I have been happy with that. If one day Shawni decides she likes me back, then we can go from there, but Angel's right. I'm lucky to have Shawni in my life, no matter what form it takes.

# THIRTY-ONE

My mom is shut away in her room when I get home, which means she hasn't noticed I left at all. Otherwise, she'd be sitting right in front of the door waiting for me to come home.

I sleep right through my alarm in the morning.

"Mija, are you up?" my mom asks, tapping on the other side of my door. Then she opens it, barges right in, and sits at the edge of my bed. She looks at me all sad like *I'm* the one who grounded *her.* "What are you doing after school today?"

"Literally nothing. I'm grounded, remember?" I snap.

"Yes, well, maybe we can do something? Want to spend some time with your mami? We haven't had one of our little talks in a while."

I have to resist the urge to roll my eyes. "I'm just tired, Mami. I don't want to do anything . . ."

She sighs. "Okay, mija. Maybe tomorrow. I'll check in another time. Now get dressed, you'll be late for school!"

She gets up and leaves my room to get ready for work. But

instead of picking out an outfit and going to school, I throw on a hoodie and take a walk around the block until my mom leaves. It's like I said, I'm just tired. Don't want to do anything, and school falls into the category of "things." I'm not really sure why I'm so anti doing things at the moment. Last night I was all about going to D&D, but now I think I'd rather sit on a thumb tack than have any kind of social interaction.

I do the same thing the next few days, leaving the house and just going for a walk around the block until Mami leaves for work, then coming back home. She hasn't caught on so far. I tell myself I'll go back to school next week, since I know I can't keep this up forever. Shawni's been messaging me on Tumblr to get well soon every day since Tuesday, since my mom has my phone and I told Shawni the reason I didn't go to school was that I didn't feel well. Which technically is not a lie.

On Thursday, Mami comes home a bit late. I'm sitting on the couch petting Boo when she walks in with red puffy eyes, sniffling. I'd ask what was wrong if she weren't on the phone.

"Who are you talking to?" I ask, half out of curiosity, half out of feeling protective of my mom, wondering who made her cry.

"Do you want to say hi to Ari?" she asks her phone, then hands it to me.

"Hi, mija." My dad's voice comes through the other end, surprising me. His tone is hard to read. Is he mad? Sad?

"Hi, Papi. What's going on?" I ask.

"It's nothing for you to worry about, okay, mija? I'll be coming home as soon as I'm ready, but I just need a little more time. Can you hand the phone back to your mami?" he asks, actually sounding like he wants to talk to her. I reluctantly hand the phone back and Mami takes it into her room.

The next day, instead of walking around the block and coming back home, I impulsively decide to take the bus all the way to Glendale. My dad usually doesn't start work until the afternoon while I'm at school, so I want to catch him before he leaves.

It's my grandpa who opens the door when I knock. I haven't seen him in years, since he's really not that close to my dad. Which means things are pretty bad if my dad decided to come here. He looks me over and raises an eyebrow.

"¿Por qué no estás en la escuela?" he asks without bothering to say hello.

"There's no school today," I lie, knowing he doesn't care enough to call my mom and snitch. "Is my dad here?"

"Emiliano!" he calls out, stepping back in the house and gesturing for me to follow.

My dad walks out of his childhood bedroom in a blanket burrito. His usually clean-shaven face is all scruffy, and his hair is a mess. His bloodshot eyes widen when he sees me.

"What are you doing here, mija?" he asks, shedding the blanket and throwing it on the couch as if that makes him look more presentable. I've never seen him looking so un-put together, but I understand why.

"I'm staying here for the weekend," I announce. I do not want to spend a weekend alone with my mom. My grandpa just shrugs and walks back into his own room, leaving me and my dad alone. A bit of my confidence fades at the sight of my dad. He probably really wanted privacy right now. "Is . . . is that okay?"

"One night," he says, sighing. "Only because I don't feel up to driving today. I'll take you home tomorrow. I'll sleep on the couch, and you can sleep in my old room." Then he opens his arms for a hug. "Can I?"

I rush into a hug before I realize I'm not sure if I even want to talk to him. He yelled at me when I had a bloody nose without even asking if I was okay. He never yells at me. But then it's like he read my mind.

"I'm sorry I yelled at you, mija." He kisses the top of my head before letting me go.

"You take the bed. I'll take the couch," I insist. It's the least I can do with what he's going through, and the fact that I just showed up uninvited.

"So, what brings you here, mija?" he asks curiously.

Isn't it obvious? Papi's been gone. Why wouldn't I come to see him? But also . . .

"I'm mad at Mami. You're mad at Mami. Figured we could be mad together."

"Does your mami know you're here?" he asks, and I shrug. "Ay, okay, I'll text her."

He gets out his phone and shoots a quick text, then sits down on the couch and pats the space next to him.

"So what's on your mind?" he asks, sounding like Mrs. Jones.

"Mami is annoying the shit out of me. She won't leave me alone, and I'm so tired of—"

"That's enough," Papi interrupts. "What we're not going to do is talk poorly of your mother while she's not here."

"Why not?" I roll my eyes. "We both know she fucked up."

He shoots me a warning look at my use of the f-word but drops it. "Your mami has made some mistakes, yes, but that doesn't make her a bad person. She's been through . . ." He clears his throat, "a lot."

"Like what?" I ask, not feeling any pity. *I've* been through a lot.

He just gives me a sad smile. "That's nothing for you to worry about, okay, mija? Just know we're all trying our best with the cards we've been dealt." I roll my eyes, and my dad exaggeratedly rolls his back. "Don't you get a headache doing that all the time?"

I roll them again, and he laughs.

"Well, this is my decompression time, so I'm afraid I won't be very entertaining this weekend. We can watch Netflix if you want, but other than that I'm pretty much out of commission."

So, we watch Netflix.


That night, I pretend not to hear my dad crying in his old room, and anger at my mom bubbles up in my chest. I've never seen (or heard) my dad cry before. I've never seen him this heartbroken. I don't understand why he keeps defending her.

When my dad takes me home on Saturday, I go right to my room and go to bed, but my mom wakes me up by crawling in my bed with me. I groan and roll over so I'm facing the wall. She reaches over me and places my phone down in front of my face.

"You're still grounded, but you can have this back."

I grab my phone before she can change her mind. It's already one in the afternoon. Looks like Shawni, Angel, Nina, and Jasmine have all texted to check in on me. I let that warm my chest for a brief moment before it turns bitter as I remember why my phone was taken in the first place.

My mom's voice eventually brings me back to the present.

"Why don't we go get lunch, huh? Just me and you, like you and your papi do."

I don't answer her. I've been short with her ever since she didn't let me go to Nina's to play D&D, but it seems like she hasn't taken the hint. Then I realize she has the power to take my phone back any time she wants.

"Not hungry," I mumble, hoping that'll be enough to keep her from taking my phone.

"Cochina, I can see your bra strap." She pulls my bra strap under the strap of my blue tank top. When her fingers brush against my shoulder, I'm suddenly brought back to that party. That room. Alone with Luis as he tugs at my bra strap, hungrily kissing my pursed lips. My body moves on its own, and I throw myself off the bed.

"Don't touch me!" I scream at my mom and run to the

bathroom. I don't know why I overreacted the way I did. But I feel dirty all over again.

Instead of going back to my room to face my mom, I step in the shower. I scrub my body all over, just as thoroughly as I did the night of that party, but I still feel unclean. Even *thinking* about what Luis did to me makes me feel like I'm right back to that night, with his smell impossible to get off my skin.

I cry silently in the shower for who knows how long. My mom doesn't bang on the door telling me I'm wasting water like she usually does when I take over-fifteen-minute showers. I know it's not a big deal to her, but I still hope she feels bad about touching me. I wish she could understand how big of a deal it really is to me.

When I finally dry off and go back to my room, my mom's no longer on my bed. I grab my phone and quickly shoot the group a text saying I got my phone back. Then I bundle myself up in a hoodie and sweatpants and wrap my comforter around myself snugly as I plop down on my bed to sleep for the rest of the day. Just when I close my eyes, my phone rings. I sigh and reach for it.

Shawni.

I can't bring myself to talk right now, so I swipe the red ignore button with my index finger. Only a few seconds later, she texts me.

Shawni: Are you feeling better? My dad said he can pick you up for Pride if you want to come!

Shit. I completely forgot about Pride. I'm still grounded, and there's no way Mami would make an exception for Pride.

Ari: I can't go, I'm sorry.

Shawni: Oh, okay. I hope you feel better.

I can't help but feel even shittier than I already did. Sure, the sounds and the crowd would be a lot for me, but I was starting to really look forward to going to Pride, and going with Shawni. I hope she's not too disappointed.

Whatever. I would have hated Pride anyway. The crowds, the noise, the smells . . . Maybe it would have been way too much for me. I let myself think about how terrible and overwhelming of a time I would have had to make myself feel better for staying home. Instead, I throw a one-person Pride party for myself in my room.

I make popcorn and hot chocolate and play *Love, Simon* on my laptop. My door is closed, so Mami should get the hint that I want to be alone. I'm afraid of how she'll react if she realizes I'm shutting her out again, but right now I don't care. I only wish the rest of the group could share this with me, but I'm sure they'll have way more fun at the parade. Instead of crowds and confetti, I get to cry over that scene when Simon and his mom have their talk. When she tells Simon that he finally gets to exhale.

That part has me bawling. I feel like I've been holding my breath since that party. No, since before that. Since I even met Luis. I would give anything to be able to stop holding my breath. To finally be able to exhale.

# THIRTY-TWO

My door opens without a knock, and I slam my laptop so hard I almost fall out of my chair. My mom walks in and sits at the foot of my bed, and I stay in my desk chair.

"How are you, mija?"

"Great," I answer, too quickly, since I'm not at all great. Being grounded sucks. And that is definitely, one hundred percent the only thing that is bothering me.

"Really?" she asks.

"Yeah," I say sharply.

Just then, another tap on the door makes me practically jump out of my seat.

"Papi?" I blurt out when I see him peeking through the cracked door.

"Is it okay for me to come in?" he asks, and I turn to my mom, who's looking at me for an answer. She knew he was here?

I nod, not bothering to hide the look of confusion on my face.

He comes in and sits next to my mom on the foot of my bed, and I swivel around in my desk chair to face them.

"So, you're back?" I ask. Could they have possibly already made up?

My dad nods. "I'm back, mija."

Then Mami clears her throat. "We wanted to talk to you about something important, actually."

I feel my chest tighten as the tension in the room thickens, making it harder to breathe.

"I talked to your papi," she says after a moment of silence.

"He's not still mad at you for cheating on him?" I snap. I really don't want to get in more trouble right now, but I'm just so unexplainably angry, now and all the time these days, that it just comes out.

"No, mija. I forgave your mami about that," my dad says.

"Really?" I find that hard to believe.

"Mija, there are a lot of things about your dad and me that you don't know," Mami says. "We've had our struggles for a while now. But he knows now about my . . . unhealthy coping mechanisms."

"What do you mean? Is sex like . . . a coping mechanism?" How have I never heard of my mom's coping mechanisms before? I thought she told me everything.

She's crying before even saying a word.

"I'm going to tell you because I want you to know that you're not alone, alright?"

"What are you talking about?"

"Your dad told me something happened with a boy."

"It's not your kind of boy drama, Mami," I say sharply, and immediately feel bad.

She turns her head, like I just slapped her in the face.

"Ariana," Papi scolds, but Mami waves a hand to quiet him.

"I hope not," she says, "but I have a feeling . . . mija, you know I'm like this for a reason, right? I don't like that I'm like this. And I wish I could stop, for your sake. I'm *really* trying to stop. And I pray I'm wrong about you, truly, I hope I'm wrong. But I've seen how you've been acting ever since that party, and mija, I don't think I'm wrong."

"What are you talking about?" I ask, the air almost unbreathable now.

"Sometimes boys don't listen. Even when you can talk, sometimes they don't listen." Tears flow freely down her cheeks, and mine get hot. How does she know what Luis did? "The point is that your dad has always been there for me. He deserved to know why I've been sleeping around, so I finally told him what happened to me. The real reason I had to leave my old job. And I know it's not an excuse, and I'll work harder to do better, I promise. Just know you can talk to us."

I'm quiet for a while. Is she saying she was raped too? Is *that* why Papi was crying last night? This whole time, that's been why she kept cheating, why she never wanted to be alone . . .

"Okay, Mami," I say softly. I want to hug her. She reaches out a hand for me and I take it and squeeze. Then Papi takes my other hand.

"Mija, just know you don't need to worry about your papi and me, okay? *We're* the ones worried about *you*. But first, mija, we really need to know. Did someone rape you?" Mami asks, and the question being asked outright for the first time has me bursting into tears. My sobbing is all the answer they need. They just let me bawl and hold onto my hands until I can catch my breath. My dad uses his free hand to wipe tears of his own. My closed-off dad is crying openly in front of me for the first time in my life.

"I'm so sorry, both of you. I feel so helpless," he whimpers. "Please, is there anything we can do to help support you through this?" he asks, and I just shrug. I have no idea what I need.

"Will you tell us who did it? Should we call the cops?" Mami asks.

I shake my head hard at that. "No cops. It's not like they'll believe me. I don't want to go through a whole humiliating trial just to get told I was dressed too slutty so I was asking for it," I say bitterly. No, I'll handle this myself. Which means I'll have to tell my friends what Luis did to me. But if I can talk about it with my parents of all people, I can talk about it with my friends.

"Just know we're always here for you, okay, mija? No matter what, you can always come to us about anything," my mom says.

"Thanks, Mami."

"We're really just supposed to do nothing then?" Papi snaps

at Mami. "Our daughter was *raped*! *You* were raped! Don't you want some kind of justice for that?"

I want to tell him I'm getting retribution. I'm just doing it my way. But there's no way he wouldn't just freak out more.

Mami gives my hand a squeeze and looks at us sadly. "We have to respect Ari's decision here."

Dad clenches his jaw. "I don't like this . . . but I get it. You've both been through enough, and I don't want to add to it. But just know if you ever change your mind, I'm happy to go with you to the police and we can do it together. You're not alone in this," Dad adds, but I just shake my head again.

It's a little while before anyone else says anything.

"I'm really sorry I yelled at you, mija," Mami says. "None of this is your fault."

"Yes, it is," I say. I don't know if I'm talking about the fact that I didn't tell Dad about Tom, or if I'm talking about what Luis did to me. Either way, it feels like the truth.

"No, it's not," Dad says firmly. "Never think that. You're just a kid, okay? You shouldn't have to worry about any of this."

"Your papi's right, mija. I should never have involved you by telling you about Tom, and for that I'm so, so sorry."

"Oh . . . thanks," I say. She's never apologized for involving me in her drama before. It actually feels really good to hear her acknowledge it. "I'm sorry, too," I say. I have to admit I've been really hard on my mom recently, when all she's done is try to hang out with me.

"No, no, you were right before. I'm not your friend. I need

to start being more like your mom. I'm going to work on that, too, I promise."

"So . . . does that mean I'm not grounded anymore?" I ask, and my mom nods.

"You're un-grounded."

"Yes! Thank you!" I throw myself into a hug with her, which makes me realize how long it's been since we've done this. When I pull away, there are tears in her eyes again.

"Your friends are really helping you, aren't they? With everything?" Dad says.

"Yeah, they are," I say honestly.

"I'm glad," Mom adds, to my surprise. "I mean, I'm sad for me, but happy for you."

"Why are you sad for you?" I ask.

She sighs. "Because I can't fool myself into thinking you need me anymore. It was always me that needed you. I think you figured that out way before I did. Being alone is . . . it's hard for me, you know? But I want to be a good mom to you. I've been thinking about what you said. About therapy. And I've decided that I'm willing to give it a try. For you, and for me. For the family."

"Oh . . . that's good!" I don't really know what else to say. I kind of always just thought my mom was a little needier than other people's moms. I hadn't realized she was trying to keep from being alone. I feel so relieved that she'll be getting a real therapist, though. "Do you think . . ." I pause, nervously chewing on the inside of my cheek. "Maybe I could get a therapist too? Maybe an online one, so I don't have to talk?"

She looks at me and her eyes are welling up again. Is she going to tell me I'm not "crazy" enough to need therapy?

"I think that would be great, mija." I let out a breath, relieved. She looks at my dad hesitantly. "Maybe we can do this therapy thing together too—the three of us."

I relax my shoulders, relieved.

"*But* I'm really glad you have other friends now, mija. It seems like they make you happy, and I can't hold you back just because I have trouble making friends of my own. That's selfish." She smiles. I think there's a sadness in it, but it's hard to tell. What I can tell is that she's really trying.

I smile back, thinking about Shawni, and how much I miss hanging out with her and the rest of my new friends.

"They do make me happy."

# THIRTY-THREE

I'm lying down in my bed smiling up at the ceiling when there's a knock on the door.

"Ariana, can you get that, please?" my mom calls out, sounding way too happy for what the situation calls for. I look at her suspiciously, then slink out of bed and walk over to the door, opening it lazily.

But I freeze when I see Shawni, Nina, Jasmine, and Angel standing on the other side.

"Hey, Ari!" Shawni says. She, Nina, Jasmine, and Angel are all wearing different variations of rainbow something or other, which reminds me they should be at Pride right now.

"What are you guys doing here?" I blurt out.

"Your mom invited us," Shawni says. "Please don't be mad at her. She thought you'd like it if we came over."

"What about Pride?" I ask.

Shawni just smiles. "We stopped by, but it wasn't the same without you."

I smile so big it hurts my cheeks. I quickly take them all to my room. "Love you, Mami!" I call out.

After everyone's inside, I close my door, and we all sit in a circle on the floor. It's quiet for a bit. I don't know what to say, and from the looks of it, neither does anyone else.

"So . . . this is nice," Nina finally says.

Jasmine bursts out laughing. "What are we supposed to talk about?"

Shawni maneuvers herself so she's laying down on her belly and props her chin up by her elbows. "We can get to know each other?"

"I . . . um . . ." Angel stops picking his lock and scratches his chin for a second. "Red's my favorite color."

"She didn't mean it like *that*." Jasmine pushes Angel's shoulder and laughs.

"I meant like, more . . . you know, more *real*," Shawni says.

"Oh! I know a game we can play!" Nina exclaims. "It's called secret or dare. It's like truth or dare, but instead of a 'truth,' you just tell any secret you want."

"I love that! Let's do it!" Shawni says.

"Wait wait wait wait wait," Jasmine interrupts. "We need some ground rules. Like, if I get dared to do something nasty I can say no."

"How 'bout this," Shawni starts, "anything goes for dares, but if it makes anyone uncomfortable, you can get a different dare, no questions asked. And we'll go around in a circle instead of choosing who to go next so no one gets left out," Shawni suggests.

"I'm down for that," Angel says.

"Okay, Angel, you first: secret or dare," Nina says. I lean forward, eager to hear his answer.

"Well, I don't have any secrets, so, dare, I guess."

"Bullshit," I cough out, and everyone laughs. Probably more because they aren't super used to me talking yet. Still, my lips pull into a prideful smile.

"I *don't!*" His face reddens as he avoids my gaze. "I choose dare."

We all look at each other trying to come up with something good, when Jasmine speaks up without hesitation. "I dare you to tell us who you like."

I perk up. I feel like I'm in the middle of a reality TV show. This is his chance to finally tell Jasmine how he feels.

Angel's face turns completely red, and his fingers freeze up from picking his lock, shaking slightly. "Isn't that a secret?"

"I thought you didn't have any secrets!" Nina points at him with an eyebrow raised.

"Um . . ." He attempts a laugh. "I get to pass on a dare, right? Give me a different one."

Jasmine looks him in the eye. "I dare you to tell us if your crush is someone in this group." She leans forward.

"Um . . . I . . ." Angel starts nervously picking the lock again. "Yeah, it is," he says, his voice so soft I can barely hear him. Nina looks around, sizing us all up. Angel won't make eye contact with me or anyone else. Jasmine bites her bottom lip like she's hiding a smile.

"Okay, moving on," Angel says. "Nina, it's your—"

"Secret," Nina exclaims, not even waiting for him to finish. Then she scooches closer and drops her voice lower. "I've been wanting to tell you guys for a while now actually. I'm . . ." She pauses and lets out a shaky breath, which feels so un-Nina. "I'm nonbinary. I would really like it if you used they/them pronouns for me from now on. At least in this group. No one else knows, so you can keep calling me 'she' when we're in public. But when it's just us . . . they/them, please." I would have thought Nina would be shy having just come out to all of us, but they're smiling bigger than ever. "Whew." Nina's shoulders relax as they smile at all of us. "It feels so good to get that off my chest!"

"Are you still okay being called Nina?" Jasmine asks, and Nina nods.

"Thanks for asking! Yeah, I like my name. I just don't like being called a girl or a she. Everyone online knows I'm nonbinary, but no one in real life. So, I hope you're all cool with that."

"Of course we're cool with it!" Shawni says, and squeezes Nina's shoulder. "Thanks for telling us."

"We support you," I say and hold out my hand for a high five, since it's the only comforting gesture I can think of. Nina high fives me back.

"Awesome." They sigh in relief and lean on Jasmine. "So, Jasmine, secret or dare?"

"Dare."

This time, Nina is the one who speaks without hesitation. "I dare you to tell us who *you* like."

My eyes widen. Has Nina put it together, too? Jasmine's face is all flushed, and Angel is leaning in, waiting for her answer.

"I don't like anyone," she says coolly.

Dammit. I have to admit it would have been kind of cute if she admitted her feelings right here and now, but I guess I can't blame her for not wanting to do it in front of us. I look to Angel, who's now staring at the floor looking like a kicked puppy in the rain.

"Seriously?" Nina asks.

"Yup. I don't like anyone. Next. Shawni, secret or dare?"

Nina frowns, but they don't keep prying. I can't help but feel disappointed, too. Poor Angel.

"Dare," Shawni says.

Nina pulls Jasmine and Angel into a quick huddle. I try not to take it personally that they left me out of it. It feels like they're talking forever before they all finally pull apart.

"Okay, we dare you to kiss Ari," Nina says.

"What?" Me and Shawni say at the same time.

"You heard them." Jasmine smirks.

Nina must be really into playing matchmaker tonight. I look to Shawni to see her reaction, but it's hard to read. Her lips usually look super soft and honestly very kissable, but right now they're pulled into a straight line.

"Why do I always have to get these kinds of dares? Is it 'cause I'm bi?"

Jasmine's eyes get all wide. "What? No! You don't have to—"

"I don't mind," I blurt out. Why did I say that? I mean, it's true. I really wouldn't mind kissing Shawni right now. But do I really want her to *know* that?

"Wait . . . really?" Shawni asks.

My face immediately gets hot. Could I be brave enough to say it twice? I feel like the sea witch is back for my voice again. My face is red hot as I nod my head yes.

*Yes, please kiss me.*

I can feel Jasmine, Nina, and Angel staring.

"Um . . . I don't know . . ." Shawni says, and I feel like I'm about to burst. Why did I have to say anything? Now she has to reject me in front of everyone. The pause is too long, and I'm about to explode.

"I . . . I don't want to do it this way," she says. I feel like I just got sucker punched in the gut. Now I know how Angel must feel. "Okay, instead of doing another dare, can I just switch to secret?"

I'm glad she changes the subject quickly so I don't have to dwell on the rejection.

"Yeah, why not," Nina says, "but make it good!"

Shawni takes a moment, either trying to come up with a good secret or trying to figure out how to say what she wants to say.

"Okay, I have one." She takes a deep breath before spilling. "My mom's a dancer."

I've never heard Shawni talk about her mom before. I would have never assumed she was a dancer. Maybe that's why Shawni's so good.

"That's it? How's that a secret?" Angel asks.

Shawni rolls her eyes. "I'm not done. She travels a lot for dance. Right now she's on tour with Lizzo."

"That's so cool! Oh my God, do you get to meet Lizzo?"

"No, I don't get to go on tour—that's just my mom. I don't really see my mom, like ever. She lives in New York when she's not traveling, since there's more gigs over there."

"Does she at least visit for holidays?" Nina asks.

"Sometimes. Not for Christmas or New Year's or anything big like that, since she usually has gigs. But for me and my dad's birthdays she tries to come, and we get to visit her on her off-seasons."

"Is that why you dance?" I ask, not realizing how blunt it is until the words leave my mouth.

"It makes me feel more connected to her." Before anyone else can comment, she changes the subject. "Okay, your turn, Ari. Secret or dare?"

"Secret," I blurt out before I realize what I've just done. There's only one secret I can really think of, but do I really have the guts to say it? I don't realize I'm sucking on my knuckles until Jasmine says something.

"Are you okay?"

I nod quickly.

"Whatever it is, you can trust us," Angel says.

"We'll be here for you no matter what, okay?" Shawni reassures me, as if she knows what I want to say. Does she?

Everyone stares at me while I hesitate. Everything in me

says I shouldn't tell them, but I feel like such a terrible friend for keeping it a secret. I decide I need to. If they hate me for lying all this time, then I'll just have to deal with it. It's what I deserve. And *they* deserve to know the truth.

"I lied when I said nothing happened with me and Luis."

"What do you mean?" Shawni asks, brows knitted together in an expression that's hard for me to read. Anger? Betrayal?

"Something did happen . . ." I start, but I swallow the rest of my words.

"So . . . you did have sex?" Nina asks. "Wait, so why are you trying to get revenge on him, then?" Again, everyone's staring at me.

"Because he raped me!" I shout, then immediately cover my mouth with my hands.

"He fucking what?" Angel's face is turning red. Is he mad at me?

"I mean . . ." My voice gets so much softer, I can barely hear myself. "*It's not like she can say no.*" I repeat Luis's words. "He said that about me. He knew what he was doing."

No one says anything. They probably all hate me now that they know me for the liar I am. I feel tears stinging at my eyes because I don't want to lose my friends.

"So yeah, something did happen between me and Luis at the party. But it wasn't anyone's business, so I lied." Tears are spilling from my eyes and I can't slow the words. "He didn't ask if I wanted to have sex. He just sort of . . . did it. And he was right, I couldn't talk then. He knew exactly what he was doing!

It wasn't my fault!" I cover my face with my hands and cry into them. I'm too ashamed to look anyone in the eye. "It wasn't my fault," I repeat again, words muffled by my hands.

"Ari . . ." Jasmine's voice.

"Sorry . . . I'm really sorry . . ." I plead. I rub my chest to soothe the racing in my heart. I think deep down I wanted to believe that what Luis said to his friends about me not being able to say no was just guys being assholes, but it wasn't. He picked me for a reason. He knew I was lonely and desperate for someone to notice me, and he took advantage of it. This whole time I thought I wasn't really over him. But what I'm really not over is what he did to me.

"Can I hold your hand?" Shawni asks. The question makes me cry harder, because why would she want to touch me now? I nod anyway because I could use the comfort, even if she probably hates me. I don't know why she wants to hold my hand, but I also want to hold hers more than anything, so I let her. She carefully pulls one of my hands away from my face and squeezes it. "Ari . . . of course it wasn't your fault . . ."

A choked sob escapes me. "If it's not my fault then why do I feel so guilty?"

"Because you want it to be your fault," Jasmine says matter-of-factly.

"Wh—what?" I ask. Everyone's looking curiously at Jasmine now.

"You want it to be your fault. If it's your fault, that means you could have done something different. That means you can prevent it from happening again in the future. But it wasn't your fault . . ." Jasmine is crying now, too. "It wasn't either of our faults."

What? Is Jasmine saying Luis raped her, too?

"Jas, you don't have to—"

"I want to, Angel. I'm okay, I promise." Then she looks back at me with tears in her eyes. "There's nothing we can do to prevent it from happening again. Because it *wasn't* our fault. And that's the scariest part of this whole thing." She wipes her eyes, and Angel's hand twitches like he wants to grab onto hers, but he crosses his arms instead, looking like he wants to cry, too.

"It wasn't our fault, but that doesn't mean there's nothing we can do." I surprise myself by how strong I sound. "We can make him pay. For real, this time. Luis isn't just a cheater and a liar. He's a fucking rapist, and everyone should know it."

Nina has tears in their eyes, too. Angel's fists are balled up so tight I can see the veins in his hands.

"Oh my God . . ." Nina says. "Knowing Luis, Ari and Jasmine can't be the only ones, right? Do you think that's why some of the girls we talked to didn't want to say anything about him? This is so fucking sick. Oh my God . . ."

"You're right, we can't be the only ones," Jasmine says. She's squeezing Angel's hand so hard it's red.

"We did everything all wrong," Shawni says slowly. "We didn't expose him for shit. Everyone knew he distributed Nina's nudes. Everyone knew he cheated on me. But this? He should be locked up, seriously." Shawni looks like she's ready to throw up. I can't say I blame her. Finding out your ex is a rapist can't be an easy thing to hear.

"Maybe we should go to the police," Nina suggests.

"Yeah, because that always ends in the victim's favor, right?" Jasmine says.

"Actually, it rarely ends in the victim's favor, especially when the victims are people of color," I correct her.

"I was being sarcastic."

"Of course it would be the white kid who wants to go to the cops." Angel laughs, but there's no heart in it.

"Okay, okay, no cops." Nina throws their hands up.

"You're right that he should be locked up, though. We just have to be smart about this if we're going to get any kind of justice," Shawni says. "We need to start thinking bigger picture. Ari, Jasmine, we can take care of it if it's too much for you guys."

I look at Jasmine, and I can tell she's thinking the same thing as me, as usual.

"No," she says.

I add, "Let us help."

# THIRTY-FOUR

After hours of talking about how we're going to expose Luis—and do it right this time—we finally have a solid strategy. I'm going to write another piece, but this time I'll be telling my own story. Jasmine will tell hers, and I'll interview some of the other girls Shawni originally tried talking to who seemed touchy about Luis. Who knows, maybe they'll open up when they know what we're planning. That's when Jasmine will make a landing page for my article, and then we'll post that to Twitter instead of Instagram this time. Apparently, Twitter is the place to go for a callout if you want people to actually care.

And this time, we'll get the school directly involved. Jasmine is going to send the school's Twitter account a phishing message offering a foundation to generate funds for student scholarships, which she's pretty sure they'll click on, giving her access to their passwords so we can post a link to the article right to the school's own account. They'll *have* to take it seriously then.

Once we have our plan figured out, Angel heads home early,

since his mom wants him home for dinner.

As soon as he leaves, Nina turns right to Jasmine.

"You lied about not liking anyone, didn't you?" they ask, squinting skeptically at her.

"Well, yeah." Jasmine folds her arms across her chest.

"You like Angel, don't you?" Nina asks.

Jasmine looks at me questioningly, as if she thinks I might have said something to Nina. I just shrug and shake my head to let her know I didn't.

"I knew it!" Shawni says. "You two are not subtle at all."

Jasmine sighs. "Okay, okay. I like him. Are you happy?"

I try to hide the smile on my face, because yes, I am happy. It feels good not to have to keep the secret from everyone anymore.

"Why didn't you tell him today? He obviously likes you, too," Nina says.

"It's *because* I like him that I can never tell him."

"What do you mean?" I ask. That makes no sense to me, especially since she seems pretty confident that he likes her back.

"Because he's, like . . . kind of perfect right now, you know? Like, he asks before hugging me, and stops tickling me if I say no, and doesn't think twice about leaving me alone if I need my space. But if he knew I liked him, would he want more?" She adjusts her arms so she's hugging herself. "If he knows I like him, what if he expects more than I'm ready for?"

Shawni shakes her head. "That doesn't sound like Angel."

"I know, I know," Jasmine says. "And I do trust him, but I just . . . you can never be sure. After what happened with Luis . . . it's just really hard to trust anyone again."

"You should take all the time you need," I say. "Just because you trust him doesn't mean you have to be ready. But when you are, we'll be here for you." I give Jasmine a smile, and she seems to relax a little.

"Thanks, Ari," Jasmine says. "I really, really do like him, though."

"We know," Shawni laughs.

"Okay, I get it, I'm not slick." Jasmine joins in on the laughter, and so do Nina and I.

"And hey, if you're never ready, that's okay, too. I'm sure you two would be an amazing couple, but you're also great as friends. You're lucky to just be in each other's lives," I say, glancing longingly over at Shawni before I realize who I'm supposed to be talking to. Shawni catches my gaze for a split second before I clear my throat and look back to Jasmine. "No matter what happens, it can still be a happy ending."

"I think you're right." Jasmine smiles at that. "With him, it'll definitely be a happy ending . . ."

Before I can say anything in response, my watch buzzes with a text from my mom.

Mami: Your friends can stay the night if they want to <3

"Yes!" I say with a small fist pump. "My mom says you guys can stay the night!"

"Oh, fun!" Nina exclaims. "I just have to text my mom."

"Yeah, I'm down," Jasmine says, reaching for her phone, probably to ask her parents, too.

"I wish I could." Shawni frowns. "But I have to get home soon and clean my house. My mom's coming over tomorrow! For . . . for my birthday." She mumbles the last part.

"Oh my God, it's your birthday tomorrow?" My jaw drops. She never mentioned that.

"We have to do something!" Nina claps their hands together in excitement.

Shawni gets all shy, glancing up at me from under her eyelashes. "I didn't want to make a big deal out of it. But yeah. My mom's flight is pretty early in the morning, and I want to clean and get everything ready for her, you know?"

"Happy early birthday!" I say. "Yeah, I understand that. I hope you have fun with your mom!"

"Thanks! I'm freaking nervous, but I can't wait!" she squeals, then gets up and heads for the door. "My dad's actually here to get me right now. I'll see you guys on Monday!"

"See you on Monday!" We all hug her goodbye.

After Shawni leaves, Nina, Jasmine, Boo, and I spend the next hour or so curled up on my bed watching *Los Espookys* on my laptop. The show is hilarious, but I can't focus. All I can think about is the fact that we have a plan now to finally get back at Luis. And I'm the only thing keeping us from executing it. All I need to do is interview a few people. Even if no one responds, my story and Jasmine's should be enough. But I don't want that to be it. I want to bury Luis's reputation under an avalanche of guilt that he'll never be able to crawl out of.

I get out my phone to text Ed. I want to tell him thank you. For everything. Even if he didn't actually join in on our plan, he still empowered me to tell my friends the truth. To tell myself the truth. And I really don't know how to thank him enough for that. A simple text doesn't seem like enough, so I reluctantly put my phone away, hoping we can make plans soon so I can tell him in person.

Soon enough, Jasmine and Nina are both asleep, and I've never been more awake. I gently slip out of bed, careful not to wake either of them. It's only like nine at night, but they both seem exhausted. Maybe it's from all the emotions and secrets we all spilled tonight.

I take my laptop out to the living room, where I pull up the TLOSC Tumblr account and get to work.

Nina, Angel, Jasmine, and I weren't the only ones Shawni was in contact with through the TLOSC account. I wonder how many of them have similar stories to mine and Jasmine's. I intend to find out.

My fingers tremble as I open my first DM to a girl named Tracy Chow. She's a senior, a foreign exchange student who came here her sophomore year and had a hard time making friends, other than Luis. From an outside perspective, her story is painfully similar to mine. She went to one party. After that, rumors spread that she and Luis had sex, and she got labeled a slut for the rest of her high school career.

When I click to DM her, I see the messages between her and Shawni from when Shawni first reached out. Like me, Shawni had invited Tracy to room 205, but unlike me, Tracy never showed. If Shawni couldn't get her to show up, who's to say I'll be able to? Then again, we actually have a way to take Luis down this time. And it might really stop him from hurting anyone else.

All I know is I have to try.

tlosc: Hi. My name is Ariana Ruiz.

My breath shakes as I let it out. I need to be open about who I am if I want her to trust me. I just hope this will get easier the more people I message. Since I don't get a response right away, I keep typing. I need her to know she's not alone. I need to just rip off the Band-Aid.

tlosc: Luis raped me.

My fingers shake, but I keep typing. I can't just leave it at that.

tlosc: I know I'm not the only one. We might have a way to stop him from hurting anyone else. Would you be willing to tell me your story? We're going to expose him, but you can be anonymous. No one has to know it's about you. It would really help us. And if you don't want to, that's fine, too. No pressure. I know how hard this is to talk about.

I hope my message isn't too clinical. I don't really know how to talk about Luis, and I didn't want to get into detail about what happened, but maybe I should have? No, that would have been too much. I wait about ten minutes before I get a response from Tracy.

tracych: I'm sorry he did that to you.

A few moments pass before I get another message.

**tracych:** Me too.

**tracych:** Do you really think this will work?

I take a moment to think about it. I know Tracy won't like my answer, but I also don't want to give her false hope.

**tlosc:** I don't know. But the only way to find out is to try, right?

Thirty-seven years pass before I get a response. It feels like it, at least.

**tracych:** Okay. I want to help.

After a few more minutes, I get a longer response detailing what Luis really did to Tracy at that party. I want to throw up. It's so similar to what happened to me that my brain shuts down for a minute. The words get all jumbled together so I can't read them anymore. I feel like someone punched through my chest and is squeezing my heart in their fist. *This* is what I was avoiding by not doing it sooner. My ears ring, my vision tunnels, and my limbs tingle. Everything hurts and then nothing does. The room goes black, and I can't tell if it's because I died or just closed my eyes. It's like I'm not even here anymore. I feel nothing. See nothing. Hear nothing.

But in the back of my mind, I know I have to keep going. I have to respond, and do this all over again for the next person. My heartbeat eventually slows down again, and my surroundings start to come back into view. My computer screen tells me thirty minutes have passed. I only ever lost time like that once before, when Luis . . . yeah. The word for what he did to me is so harsh, but it's what happened. And now that I'm admitting it to all these strangers, it makes it real.

*Okay, focus. Everyone's counting on you.*

I take a deep breath and start typing. I can't just not respond after Tracy just relived all of that for me.

**tlosc:** Thank you for telling me this. We're going to do everything we can to stop him, I promise.

**tracych:** I want to be anonymous. Thank you for doing this.

She thanked me? I haven't done anything yet, but I guess the thought of stopping Luis is a good one. I just have to gather enough stories so this is undeniable. And when I'm all done, maybe I'll finally be ready to tell my own.

I copy and paste the messages I sent to Tracy and send them to the next person, and the next. I feel bad copy and pasting, like it makes this less personal. But at the same time, I don't have the spoons to sit here and tell everyone what Luis did to me in a personalized way.

Once I've messaged everyone and gotten a decent number of responses, I compile all their statements into a Google document. I spend the rest of the night staring at all the notes everyone sent me, skimming the graphic ones to keep from dissociating again. My brain makes me take a step back when I read those replies, and it's like I have no idea what I'm reading. I'm still the only thing holding us back from exposing Luis right now, but I haven't been able to bring myself to start writing. Every time I look at the Google doc, I think about how my story should be in there, too. But I don't know if I'm ready.

*It's not like she can say no.*

I shake the memory out of my head. I really thought he liked me. I really thought I liked *him*. Now, looking at the notes just makes me pissed at myself over how easily I fell for him.

The sun is up when my dad comes out of the room ready to go to work. Mami wakes up from her spot on the couch when he opens the door. I know he's forgiven her, but I guess that doesn't solve all their problems overnight. She goes to change for work.

"What are you doing up so early, mija?" Papi asks.

"Couldn't sleep," I say as nonchalantly as possible. I don't want him to worry.

"Ah, well get a nap in at least, if you can," he says, and kisses me on the forehead before heading out to work.

Around ten in the morning, Nina and Jasmine still aren't awake. My phone buzzes in my pocket, and I pull it out to see a text from Shawni.

Shawni: my mom never showed . . .

Instead of texting Shawni back, I call her.

"Is everything okay? What happened?" I ask as soon as she picks up.

"I guess one of the other dancers got injured and she had to cover for them." Shawni sounds a little stuffy, like she's been crying. "She was supposed to be here an hour ago, but she never even got on the plane. Didn't even tell me until just now. I've been waiting at the airport like an asshole."

"Oh my gosh, are you okay?"

"Can we just hang out again? My dad went to work since he thought I'd be spending the day with my mom. I don't want to tell him. He'll be so mad."

"Yeah, of course. Can you come over? Nina and Jasmine are still asleep."

"I'm already here, actually. I dropped my dad off at work and took the car to pick up my mom. Want to go get food or something? My mom sent me a bunch of money since she felt bad, so it's on me. We can even pick up food for Jasmine and Nina."

"Yeah, that sounds good. I'll be right out." I write a quick note to Nina and Jasmine telling them I'm picking up breakfast. Then I slip on my sneakers and rush out of the door to meet Shawni at her car.

Shawni's cheeks are stained with tear tracks, and her throat is raw when she says, "Hi."

I can't stand seeing her like this.

"Can I hold your hand?" I ask. I don't know what else to say. Your mom sucks? Happy birthday?

Shawni answers by putting her hand palm up on the center console. I know now that means yes, so I slip my hand in hers and squeeze.

"My mom was gonna take me to my favorite breakfast place. Have you ever been to Snooze?" Shawni's voice is still raw, but she's smiling now as I shake my head. "I freaking miss that place. Want to go there?"

"Wherever you want," I say.

Snooze is apparently a breakfast place that specializes in

× 273 ×

really fancy pancakes. Instead of eating inside, though, Shawni calls in to order the food to go so we can eat it in the car. We end up going with the mysterious "pancake of the day." We get that and a few other kinds of pancakes to share with Nina and Jasmine when we get back. I think we're eating in the car because she wants to be able to talk to me, and she knows I won't be able to say a word in public.

We sit in her car with the AC blasting to make up for the March heat outside, and I try Snooze pancakes for the first time. Apparently, the pancake of the day is a pineapple upside-down pancake, which I've never heard of but sounds amazing. Shawni watches my face to see my reaction as I take my first bite.

My eyes widen. "This is really good."

Shawni laughs and takes a huge bite of her own. "I told you it would be!" she says through a mouthful of pancake.

We eat in silence for a while, letting the soft goodness make up for Shawni's heartbreak. Until the food is gone. The vibe shifts as she starts picking at her potatoes.

"Do you ever feel like your mom doesn't love you?" she asks as she sticks a forkful in her mouth.

I blink. It's a really personal question, but I feel like Shawni and I are close enough by now to talk about something like this. Especially with what she's going through.

"I mean, I don't feel like that today, because she apologized to me about how she's acted in the past. We actually had a really good talk yesterday before she invited you guys over, and I think things are going to start getting better. But yeah, to answer your question, I used to feel like my mom didn't love me. She would use me as her therapist and just like, not care if I had the emotional capacity to deal with her problems, you know? But I really do think she's trying to be better now."

Shawni nods, like she knows exactly how I feel. "I feel bad for saying I feel like my mom doesn't love me. Like, am I self-ish for wishing she'd just take a damn day off for my birthday? But at the same time, I know it's her career. It doesn't mean she doesn't love me. Like, we talk on the phone all the time. Sometimes for hours, and I don't ever feel like she doesn't want to talk to me. But I just never see her. It's hard to feel loved by someone you never see, you know?"

I nod, even though I don't know. I've always lived with my parents, so I couldn't possibly know what Shawni's going through. Still, I let her talk while I eat my potatoes, and I just listen. Our moms seem pretty opposite. Hers is never around but always wants all the updates from Shawni, always wants to know what Shawni's been up to and how she's doing. Mine is way too clingy and can't stop giving *me* all the updates about *her*. Well, I guess that was her in the past. We'll see if things change now.

"Anyways, we should get back to Nina and Jasmine before they wake up, right?" Shawni asks as she puts the car in reverse and starts backing out.

"Right," I say, trying to hide my disappointment. I love Nina and Jasmine, but it's nice to spend some alone time with Shawni, too.

When we get back home, Nina and Jasmine are sitting and talking on the living room couch.

"We got some more dirt on Luis," Nina says right when we walk in.

"Already?" Shawni asks.

"Well, not really. Basically, I gave Angel permission to share that recording he got of Luis talking about me. That way I don't have to tell my story. Luis said it all himself. He *bragged* about it. His friends might be okay with him talking about girls like that, but I doubt the school administration will."

"Today is the day I write my story," I blurt out. By now, I have all the testimonials I need, along with incriminating voice recordings of Luis admitting to what he did with pride. And if Jasmine can be okay with her story being told, then I can tell mine.

I'm ready to see him pay for what he did.

"Do you want us to leave you alone to do it?" Shawni asks.

I shake my head. "Can you guys stay? Actually, invite Angel back over, too. I don't want to do this alone . . ."

Jasmine takes out her phone to text Angel. "Of course."

I sit down on the edge of the couch with Nina and Jasmine, and Shawni sits on the floor, scooting her back onto the couch in between my knees.

I can do this.

I think about all the harm Luis has caused, not only to me but also to everyone else. And he's gotten away with it, too. Not anymore.

"Can I?" Shawni asks, hand hovering over my knee. I nod

my head, and she squeezes it reassuringly. "You can do this."

My fingers finally start moving.

*My name is Ariana Ruiz, and I need to tell you a story . . .*

I go on to confess that I lied on Instagram when I said nothing happened between me and Luis. I write my story. The whole truth, for the first time. I write what happened at the party, and about what I heard him say when he was bragging to his friends about it. Everything. And Shawni leans on my knee the whole time. Nina and Jasmine give me enough privacy by not looking at the screen, but they're all here to give me the moral support I need.

Angel shows up just before I finish the article, and it's *long*.

The odds of getting legal justice are so low that I'm not even worried about that part. Instead, I have a different goal here. We're leaving it up to the school and Twitter to decide his fate. With all the details from Luis's victims in my article, the school won't be able to ignore the accusations and the proof of what Luis has done. I want him to get expelled. I want him to lose any scholarships he has. I want him to be too afraid to hurt anyone else ever again. And I want this to serve as a warning for all the Mannys and Jesuses out there. A warning for anyone else like Luis that they won't get away with it.

Once I'm done, the five of us share a collective sigh of relief.

"My turn," Jasmine says, gesturing for me to hand her my laptop. My part is done. Now all that's left is to let Jasmine put it up on the website and schedule the Twitter posts from the school's account.

"I'm proud of you," Shawni says, turning around so she's

facing me as I hand Jasmine my laptop.

"Thanks," I say, heat rushing to my cheeks.

"You did good, Ari," Angel says. "You too, Jas." Angel's hand moves toward Jasmine's shoulder, but at the last second he clears his throat and puts his hand in his pocket instead.

After a few minutes of Jasmine clacking on the computer, she shuts it.

"Alright, it's done. Post goes live at seven o'clock tomorrow, an hour before school starts."

We all look at each other, grinning speechlessly.

It's finally happening.

# THIRTY-FIVE

Soon enough, our little hangout turns into a celebration, both for Shawni's birthday and the eve of justice. Everyone huddles around my computer to read through the website Jasmine put up with my article on it while I hide in the corner. I feel so exposed, having them read it, but at the same time, it's going live tomorrow, and the whole school will see it, so I should get used to the idea.

Shawni looks up from the computer first, wiping a tear from her eye. "Yeah, he's definitely going down . . ."

Nina squeezes Shawni's shoulder. "Well, there's no way he's getting away with this. You did amazing, Ari."

"For real, Ari," Angel says, giving me a smile.

"God, I can't wait to see the look on that asshole's face tomorrow," Shawni says.

"I'm so jealous of you guys." Jasmine looks at Shawni and me. "Y'all actually get to see his reaction. Take a picture or something for the rest of us."

Everyone laughs, and I can't help the swell of pride in my chest from their love and faith in me. It makes me feel ready to take on tomorrow.

We all move to the living room to watch a movie, but before we put anything on, Shawni excuses herself.

"Um, Ari, can you come with me really quick?"

"Oh, um, yeah." I stumble over to where she is in the hall-way.

"Do you want us to wait for you?" Nina calls out.

"No, thanks! We'll just be a minute!" Shawni calls back, then looks at me from under her lashes all shy.

"What's up, Shawni?" I ask.

"I . . ." She takes a nervous breath before going on. "I've been wanting to tell you this for a while now. Actually, it might be pretty obvious, but I thought you should know anyways."

"What is it?"

"You might have already guessed, but I have . . . feelings for . . . someone."

My stomach drops as I remember that day we were walking to class, when she shared That Look with Luis. The day at lunch I caught her staring dreamily at him . . . Not just because she knows what he did to me, but also because . . . I don't know. I thought she was over him. It just hurts.

"You're still in love with Luis . . ." I say, the words forming a bubble in my throat that might turn into a sob at any minute.

"Ari, no, I—"

"It's okay, really," I interrupt. And it is, no matter how much it hurts. "It's not like you can control your feelings. You just—"

"It's you, Ari! I was talking about *you*. I have feelings for *you*, okay? It's always been you, Ari. This whole time."

Stunned, I open my mouth to say something, but the sea witch is back. In the movies, the confession is where I'd be expected to kiss her, right? But my lips won't move, to make words or for anything else.

"I'm sorry, I shouldn't have dropped that on you. You don't have to say anything." Then she hurries past me into the living room, and before my feet can react, the front door opens and closes.

"Where are you going?" Jasmine shouts, too late.

"What happened, Ari?" Angel asks as I finally run out to the living room.

"I . . . she . . ." I stumble on my words while I fight with the sea witch for control. "Shawni has . . . feelings . . . for me?"

Everyone is staring at me now, waiting for some kind of explanation, until Angel breaks the silence. "Isn't that . . . a good thing?"

I can't bring myself to answer. Everything we've planned for is finally coming to fruition, but I can't think of anything except Shawni. Why couldn't I just tell her I felt the same way? Why do I have to be like this? I didn't even have to talk. I could have texted it to her. I still can, but . . . I can't.

"Hey Ari, you don't have to feel guilty for not feeling the same way. It's a part of life," Nina says, and I look up to meet their sympathetic gaze.

"Right. She'll understand eventually. You just have to let her know," Jasmine adds gently.

I shake my head, then surprise myself when the words come out. "But I do feel the same way."

There's a short pause before Nina breaks the silence again. "Why didn't you just tell her that?"

"Because she can't always talk, asshole," Jasmine says.

"Better late than never, right?" Nina says, shrugging.

"What do you mean? I ruined it," I say, quiet enough I'm surprised they can hear me.

"Let's just focus on one problem at a time," Jasmine says. "Ari, she's probably not mad at you. I'm sure she just needs a minute to gather up her pride."

"Okay, so Ari, do you want to tell her how you feel?" Nina asks.

"You don't have to," Jasmine adds, "not unless you feel ready." She gives me a little smile.

"I want to, but . . . how?" I ask.

"I don't know," Angel says with a sigh. "Admitting your feelings is fucking hard."

"Tell me about it," Jasmine says, looking at Angel in a way that even *I* can see is romantic, but Angel won't meet her gaze. He just pulls out his lockpicking kit and starts fiddling.

"Are you avoiding me?" Jasmine asks him outright.

"What are you talking about?" Angel responds.

"You've been acting weird since last night . . ."

"No, I haven't," he says all defensive.

"You kind of have," Nina says.

"Fine." Angel puts his kit down and looks up at Jasmine. "I know you're smart enough to know what's going on. You know how I feel about you, and you don't feel the same and that's fine. I'm fine. I don't blame you and I'm not mad—"

"Then why are you avoiding me?" Jasmine's voice gets quiet. Nina and I share an awkward look. I feel like we shouldn't be hearing this.

Angel's face goes soft. "I'm in love with you, Jas, and now you know that, and I don't want you to think I want anything other than what you want us to be. I don't want to make you uncomfortable—"

"Stop!" Jasmine interrupts. Angel looks like he just got shot in the heart, but he nods.

"Okay. I'll stop, then."

"No, don't stop! I mean—that's not what I mean—"

"What do you mean then? Just tell me what you want and I'll do it," Angel says gently.

"I don't know!" Jasmine shouts, tears coating her eyes. "All I know is I don't want to lose you." The tears fall, and she looks over at me and Nina, as if noticing us for the first time. She lets out a shaky breath. "Maybe we should go for a walk . . ." She holds out a hand for Angel, and he takes it, and they head out the door.

"*Finally!*" Nina laughs once they're gone. "Talk about a slow burn, amiright? Now all that's left is you and Shawni." They smile.

I laugh, feeling hopeful again. If Jasmine can do it, so can I. I'm going to tell Shawni how I feel. Tomorrow.

The next morning I rush to get ready for school. The tweet is up and I can't wait to see the look on Luis's face when he sees it. When everyone sees it. I rush to get ready, and get to Journalism early, hoping to see Shawni in there waiting for me, so we can have some time to talk. But she's nowhere to be seen. The minutes tick by slower and slower, until finally the bell rings, and Shawni walks in. I can't talk to her now, but I hope to at least get her to look at me. Instead, she keeps her eyes on her own desk. I want to tell her how I feel, but maybe now isn't exactly the right time.

Although no one seems to be talking about the post yet. Why aren't they? The vibe of the class doesn't change any more than usual when Luis walks in the room, and my stomach drops. Something's wrong. Is this going to be a repeat of our last failed attempt?

I pull out my phone and check the school's Twitter account. It's suspended.

Fuck. The administrators must have seen the post and reported it before anyone else saw it! My throat and stomach twist up into knots. What are we supposed to do now?

Is the school seriously taking their hacked account more seriously than Luis being a rapist? I refuse to believe it. I wait for him to get called to the office any minute.

The minutes go by so slowly, and I imagine I'm the one

getting caught and called to the office. I wonder what they'll do if they find out it was us. Is hacking the school's Twitter account an expellable offence? I try to get my mind off it by thinking about Shawni.

I find myself writing on a piece of paper.

*I have feelings for you too.*

I fold it up, but don't hand it to her. It's still not the right time. Maybe in dance class, when we'll have some time to work through it.

I excuse myself to go to the bathroom to try to focus on what to do. I can't just let Luis get away with everything after all the work we put into this.

Then the idea hits me.

I go to ExposeTheMierda and fill out their form again. This time I reframe the story, focusing on Luis's crimes and how the school is trying to cover them up. I link to the exposé I wrote. *That'll* put pressure on the school to do something.

I go back to class, hoping against hope that this will work.

# THIRTY-SIX

About halfway through class, my watch notifies me I got an email response. I discreetly tap it, even though I've run out of hope.

> Subject: Your Story is Up!
> Hi Ariana,
> Thank you so much for submitting your story to
> ExposeTheMierda! I'm so impressed with this submission!
> I went ahead and posted it on today's blog. I'd love to see
> this Luis Ortega go down for what he did.
> Speak truth,
> ETM

I can't help but let out a little squeal at that. Then I quickly clear my throat. A few of my classmates give me weird looks, but for the most part no one seems to care. It's only a few minutes before the buzzing starts. Mrs. Jones is writing something on the board, so she doesn't see the wave of students checking their phones. Everyone starts whispering and staring at Luis. I stare eagerly, too. He's checking his phone. He stares at it with his mouth wide open, then looks up.

"I never— I'm not a—" he starts, and the whispering stops.

"A rapist?" Melanie says, glaring at Luis. Mrs. Jones whirls around.

"Excuse me?"

Luis's mouth is open like he wants to keep going, but there's nothing he can say. This time, we got him. He glares right over at Shawni, like he knows she was involved.

Then there's a knock at the door, and an administrator opens it. I brace myself for my punishment, but Shawni and I don't get called to the office.

"Luis Ortega?" they call out. "Principal Matthew wants to speak with you."

Luis looks like he's about to murder the administrator, but he gets up and walks out with them. Mrs. Jones tries to get the class back on track, but no one is listening to her. Everyone keeps chattering so loud you can't hear her over all the noise. I feel bad about the fact that no one's listening to Mrs. Jones, but I also feel so, so good.

"I told you he was a piece of shit!" Melanie shouts to Jessica, whose face is ghostly pale. She doesn't respond.

"You can't seriously be buying this, right?" one of Luis's friends starts, but he's quickly iced out by everyone around him.

"You can't seriously be so far up Luis's ass that you think

every single one of those accounts is fake," Melanie snaps, and I have to resist the urge to clap my hands.

An announcement over the loudspeakers interrupts the conversation.

"As many of you may already know, our school's Twitter account has been hacked. We take this issue extremely seriously. If you or someone you know was involved, please come forward now to minimize your consequences."

The bell rings.

Shawni is the first one to rush out of the room, and I have to jog to try to see where she's going. I just want her to acknowledge me, but I can't get her attention. When we get to the courtyard, Luis comes out of the office. He's headed right for Shawni, like he's on a mission.

"You bitch!" He raises a hand like he's about to hit her.

Before his fist makes contact, I run full speed in between them and swing my knee between Luis's legs. The sound of air leaving his lungs is glorious as he falls to his knees.

"Don't . . . don't call her a . . . a bitch." The words are so soft they're barely audible, but the fact I was able to get anything out at all is a miracle. Luis falls to his knees, clutching his crotch with both hands. There's already a huge crowd around us, all cheering me on for kneeing a now known rapist in the balls. They all look like they're piecing the puzzle together. My Instagram post, the rumors, the allegations—all of it. They know now what he did to me. His face is completely flushed as he looks up at me while still on his knees.

"*You?*"

I hold eye contact with him, letting the *yes* be implied. Pride swells up in my chest at the thought of everyone here knowing *I* wrote that essay. But panic follows. What if I get caught?

"Break it up!" A teacher pushes past the crowd to see what's going on.

"She kneed me!" Luis points at me.

"He was gonna hit that girl!" someone else calls out.

"That's a lie! I didn't do anything!" he pleads, but the teacher isn't having it.

"Why are you still here, Luis? Go home," the teacher says.

Kids start booing at him, and his face goes a deep red. He grabs his bag from the ground and makes a break for the parking lot. Just as I'm about to keep walking to class, the teacher grabs my shoulder, making me flinch hard. She grabs Shawni's, too.

"Not so fast. You two, principal's office."

Shawni and I share a look. Are we caught? I guess kneeing Luis in the balls was a little conspicuous. Still, I can't bring myself to regret it. He was going to *hit Shawni*.

I slip Shawni my note while we walk. I might not get another chance. She takes it but doesn't read it. Maybe because there's a teacher walking with us, or because people are staring. I guess I don't blame her for wanting to wait, but I can't handle the suspense.

Most of the staring faces blur together, until I see Angel. He stops walking when he sees us, and his eyes go all wide. He probably thinks we're confessing. If I could make words happen right now, I'd let him know he's safe as we walk past, but I can't.

When we get to the office, a lot of the girls we interviewed are already in there. Some are walking out, and a few are walking in behind us. I make eye contact with Tracy Chow, and she grins at me shyly before averting her eyes to the floor. Are they all here to snitch?

There's a man inside Principal Matthew's office and he's clearly yelling at her through the glass doors, but we can't hear what he's saying. Shawni finally looks me in the eye, and for the first time since I've known her, she looks scared. Like, really scared.

The door finally opens and we hear him say, "You know I am one of this school's largest supporters. You might want to think long and hard about how you handle this whole *misunderstanding*." Then he turns to recast his glare at all of us, like he's not quite sure who to blame. Shawni turns away. Once he's staring right at me, I notice the man has curly black hair and gray eyes. Just like Luis.

Fuck. It's the judge.

His mouth turns into a cold smile. "You kids should know that what you're attempting to do is called defamation. And the punishment for that is quite serious indeed."

Then he walks out, and we finally sit down. Shawni's hands are shaking, and her chin is trembling. I look down at my own unsteady hands. All I want to do is hold hers and forget about everything else. I'm afraid of what Luis's dad is capable of. I'm afraid of what *Luis* is capable of now that he knows I'm behind this. But I focus on Shawni instead. She closes her eyes for a while, then finally reads my note. She stares at it for way too long, and it's hard to read her expression. Instead of looking at me, she closes her eyes again. She turns her palm up on her knee. An invitation.

I take it, and she squeezes. A small smile tugs at her lips. I squeeze her soft hand back firmly.

*We're going to be okay,* I try to tell her telepathically, since I can't take my phone out in the office. I won't let Shawni take the fall for this.

I take out a piece of paper and write my confession.

# THIRTY-SEVEN

Shawni and I get called into Principal Matthew's office together. I hand her my piece of paper, and she takes a moment to read it over. Before she gets a chance to say anything, the door swings open.

Angel practically falls over himself as he enters the room. We lock eyes, and his gaze travels to the paper, still in Principal Matthew's hands.

"Can I help you?" Principal Matthew asks.

Angel clears his throat. "It was me," he says. "I hacked the school's Twitter account."

Principal Matthew sighs, and someone grabs Angel's arm and yanks him out of the room. Then Nina rushes in. And Jasmine is right behind them.

"No, I did it!"

"It was me!"

Principal Matthew rolls her eyes and sighs again. "Shanaya and Ariana aren't here for the . . . um, hacking. But if you want to make a formal confession about that, you're going to have to get in line."

"What?" Nina asks.

"Everyone in this office is convinced they're the ones who did it. I can't do anything with this information, and frankly, I'm much more concerned with the content of the post than the fact that it exists at all. So unless you want to get in line, the three of you are free to go." She shoos Nina, Jasmine, and Angel out of the room before addressing me and Shawni again.

She sighs, then says, "So, what's this I hear about you two attacking that boy?"

I grab one of the pens in her little cup and start writing on the paper Principal Matthew put back on her desk. Before I can write down that Shawni had nothing to do with it, Shawni starts talking.

"He's not just a boy. You know what he did. He's a *rapist*. And he tried to hit me first!" Shawni doesn't try to put the blame on me, even though I'm the one who kneed him.

By the time she's done, I have my note.

*I'm the one who kneed him. Shawni didn't do anything.*

Principal Matthew turns the note around so Shawni can read it. "Is this true?" she asks Shawni.

Instead of answering, Shawni starts defending me. "She didn't do anything wrong. He deserved it!"

"Alright, Shanaya, you're free to go."

I smile wide at the thought of Shawni being let go before I realize I'm probably in big trouble. It's my second violence-against-assholes in as many months.

"Look, I'm not saying he didn't deserve it, but we can't just let violence go unpunished at this school. I'm sorry, but I can't give you special treatment. I'm afraid I'm going to have to give you . . ." She sighs and pinches the bridge of her nose, shaking her head like she's conflicted. "A warning."

I crack a smile. That's it? I assumed I'd get expelled for confessing, but I guess it helped that I didn't take the blame alone.

She takes a breath and says, "Ari, I read your post and I can't even imagine what you're going through. I want you to know that we'll be investigating this matter thoroughly."

I want to cry. She believes me.

"And, look, I know it wasn't you who hacked our account. I need you to be honest with me, alright? Luis is saying it was Shanaya. Do you know if that's true?"

I start writing again.

*I told you it was me.*

I give her a confused look, like I don't understand how it could be anyone else. She just sighs.

"Alright, Ariana, you're free to go."

Shawni's waiting for me outside the door when I come out. She takes my hand before we head back to the office together. Jasmine, Angel, and Nina are all waiting for us by the office door.

Angel looks like he's about to cry. "Can we ditch the rest of the day?" he says in a hushed whisper, so no one in here can hear. "Let's go to the park or something. I really wanna talk to you all."

Nina and Jasmine nod, and Shawni sighs. I for one am nervous about it. Not about ditching, but about this "talk." Angel looks upset, and I wonder if that means the talk is going to be about how we all need to go our separate ways now. I'm not really in a hurry to have that conversation. It's a second before Shawni says anything, too.

"I'll meet you guys at the park," she finally says, and walks out of the office, letting go of my hand.

But instead of walking with everyone else to the park, I follow Shawni. She's headed to the outside bathroom, the one no one ever uses. I walk in after her. I'm about to reach for her hand so she knows I'm here when she breaks down crying.

I play a "hey" from my watch, and she startles.

"Jesus, Ari, I didn't know you were in here!" Then she starts laugh-crying.

I show her what I've texted on my phone.

Ari: Are you okay?

I wonder if she's also worried about losing our newfound friend group.

Shawni turns around and looks down at me, wiping away her tears. "Hug?" she whimpers. I open my arms out to her, and she falls into them in a tight embrace. "We did it, Ari. We did it!" Another laugh-cry. "I didn't think this would actually work!"

Then she just laughs and laughs, and I laugh with her. She

wasn't sad crying, she was *happy*. Because we defeated Luis. I
have to admit, I had my doubts about whether it would work
out, too. But *we did it*. I hug her back as tight as I can.

When we finally pull away, she holds my gaze, and for once
I don't feel like I'm under a microscope with the eye contact. I
feel like she's really seeing me, and I want her to.

"Can I kiss you, Ari?" she asks softly.

I nod my head, wide-eyed, unsure what to do, but sure that
this is what I want.

I stand on my tiptoes to make the kiss come easier, and she
leans in, finally pressing her lips to mine. I can't help but smile
under the kiss, which inadvertently makes her kiss my teeth
instead of my lips, but she just giggles and pulls away.

I'm about to start overthinking whether I ruined the
moment, but she giggles again and reaches for my hands.

"Sorry, let's try that again?" she says, and my chest warms. I
make it a point to pucker my lips this time so she doesn't kiss my
teeth. I close my eyes, and before I know it, I feel her soft lips on
mine. I can't believe this is happening. Our lips don't part for a
few seconds, and when they do, I'm reluctant to pull away, so I
give her a few quick last-minute pecks on the mouth, and she
starts giggling again.

"God, you are so fucking cute."

I blush as I type.

*So are you*

She gives me the cutest smile ever with her cute face, and I
return it with mine.

"Ready to go to the park?" she finally asks, and I nod.

We sneak off campus walking to the park hand in hand. When we get there, we see Nina, Angel, and Jasmine sitting at the park table laughing. As soon as they notice us they look at our hands and smile.

I remind myself that our future is still unclear. Who knows if we'll all still be friends after today, since it could increase everyone else's odds of getting caught with me. I should enjoy this final hangout while it lasts.

Shawni and I sit at the table, and Angel clears his throat.

"I love you guys," Angel says, wiping his eyes. Jasmine puts a comforting hand on his shoulder. "I know we said we had to keep a distance from each other to avoid getting caught, but . . . do we have to?" he says, asking exactly what I'd been thinking.

"I mean, you all kind of outed yourselves as our friends when you busted into the principal's office to defend our honor, right?" Shawni laughs.

"Sorry . . ." Angel says, rubbing the back of his neck.

"I'm not," Jasmine says.

"Me either." Nina grins. "It kind of worked out perfectly, with everyone confessing. They can't get *everyone* in trouble, so no one gets in trouble."

"Oh, thank God." Angel drops his head down on the table in relief.

"Friends for life." Jasmine grins and throws her arms around Nina and Angel's shoulders.

"My ride or dies." Angel grins at Jasmine, then at everyone else.

My phone buzzes, and I open it to see a text from Ed.

**Ed:** I was wrong. You did good.

"Hey, guys?" I say with a smirk. Everyone looks up. Even if Luis's dad comes after me, I can at least do one last thing for Ed. "Can we maybe add one more person to our group? There's someone I want you all to meet."

# THIRTY-EIGHT

I can't stop thinking about Luis's dad and what he could do to me—and to my friends. But I don't say anything to them. They deserve to celebrate after everything. *I* deserve to celebrate. I deserve to enjoy the moments between now and when I get in trouble. Who knows what comes next. Juvie? Probation? I don't know what the consequences of "defamation" and "slander" are, but I'm sure I'll find out soon enough.

When I turn the corner to my apartment complex, "soon enough" threatens to come way faster than I'm ready for.

Luis is waiting for me at the bottom of the steps to my apartment. I quickly turn around and slip back around the corner and press my back against the wall of the laundry room. What is he doing here?

My heart pounds against my chest, and I press both hands over it to soothe myself, but the beating doesn't slow. I close my eyes and focus on my breathing instead.

In. Out. In. Out—In—in in in.

"You don't really think I *raped* you, do you?" Luis says, and my eyes shoot open to find he's right in front of me. My brain shoots into overdrive, and instead of fight or flight, I freeze. I pin my arms to my sides—because I'm nervous, but also so I can have easy access to my pocketknife. There's no way I can make words happen to answer him, but he doesn't seem to care what I say anyway.

"I mean, it's not like I *raped* you. You went into that night wanting me. I know you did. With that skimpy little black dress. You were flirting with me." He eyes me up and down, as if imagining that dress on me again. "You can't put all the blame on me, you know."

I just glare at him, and he throws his arms in the air, making me flinch.

"Did you really think you'd be able to get away with dragging my name through the mud? You think you're so smart with that stunt you pulled, but I know you. You're like a nervous little stray."

He takes a step closer, and I inhale sharply, brushing my fingers against my pocket to remind myself I have protection.

"*Innocent.* You think you're so funny, don't you?" he scoffs, and I remember the posters I put around the school with Ed's mugshot. Luis starts laughing. "Ed tried to fuck with me, and look what happened to that little bitch. I'd hate to see something bad happen to this one . . ." He reaches a hand out to touch my face, but I swat it away. "I don't know if this little stray can take juvie." Then his expression turns to ice. "My dad's a judge. You think I can't get you put away for this?" I picture myself pulling out my knife and using it. If I'm going to jail anyway . . .

"What do you want?" I mouth the words, since I can't bring myself to speak them, but he understands. His eyes narrow on mine, and it takes all my willpower to hold his gaze.

"You're going to tell everyone you lied. You'll tell them you made it all up. That all of you did. And you're going to publicly name every bitch involved. Otherwise, I'll do to you what I did to Ed." He smiles. "Either that, or jail. It's your choice."

Then he walks away.

It isn't until I see him get in his car and drive away that I take a steadying breath to remind myself I'm safe, look down at my watch, and end the recording.

# EPILOGUE

## *Four months later*

"I'm gonna tell him tonight," Jasmine whispers in my ear as she, Angel, Ed, Shawni, and I all sit in Nina's backyard waiting for them to come out from inside for their big quince debut. I look to Jasmine, who's staring at the door waiting for Nina, as if she hadn't just told me the biggest news I've heard in months. She and Angel have been "taking it slow" for the last few months. Back when they confessed their feelings to each other, she said she'd tell him when she was ready to have a boyfriend.

"Good luck," I whisper back. Then I look around, smiling at the fact that every chair outside is filled. Nina had thought we'd be the only ones to show up, but in the last few months, we've gotten much closer to a lot of the others who confessed to our "crime" the day we exposed Luis.

The door finally opens, the song "Born This Way" by Lady Gaga plays as Nina dances their way out in a tuxedo bedazzled in the trans flag colors. We erupt in a roar of whoops and cheers. Nina beams, throwing all of us a double thumbs up with a contagious grin. They bow, soaking in the applause. Then the music changes, and they gesture for us to join them on the makeshift dance floor.

Shawni of course doesn't hesitate. She holds her hand out for me, and as soon as I take it, I'm being pulled up to dance. Ed, Angel, and Jasmine aren't far behind. We all practically stumble over each other as we make it to Nina and barrel into a group hug.

The outside air gives me enough space that I don't feel claustrophobic or overwhelmed by the music and the people. Instead, I'm filled with laughter as we all dance to our hearts' content. After a full year of dance class with Ms. M, I'm still not skilled in any way, shape, or form. But that doesn't stop me from whipping my hair around, throwing my limbs wherever they please, and going wild in the cypher we've started.

Once the music changes to something slower, Shawni holds her hands out to me, and I take them. She gently places my hands on her hips.

"This okay?" she asks, and I nod enthusiastically.

Shawni and I have been dating ever since the day after we exposed Luis, but I don't think I'll ever stop feeling giddy at her every touch.

Then I see Jasmine and Angel from the corner of my eye, and I can't help but watch as inconspicuously as possible. Jasmine is whispering something in Angel's ear. Is she telling him right now?

Judging by the ear-to-ear smile on Angel's face, I'd say that's a yes. And if that wasn't enough of an indicator, Jasmine pulling him in for a kiss definitely seals the deal.

Shawni follows my gaze, then squeezes my hands and squeals, "Oh my God, *finally!*"

"Right?" I laugh, and Shawni pulls me closer. I mirror her wanting smile and we simultaneously go in for a kiss of our own.

I melt into the kiss, smiling through it like I almost always do.

"You are so cute. Do you know that, Ari?"

I just giggle in response and nuzzle my face into Shawni's shoulder. "I love you," I blurt out. The words were unexpected, but I don't regret them. While part of me is scared of what she might say back—or even worse, what she might not say—I'm more eager than afraid to hear it.

Shawni's surprised expression turns into a happy smile. "I love you, too."

My shoulders relax, and we wrap our arms around each other, just holding each other and swaying to the music until the song fades out.

An upbeat song plays next, which pulls me out of the moment a bit. Shawni, on the other hand, seems more than happy to keep dancing. I look over to the tables and see Ed sitting down alone.

"I'm gonna go sit down for a bit, okay?" I say, and Shawni squeezes my shoulder as an okay before running over to Nina, Jasmine, and Angel to dance with them.

I go straight for the table where Ed sits in alone.

"Hey, Ari," he says. I was worried he might have been alone

because he was sad or feeling left out, but he sounds content, and he's smiling.

"Hey," I say back. Then I hear people talking about Luis at the table behind us. His name used to make my skin crawl, but now I tune them out after hearing the topic of discussion: that his dad finally cut him off after he confessed to his crimes. His court date just passed. He's a registered sex offender now, and he's getting put away for what he did. All of it, including . . .

"You're in the clear, then?" I ask, knowing Ed is also overhearing this conversation. Though he must have already known.

He smiles. "I was going to tell you after the party. Record's all clean. I'm gonna go to school to get my GED!"

"That's amazing!"

Ed looks at me and smiles. "Thank you, Ari."

I shake my head. "Thank *you*. I wouldn't have had the strength to do any of it if I didn't know someone like you existed out there."

"Okay, so I guess we both are pretty awesome, then." He laughs, and I join in.

It strikes me that I felt nothing at the mention of Luis's name when I heard it. I feel completely free of him now. And that's magical.

I have Nina. I have Jasmine. I have Angel. I have Ed. And most of all, I have Shawni. The weight on my chest is gone once and for all.

I can finally exhale.

If you or someone you know has been a victim of sexual assault, here are some resources that may help:

RAINN:
*www.rainn.org/about-national-sexual-assault-telephone-hotline*

The National Sexual Violence Resource Center:
*www.nsvrc.org/survivors*

# ACKNOWLEDGMENTS

There are so many amazing people I want to thank for helping me get to where I am and helping this book to exist in its current form.

To my editor, Alessandra Balzer, for helping me fall back in love with this story after I had struggled for so long. It was one of the hardest books to edit, but you helped me find the reason I started this book in the first place. To my agent, Alexandra Levick, for championing me and my work all this time. To Jessie Gang for designing such a stunning cover and to Be Fernandez for bringing it to life. To everyone on the HarperCollins team who has touched this book and helped to get it where it is today, especially Caitlin Johnson, Shannon Cox, Audrey Diestelkamp, Lauren Levite, Patty Rosati, Mimi Rankin, Almeda Beynon, Laura Harshberger, Mark Rifkin, Vivian Lee, Andrea Pappenheimer, Kerry Moynagh, and Kathy Faber, some of whom are, as of the moment I'm writing these acknowledgments, currently on strike for a fair contract and better pay. Thank you for everything you've done and are doing.

I also want to thank my mom, as always, for your undying support. To all my family who have cheered me on throughout all of this. To all my friends, both irl and internet-made, for continuing to be there for me through the highs and lows of drafting and revising. Thank you.

And lastly, to all the real-life Luis Ortegas of the world: I hope you fall dick first on a cactus. I hope you choke on Cheetos dust. I hope every time it's really hot at night and you flip your pillow to feel the cool side, I hope it's hot on that side too. I hope your spoon falls all the way in your soup. I hope you hear about this book, and I hope it haunts you.

AUTAUGA PRATTVILLE
PUBLIC LIBRARIES
254 Doster Street
Prattville, AL 36067